THE TUNNEL

CARL-JOHAN VALLGREN

Translated from the Swedish by Rachel Willson-Broyles

Quercus

First published in Great Britain in 2016 by:

Quercus Editions Limited
Carmelite House
50 Victoria Embankment
London EC4Y 0DZ

An Hachette UK company.

A CIP catalogue record for this book is available
from the British Library.

TPB ISBN 978 1 78429 863 0
EBOOK ISBN 978 1 78429 277 5

10 9 8 7 6 5 4 3 2 1

Typeset by Jouve (UK), Milton Keynes

Printed and bound in Great Britain by Clays Ltd, St Ives plc.

PART I

Stockholm, September 2013

He was sitting on a bench in Midsommarparken, hyper-aware of every movement around him. Nothing suspicious since he'd left the apartment half an hour earlier. A few nursery school children in yellow reflective vests were making a racket in the playground. He shifted position, moving into the shadow of a tree. He rubbed at a stain on his trousers. No idea where that came from. Lunch, when he fried two eggs in oil?

On the corner of Svandammsvägen was the pub he liked to go to. Tre Vänner, it was called – Three Friends. The chairs inside were upside down on the tables. The pub wouldn't open until evening; he could go there later and think through the middleman's information. He liked the place. He had a glass of Murphy's Irish Stout there on occasion, but his visits were irregular and he never went more than once a month. He didn't want people to recognize him.

That was one of the difficult things about his job, he thought. You could never tell anyone what you were working on. The fewer people who knew, the less risk of trouble. That was why he'd only had to pay for a fraction of all the stuff he'd done.

His eyes roamed towards the metro entrance. A woman walked out of the doors: the Thai girl who'd moved in with his upstairs neighbour a few months earlier. She was black and blue and her right eye was swollen shut. He ought to do something about it. Their fights had escalated in recent weeks. The other neighbours were afraid of the guy. And his girlfriend seemed so helpless – she didn't speak a word of Swedish and hardly seemed to know which country she was in.

He looked at the clock. One hour and ten minutes left. Time to take off, if he wanted to be on the safe side.

He bought a sandwich at the kiosk before heading down to the tracks. He swiped his SL card across the reader and passed through the turnstile as he ate. The green tile walls around the escalator reminded him of prison . . . Zoran would be executing a similar manoeuvre, but up in Tensta, on the other side of the city. Zoran had been out of the business for nearly a decade. He had taken classes to become a massage therapist, married a woman who didn't take any shit, and settled down on the straight and narrow. Two little kids at home. Six and three. Crime was no longer his thing – he changed nappies. Fried up *falukorv* for dinner. Had a real life.

Jorma had known him for over twenty years, since his days as a bouncer at the underground nightclubs in Hammarbyhamnen. They had done break-ins together, dealt in stolen vehicles, robbed four armoured trucks. But that was a long time ago. Zoran had vanished suddenly, and he hadn't heard from him again until three weeks ago. Zoran had called to pass along the middleman's idea.

He had reached the tracks. He took a right, heading towards the platform for northbound trains.

As he waited, he discreetly studied the other travellers. He was being paranoid for no reason. An old woman with a cane was reading the timetables on the wall. Further along, a teenage couple were kissing. On the bench closest to him, a Finnish man in a pinstriped suit was talking on the phone. He could hear fragments of the conversation, something about a meeting with an IT firm and a business lunch later that day.

He shuddered as he suddenly thought of his father, Harri. How he had spent his time boozing on park benches throughout the last few years of his life, before dying of a heart attack at barely fifty. A stereotypical Finn. Jorma had run into him now and then in Vällingby city centre, with his sheet music and a bottle of dessert wine next to him on the bench, so smashed that he didn't even recognize his own son.

The train towards T-Centralen thundered onto the platform. He walked up to the first carriage, looking over his shoulder even though he knew everything was fine. No one was tailing him. The doors opened and he stepped into the half-empty carriage. One minute later, the train had passed through the tunnel to Liljeholmen.

He was the only passenger to get off. The train from Norsborg came in on the opposite platform. It was crammed full of people from the outer suburbs. A babel, he thought as he crowded his way onto the train: people were speaking a dozen languages. There were young guys with African roots, two women in niqabs, an older Arab man with a hookah in a plastic bag on his lap. Poor people. Like the Finns back in the day, at the bottom of the social hierarchy.

The journey went faster now. Hornstull, Zinkensdamm. Inner-city kids filled up the train, *gymnasium* students in super expensive brand-name clothing, or deliberately dressed down. There was hardly another city in the world where the class differences were as obvious as in Stockholm.

A man in a yarmulke was standing next to the escalators at the exit towards Mariatorget; he seemed to be waiting for something. The guy looked like Katz, Jorma thought, the few times he'd seen his oldest friend wearing a skullcap. Katz had left half a dozen messages on his voicemail in the last week, as if he sensed what was up and wanted to convince Jorma to bail out.

In the past year, Jorma had seen his friend more often than usual. Last summer's incidents had brought them closer together again. The Klingberg Affair. Katz had been falsely accused of murder; Jorma had tried to help him. Eva Westin, their mutual friend from their days in Hässelby, had been dragged into it as well, as had her daughter. Everything had worked out in the end; everyone made it through and Katz's name was cleared. But it seemed they had all felt a greater need to see one another since.

He changed trains at Östermalmstorg, peeking back over his shoulder again before he continued towards Ropsten. He made a note of the deserted platforms; no one was boarding. The only people who used public transport around here were the people who worked in the neighbourhood, the *servants*.

He had a bad feeling again as he rode the escalator up to the Gärdet exit. He looked around cautiously. Two men in tracksuits were following ten metres behind him. The guy closest to him had a pair of headphones around his neck. Looked like a cop. He felt his heart beat faster.

He started to walk to see how they would react. He pretended to be looking at the advertisements on the walls, and out of the corner of his eye he found that they were keeping pace with him. Police, he thought, or just a coincidence . . .

As he approached the ticket hall, he thought about calling the whole thing off, going back home and telling Zoran that someone was tailing him and it would be best to lie low.

He could see the turnstiles now, and the Pressbyrån shop on the other side. The escalator stairs flattened out; a few pigeons that had lost their way in the pedestrian tunnel were flapping up around the ceiling in fear. He took a left towards the lift and bumped into an old man with a Rollator; he mumbled an apology.

The lift door was open. Without turning around, he stepped in and pressed the 'down' button. As the door slid shut behind him, he turned his head. False alarm: the men in the tracksuits had passed through the turnstiles; they were laughing at something, conversing loudly, then they jogged off through the pedestrian tunnel. On their way to Gärdet, he thought, just as he was, but not to plan a robbery – to go for a run.

They had set the meeting for three o'clock. Jorma arrived half an hour early. The sports fields at Gärdet were the perfect spot. There was a good view in all directions. Nowhere for cops to hide.

He followed the pedestrian path above the fields. He was sweating when he sat down on a park bench. The enormous green below him was nearly deserted.

A few joggers ran past, young upper-class girls with anorexic role models. A bald man with a dachshund on a lead disappeared into a grove of trees. He gazed out at the brick buildings of the Swedish Defence Materiel Administration on the other side of the fields. No suspicious movements. From a distance, the cars on Lindarängsvägen looked like toys.

What was he *doing* here? Was he even sure that this was what he wanted?

One year earlier, he had decided to quit. He had money saved up from old jobs. He'd been thinking of going back to work in construction again, maybe starting his own company. His third talent, alongside committing crimes and playing the piano: he was a skilled craftsman. *I already made my decision*, he thought. *No more robberies.*

He had made himself unavailable: he changed addresses and no one knew where he lived. He had no home phone and could only be reached by email. He had slowly started to phase out his old life and the very thought of a continued criminal existence. And then suddenly Zoran contacted him.

In the end he had said yes, and he knew why. Because he missed it. Because life had grown boring. It was so banal. He missed the excitement, planning the minute details of a job, the feeling of being in control in the midst of a chaotic situation.

What about Zoran? he thought. *What were his reasons? The dream of the perfect heist? Money troubles? Or was he bored and in it for kicks just like Jorma?*

A man walked in from Värtavägen to stand by one of the football goals on the field. The middleman. He recognized him: Hillerström. He had contacted him about robbing a cash depot last summer. But it had never come to fruition because Jorma had decided to pull out.

A dot in the distance started moving towards them from Lindarängsvägen. He could tell by the way it moved that it was Zoran. Confident, but still on guard. There were a certain number of chickenshits in the business, people who lost it when things got hot, but not Zoran. He would rather take a bullet.

'I have an insider at a cash-in-transit company,' Hillerström said after they'd made it through hellos. 'The guy seems dependable and the job has to be done soon for various reasons. The way I see it, it's a great opportunity. The haul is somewhere between five and eight million. 10 per cent goes to me, as a fee.'

Neither Jorma nor Zoran said anything, and Hillerström seemed to know what they were thinking.

'I know. People claim it's not worth the risk these days. The new trucks have immobilizers and security cams, bags are better at self-destruction. But this is going to work . . . The company is called Trans Security. It's been around since 2002 but hasn't made much of a splash. They deal with the same sort of thing as Loomis and Falck, but on a smaller scale. They handle cash and they pick up and deliver night deposit boxes. Apparently they've never been targeted in a robbery, but there's a first time for everything.'

One month earlier, the company had suffered a garage fire. The owner had been sloppy with fire prevention regulations. Two vehicles were completely destroyed and the company would have to rely on old trucks until mid-September, when new vehicles would arrive from Germany.

'The cash boxes are the old kind: they have an inaccessible GPS. But it's possible to break through the lock with a regular old axe, if you hit it in the right spot. We'll have to transfer the cash to our own bags on the scene. The dye packs won't destroy more than twenty per cent of the bills, if they go off at all, and some of them will be washable. What can they do?' Hillerström went on, lighting a cigarette and blowing smoke out of his nose in two columns. 'Call their customers and say, "We accidentally burned up our trucks and unfortunately we can't pick up your night boxes until the middle of next month"? Doesn't sound very confidence-inspiring to my ears.'

'Where did they get the old trucks from?'

Zoran's question. As detail-oriented as in earlier years.

'They belong to the same company. They're ones they used to use years ago. Apparently they were just left sitting around in a garage somewhere.'

Hillerström glanced at the grove of trees two hundred metres away. There was a slight bulge in his jacket at his chest and back, as if he were wearing a Kevlar vest underneath.

'And who's the insider?' Jorma asked.

'A logistics guy at the company. A real square. A former security guard turned office drone. This guy plans the transport schedules. The drivers don't find out which routes they have until they get in their trucks in the morning. But this guy knows . . . and he'll make sure that at least one of the older vehicles is loaded with cash. The man is in debt. He wants a third of the haul, he says, but he's not gonna get it. I'll renegotiate with him once the job is done. This deal is yours, if you want it. But don't wait too long. I have a couple of other interested parties.'

Hillerström looked at them. The sleeve of his jacket had slid up a bit; a watch worth somewhere in the ballpark of one hundred thousand kronor clung to his wrist.

'We'll have to meet this guy before we can make a decision,' said Jorma.

'That's fine with me. When?'

'Tomorrow evening.'

'Sure. Just name the place, and I'll make sure he's there.'

Five minutes later, they separated, heading in two different directions across the sports fields.

'What do you think?' Jorma asked as he and Zoran walked towards the old industrial neighbourhoods above Värtahamnen.

'Sounds almost too good to be true. But I believe in this deal. Just have to check a few things with the insider.'

The Helsinki ferry was visible far away in the channel. When this job was finished, it would be time to go on a trip, Jorma mused. Maybe to Finland. Take Katz along to see if he still remembered the language. Jorma had taught it to him when they were teenagers in Hässelby. Katz was like a sponge when it came to languages: he could absorb them in no time.

'With any luck the meeting will happen tomorrow. Hillerström was going to check and let us know within the hour. Just one thing, Zoran: why are you doing this?'

'Why do you ask?'

'You have two kids at home, a perfectly decent day job, and you haven't been in the business for a long time.'

'I need the cash. And Hillerström showed up with this tip at just the right time.'

Zoran was giving him an odd look.

'It's just that it might not be the right thing to do,' Jorma went on. 'What'll happen if we get nailed?'

'We won't. What the hell is up with you?'

He looked away.

'Nothing. I'm going home now. See you later.'

A rollerblader whizzed by on the pavement. Jorma felt like he was being observed from a point behind him, but when he looked around there was nobody there.

When he arrived at Lill-Jans Park he turned on his phone. He hadn't wanted it to be on during the meeting or his trip there. The cops were ahead of the game when it came to phone surveillance. But Zoran had gone home, and so had Hillerström.

He called his sister as he turned onto one of the riding paths that led over to Östra station. He listened to the phone as it rang, knowing exactly what it sounded like at her end: the *Sopranos* theme song. Fitting, he thought. Leena had always stood by him. She had kept mum each time the cops came by to ask questions about her brother. She had covered for him, hidden things for him. The safe deposit box in Huddinge where he kept his savings was in her name.

He let it ring eight times before hanging up. She was probably at the school where she worked helping students with concentration problems. Or in the allotment garden that she had made her life's work. Or, as he hoped, at her son's place, with her phone on silent. Kevin was nineteen and had just moved out. And Leena would not have been the sister Jorma knew if she didn't spend every free hour at Kevin's new apartment helping him.

He thought about calling his mother, Aino, instead. The nearly eighty-year-old woman lived at a Finnish retirement home in Nacka, had been wheelchair-bound for the past few years, and had 'a touch of the Alzheimer's', as she herself put it. But it was lunchtime, and he knew she would be in the cafeteria with a hundred other half-demented elderly people, unable to talk to him until she was back in her room.

He turned off his phone again. He thought about the life he had lived and wondered why he'd never felt any remorse.

The late eighties, working as a bouncer at the underground nightclubs in Hammarbyhamnen, the network he had started to build, only twenty years old. He had worked as a torpedo for older criminals, beating people up until they barely survived, and back then he hadn't been ashamed – he'd thought they deserved it.

Later he had started working as a debt collector. Same thing there – no remorse. Those he extorted money from were no law-abiding citizens, they were criminals trying to screw other criminals out of their money.

He remembered the days after his first bid – he'd been a new member of the Hell's Angels; he had just started working as a bouncer again and reported two men to the police for threatening him with a sawn-off shotgun in the queue for a bar. Two prospects from a competing motorcycle gang. He had to pick them out from a photo line-up at the station, and once the papers came in from the prosecutor he had their names and personal ID numbers and could bide his time. Just as he'd planned, the preliminary investigation was closed when he withdrew his report. He looked up their addresses in the national register . . . and served his revenge up cold a few months later. One of them still couldn't walk.

He had stuck with his life of crime because it suited him, wasn't that so? Because he was equipped for it. Good at it. He lacked a conscience. He'd made enemies, of course, but at least as many friends. He had drifted in and out of various networks, but still he had retained his freedom of movement. His most enduring affiliation had been two years with the Hell's Angels – the longest he had gone along with taking orders from other people. He had been nosing around a position as sergeant-at-arms before he left the club in good standing. In fact, he was one of the few to manage that trick. Because he had lost his taste for it, and because the president knew he could be trusted: he would never reveal anything, never breathe a word of what he had seen, heard, or done to an outsider, not even Katz.

Regret? He had never allowed himself to feel anything like it.

And now, suddenly, a cluster of memories demanding the opposite: Aino's despair when she picked him up from the police or social services, just thirteen years old. The fear in the people he'd threatened, men who were fathers, siblings . . . children themselves. The pain of a person whose leg he'd broken or whose jaw he'd smashed. The victims he'd robbed, pissing themselves in fear. He hadn't dared to look at what he'd done through their eyes. He had thought that something would burst inside him.

It was eleven at night and they found themselves in a forested area on the island of Ekerö. The insider was already there, in his own car. This was the only direct contact that would occur between them, and the less the insider knew about them, the better. No names. No faces. The guy looked terrified when he saw them coming down the gravel path in ski masks.

'Jesus, you scared me,' he said. 'Is it Halloween or something?'

'Come on. Let's take a little walk.'

They walked into the forest and stopped in a glade ringed with birches. Faint moonlight filtered through the treetops.

The guy spontaneously began to tell them about the vehicles, giving them info about times and the guards' routines, his nerves causing him to stammer as he suddenly started talking about the haul.

'With a little luck, we're talking eight million. But I want a third of it . . . or else I'm out. After all, I'm risking a lot here, like my job, for example.'

A snitch type, Jorma thought as he handed him a cigarette. Ratting people out for money, betraying his colleagues; he didn't know the meaning of honour.

He let him light the cigarette before boxing his ear. The guy's hand flew to his cheek.

'What the fuck did you do that for?'

He didn't respond, just hit him again, and harder.

The guy was trembling all over. He looked like he wanted to run away.

'You don't get to make demands in your position. You can work out your deal with our mutual contact. And starting now, you will not back out. It's too late. You're past the point of no return, got it?'

The guy nodded.

'Good. Then we're going to ask you some questions, and you will answer them in as much detail as you can, is that understood?'

He began to relax as they grilled him. He seemed to have swallowed down his reaction to being struck. Maybe he'd even realized that he deserved it, that he needed to be more alert from now on.

'What kind of transports does your company do?'

'All sorts. Mostly cash. Class four – that is, a minimum of two million in each vehicle.'

'For banks?'

'No, for businesses. Furniture stores, superstores, appliance chains. We pick up their daily cash and transport it to our vault. The larger secure-transport companies more or less have a monopoly on ATMs.'

'What do the trucks' cargo areas look like?'

'There are control panels for the alarms and time locks right at the back. Safes that can be opened with codes. Space for the bags. The money is sorted by denomination: thousand-kronor bills and five-hundred-kronor bills are in grey bags, and they're in the right-hand safes.'

'How many people ride in the truck?'

'Two. One is trained in valuable-goods transport, and the other is trained as a security officer.'

'Is there an escort?'

'Sometimes. A security officer in an unmarked car will follow them and keep in radio contact with headquarters. But I think I can avoid having one.'

They nodded, jotting everything down in their mental notebooks.

'We need photos,' Zoran said. 'Of the truck interior. Can you arrange that?'

'I've already taken care of it. I secretly took pictures last week; they're in the glovebox. You can have them later on . . . I'm pretty sure I've thought of everything. Including where the suspicions will fall if the boss gets it into his head that an employee is involved. I'm going to make sure a certain guy is driving – Göran. This guy visits Polish whores. At an apartment bordello in Huddinge. He told me about it once when he was drunk at a staff party . . . he wondered if I wanted to come along. The police will believe that he's involved, that he was blackmailed or something.'

The first thing the cops would do was check out who planned the run, Jorma thought – *that is, the logistics guy.* That poor, stupid devil was going to go down for this; he wouldn't last two minutes in an interrogation. But by then they would have vanished with their spoils, and he wouldn't be able to identify them.

'There's just one problem.'

'What's that?'

'The job has to be done within the week. The new vehicles are arriving from Germany earlier than expected. The boss managed to rush the supplier. If you want to get at the big money, it has to be Monday, right after the payday weekend.'

He looked at them like a little kid expecting praise.

'I'll make sure that Göran gets the run in one of the old trucks. There will be night deposit boxes from Södertälje, among other places, cash from a large vegetable market and from the shops at Kungens Kurva. They'll go in the same load. The truck will make its final stop in a secluded spot by the shopping centre in Skärholmen city centre. You can get it as it's driving out.'

'There's a police station around the corner there,' Jorma said.

'I've checked that out too. It's closed for three months due to a flooded basement – a broken pipe or something. They've moved to a temporary location in Älvsjö.'

Have to double check that, he thought. *Four days to work with; the window of time has shrunk . . .*

He gave the security guy an expressionless look. The kid was sweating, even though it was chilly out. He was thin, Jorma realized, rail-thin. His face was gaunt. *He's sick,* he thought, *though maybe he doesn't know it yet himself.* He wondered how he had ended up in debt . . . Gambling? Drugs?

A twig snapped in the forest behind them, and once again he had a bad feeling.

'Wait here,' he said.

He felt like an idiot as he walked towards the sound. Cop paranoia. And apparently he couldn't control it.

He stopped after thirty metres, next to a cairn. He heard something run off through the trees. Nimble steps. A deer, he thought; there were plenty of them outside the city.

Then he walked back to the glade. It was always like this at the start of a plan. You saw cops and problems where there were none, imagined things because your subconscious wanted you to. Being suspicious was about minimizing the risks. Both he and Zoran were good at that.

Early morning, and they were sitting in a car in the multi-storey carpark in Skärholmen city centre. His anxiety had finally started to dissipate. His gut was telling him that this job would go just fine.

'Should be a piece of cake,' Zoran said, handing him the binoculars. 'We'll stop the truck when it drives out, block its way between the pillars. Someone can come up behind it so it can't back out.'

The loading dock was a hundred metres away. Ordinarily they would have done recon at least a month in advance because security camera footage was only saved for four weeks, but this time they had to improvise. The Toyota they were sitting in had fake plates. Jorma had been lying on the floor in the back seat since they'd left the city to avoid being seen by the traffic cams.

'We need one more driver. And a man to keep an eye on the guards while we open the truck. Another person to take care of the escort car in case our insider doesn't manage to avoid having one. We'll use plastic explosive on the door, break open the security cases, and repack the bills into our own bags. We'll give ourselves a max of four minutes to do the whole job. We can concentrate on the bags with thousand-and five-hundred-kronor bills, pack the money, and get out on my signal, even if we haven't got it all.'

'What about the escape route?' Jorma asked.

'We'll check it out in a bit.'

At least the police station was really closed, just like the insider had told them. They had driven by to check. If the cops came from the city, they would take the Kungens Kurva exit. So it would be best to scatter the caltrops there and make their getaway to the south-west, away from the motorway.

'How are things on the family front?' Jorma asked. 'The kids . . . are they good?'

'I think so. I'm not really sure. I've been staying at friends' places for a while.'

'Problems with Leyla?'

'Not really. It's a long story.'

Zoran wouldn't look at him.

'We're thinking of moving. Changing hoods. Things are going downhill in Tensta. I love the suburbs, I was born and raised there, but you can't trust anyone anymore.'

Something about his voice . . . Jorma couldn't put his finger on what it was.

'You still haven't told me why you want to do this.'

'Neither have you.'

A security car with a Securitas logo came down the ramp to their level of the garage. They unconsciously sank down in their seats while the vehicle passed at a distance of ten metres. Its windows were tinted; it was impossible to see in. Then it turned off towards the steel door that hid the loading dock.

'Damn, we just got a lucky break. Time it, Jorma. I want to know how many seconds it takes for the door to open and close.' The electronically controlled door slid open, and they caught a glimpse of the secure area on the other side: a security camera angled down – no way its reach could extend more than twenty metres – and two guards from the shopping centre waiting at the ramp. Then it closed again with a metallic whine.

'Thirty seconds.'

'Then that's what we have to work with. Get back on the floor of the car. We've been here long enough.'

They left through the back exit. Zoran turned onto Ekholmsvägen and drove to an intersection. Aino had lived in this neighbourhood for a few years in the late seventies. Dreary rental apartments. Buildings covered in graffiti.

A drunk woman with a pit bull was standing outside the Vårberg newsstand, talking to herself. He thought he recognized her.

They turned south on Svanholmsvägen and drove towards Vårby Gård. A few minutes later they stopped at a car park.

Jorma looked around. Hardly any vehicles, free parking. No windows facing the area from the nearby buildings. They could leave a getaway car there the night before the robbery, and no one would notice it in the morning.

'What do you think?'

'Should work. We'll switch cars here and keep heading south.'

The car park was hidden from the larger road. There was a wooded area five hundred metres behind it.

Zoran kept driving. Backgårdsvägen. Walkways linked the red-brick buildings that flanked the street. The road narrowed around speed bumps. They should leave caltrops here too, as a safety measure – a single punctured tyre would cork up the whole thoroughfare.

Vårby Allé. The neighbourhood where he had begun his life of crime. He had lived here for a year, when he was thirteen. With a foster family, while Aino couldn't handle him. Harri had been out of the picture by that point; he had packed up his few belongings and moved to Vällingby, where he bankrolled his alcoholism by teaching piano lessons at the community music school.

Aino had come to visit him in his foster home each Sunday, and she never wanted to let him out of her embrace when it was time to go. Social services had determined that his placement would last no longer than a year; she needed a relief period and Jorma would move home again as soon as her situation had improved. But instead he sank deeper and deeper into crime, until the authorities gave up on him and placed him in a youth home in Hässelby. That was where he'd met Katz, just as hopeless a case as Jorma. He could picture Katz, the first time they'd met. His vaguely Middle Eastern features from his father's side, Jews who'd moved to Sweden before the war; his dark eyes, full of sadness and frustration. He had lost both his parents in quick succession. He had taken revenge on the world by fighting and doing drugs. The two of them clicked right away.

'We'll head for Botkyrka,' Zoran said. 'The cops will have lost us, and from there we can go whichever way we want, through Huddinge and back into the city, or back up on the E4 again, in the opposite direction. We just have to find a good hideout. Lay low for a couple weeks.'

They passed Vårby school, where he'd officially spent his last term when he'd lived here. In practice, he had never set foot there; instead he had hung around with the gangs in Fittja or gone into the city to rob kids his own age of their money. Unlike Katz, he had avoided drugs, but he had other vices: theft, break-ins, muggings, all kinds of shit that had presumably ruined people's lives.

Regret? Maybe . . .

Lake Mälaren unfolded below them. More memories returned to him. His foster family. They had taken him in because of the money. The mother in the family disliked him; the father pretended he didn't exist. He'd had foster siblings, two younger girls, Maria and Lotta, maybe eight and five, with whom he'd played now and then. But he hardly remembered them anymore; the agony he had felt must have erased them from his mind.

They were driving along the shore by now. The lakeside allotment gardens and steamboat docks. The luxury homes on the other side of the road, with views of Lake Mälaren. They passed Spendrups – *that old Vårby brewery*, he thought. They had sat on the dock one summer drinking beers someone had managed to steal from the trucks outside; little kids, all of them, but their future had already been written. Half of them were dead now.

They arrived at the high-rises on the other side of the highway. Fittja made him think of a foreign, destitute country, the outskirts of an African city; all that was missing was the heat and emaciated beggars.

'If we make it here, we're safe,' Zoran said. 'So, we have four days to get everything ready.'

He looked over at the endless rows of unwelcoming buildings. Mälaren, glittering in the sunlight. *It will be just fine*, he thought. Just one last job. Then he would be done with this life.

Katz had called again, he noticed when he arrived home. His mobile phone was on the kitchen table. Two missed calls, which he had no intention of returning.

He made a cup of espresso from the machine and took it out to the balcony. He started to flesh out the most crucial parts of the job.

They needed a safe apartment, or preferably a house, where they could lie low after the robbery. The first few days were the worst, as he knew from experience. But the manhunt would then begin to slacken off. It was all about momentum.

They needed at least three cars with fake plates; one of them would serve as a command centre. And then another getaway car waiting for them in Vårby Gård. He knew a couple of trustworthy strawmen who dealt in cars, so on that front he couldn't see any problems.

They also needed bulletproof vests and weapons. At least a couple of automatic weapons and smaller guns. If push came to shove with the cops, they had to be able to defend themselves.

He turned the page in his mental notebook and scribbled down the word 'bomb'. A dummy would have to do; he didn't have enough time to make a real one. They would have to put it somewhere highly visible at the crime scene in order to divert the first patrol. They wanted to force the cops to stop and deal with the bomb, but the blasting charge would have to look real if the ploy were to work.

He took a sip of espresso. *New burner phones.* They couldn't be used until the job and would have to be thrown away immediately afterwards. And zip ties to restrain the guards in case they resisted, and bags to transfer the money into. *Duffel bags,* he thought, *seven or eight of them.* They should buy them from several different sports shops so as not to raise suspicions. The whole city was full of security cameras; you couldn't walk one metre without being caught on film.

The hideout would be the hardest thing to arrange on short notice. It would be best to take care of it via a front-man. Maybe a summer cottage close to the city. But Zoran would have to deal with that.

The espresso had cooled in his cup. He peered down the street. The afternoon rush hour was starting. Normal people, coming home from normal jobs. The abusive boyfriend upstairs had started playing Bob Marley on the stereo.

He walked back into his apartment, sat down at the piano in the living room, and looked at the sheet music on it. A Kurt Weill piece. Art music, just as difficult to play as a composition by Mahler. Sudden shifts in tempo, intricate left-hand moves, and advanced disharmonies. He struck the first chord but stopped as he heard the first notes of 'Buffalo Soldier' one floor above. They were fighting again. The woman screamed something in broken English, and then the man's voice: 'Shut up, you fucking Thai slut, I'll fucking sew your cunt shut . . . Shit, you're just awful . . .'

Jorma shut out the noise, walked into the kitchen, and continued his checklist.

Gloves, so they wouldn't leave fingerprints. One more driver, and an extra person to put out caltrops on the exit off the E4.

He took the envelope of photographs from his jacket pocket. The insider's pictures of the armoured truck's interior.

Nothing strange there. It was the old style, the kind

Loomis and Falck had got rid of in the early 2000s because they were far too easy to open. On some of them, it took nothing more than a motor-driven angle grinder to cut open the door.

The photos had been taken with a flash, probably late at night when the guy was working late. Two cabinets on the right side were open; they contained grey bags, the ones holding the larger denominations. They were the type of plain old metal cabinet that could be jimmied with a crow-bar. On the left was a storage area for bags full of lower denominations. At the very back was an instrument panel for the time locks and the alarms. There was a camera mounted in the middle of the ceiling.

Was he wrong about this? There was still time to back out.

He still had money left over from earlier jobs. He could loan it to Zoran, whatever he needed it for.

The fighting above him had moved closer. He heard the woman crying in the kitchen, the sound of something break-ing, a chair hitting the floor, it sounded like . . . and then the man's stoner voice as he called her a cunt, a whore, a Thai slut.

Gotta start calling around, he thought as he walked to the hall and put on his shoes. From a secure line. Arrange a meeting with some people to sell the job.

He met Micke Fredén and Stefan Lindros at the Ringen Centre in Skanstull. They were waiting for him in the food court with their respective combo plates of yakiniku and sushi. They seemed happy to see him; it had been a few years.

He had got to know them in the late nineties, during one of the few times he'd been to prison. They had been planning an escape and Jorma helped them with a few favours. But both of them had been relocated before they were ready. Each had been transported suddenly, in the middle of the night, as if the COs suspected what was up. They served out their sentences in different facilities but contacted him once they were free again. They did some stuff together around the turn of the millennium. Blasting ATMs, among other things. With red plastic explosives, he remembered with nostalgia – that damp, cold surface, and the smell of it, like vanilla.

As far as he knew, neither of them had spent much time on the inside. He didn't want to take any risks by working with people who were listed in the surveillance database. And no suburb kids or gang members. He was too old for that.

They made small talk for a while, telling each other about their lives since they'd last met. Lindros had done some business in Spain, buying up half-finished apartment buildings in bankruptcy estate and selling them on to people in the construction industry who needed to launder money. Fredén had worked as a bouncer at bars, doing some carousel crime on the side: he imported fizzy drinks and cigarettes from Germany and sold them in Skåne without paying VAT or the tobacco tax.

'But that's not why we're here,' he said. 'You had a job in the works. Maybe we should go somewhere where we can chat.'

They left the Ringen Centre and walked down to the Hammarby canal. Young couples with prams were strolling in the sunshine. A gang of teenagers was skateboarding alongside the quay.

'What kind of job is it?' Lindros asked.

'An armoured truck . . .'

He told them about the middleman and the insider and explained the task.

'So, old trucks. Sounds like child's play.'

'Aside from the timeline. It has to be done in three days.'

'How many people do you need?'

'Four or five, including me and Zoran.'

They had sat down on a bench by the water. A ferry was gliding away from the quay, setting course for Hammarby Sjöstad. Images from prison flickered through his mind. Life in a shrinking cell. The sense of claustrophobia that just got worse as years went by. Walking around with eyes in the back of your head to protect yourself from people who actually belonged in a psych ward but were instead dumped in a prison because society thought it was a good way to save money. His last turn had been at Österåker. Accessory to aggravated robbery. He hadn't said a word during the trial; he had kept quiet as a mouse so as not to compromise anyone. He had only planned part of that job, obtaining weapons and doing a little recon, but he ended up getting nailed for the whole thing. He hadn't grumbled or made an effort to get his sentence reduced. In reality, he had done time for other people, and once he got out he got his share, plus interest. But had it been worth it?

'You said Skärholmen city centre . . . Have you been down to check it out?'

'Twice. Once with Zoran, and once by myself.'

'How does it look?'

He took a drawing from his jacket pocket to show them where the loading dock was, where they would stop the armoured truck, the escape route, the position of the lookout who would stand guard by the E4.

'What kind of money are we talking?'

'Between five and eight mil. We'll divide it up based on risk.'

The conversation flowed on. They discussed people who might be interested. Fredén had a bouncer colleague who needed cash. Jimme Gårdnäs. Lindros had an acquaintance from Uppsala he thought would be a good fit.

They had made up their minds without stating it. Jorma went through the times and the positions of the cars. The command centre. The car that should be waiting at the Statoil station. He explained how they would get to and from Skärholmen city centre, and how they would contact each other once the job was done.

'Let's have another meeting tomorrow,' he said. 'To go through all the details.'

'Your insider . . . you're sure he can be trusted?'

'He's so mixed up in this, he can't back out.'

A woman walked by them on the quay. She was dressed like a plainclothes cop. Baseball cap. Motorcycle boots. Sunglasses. She sat down on a bench twenty-five metres away.

'Come on,' he said. 'Let's go.'

A couple of workers were putting up scaffolding in front

of a building. They laughed at something, handing each other tools. *I could have been one of them*, he thought. *Done something constructive, instead of this.*

He looked over his shoulder as they walked towards Barnängen station. The woman with sunglasses was still sitting on the bench. His mind played him another reel of prison memories. The psych eval he'd undergone during his last turn, a so-called 'short psychiatric evaluation', as required by law. *Anti-social tendencies with elements of paranoia.*

He had just laughed at it back then, but maybe there was something to it after all.

The forest they found themselves in was just west of Rön-ninge. There were no houses nearby, only a deserted gravel pit.

They had come in different cars, spacing their arrivals at ten-minute intervals, meeting up at a turnaround where the forest road ended. Thistles and small shrubs sprouted from the ground. The sky was grey as a corpse.

Jorma opened the boxes and put a SIM card in each phone, his hand shaking in a way that was unlike him. *A bad feeling,* he thought. Ever since he woke up . . . ever since they started planning this job. He couldn't explain it.

He tested the phones by calling them. No problems. He turned them off again.

He saw Zoran's determined face out on the turnaround.

'It'll all work out,' he said. 'We've done this before, Zoran, haven't we?'

Jorma climbed out of the car and walked over to Lindros and Fredén and the friend they'd brought along, Gårdnäs. A psychopath type. Jorma could tell just by looking at him. That was one more reason to worry. This guy might lose it if the cops showed up. He said he had spent the last year steal-ing cable from construction sites. He would go out at night with a stripping knife, a car and trailer, and a couple of grams of speed. If he was lucky, he could collect a hundred kilos in one night with his ulcerous, cable-blackened hands. It was a big step forward to be included in a robbery, he explained.

'Listen. Everyone takes a phone. The numbers are in "recent calls". The first one goes to the command centre – that is,

Zoran. Use them only with gloves on and toss them right after the job is done. Zoran and I will take the loot to the safe house. We'll contact you, not the other way around, but you can count on it taking a few weeks for everything to calm down.'

A grey, misty morning. Birdsong in the distance. No audible sounds of people or cars. They were a kilometre from the closest main road.

'I'm super stoked for this!' he heard Gårdnäs say. 'It's making me fucking horny. Makes me wanna fuck, you know? Fuck!'

Jorma walked into the woods to take a piss, and he could smell the sulphurous smell of his own urine. When he came back to the turnaround, Zoran was standing next to the boot of the Audi, unloading weapons: a few hand grenades, two Uzis, an AK-5, and a Czech M-23 submachine gun.

He smothered the bad vibes he got from the grenades.

'What's wrong with you, Jorma, are you nervous?'

Could they see it on him, his anxiety?

'It's fine. I'm focusing.'

Zoran opened the passenger-side door and took a pistol from the glovebox: a Tokarev 7.62.

Jorma's pulse increased as Zoran handed it to him. The butt against his palm. The chill of the barrel. It was incredibly light. He had used a similar one during previous jobs. Could it be the same weapon? Some of them went around and around in circles.

'Take these too. In case we're separated.'

The keys to the apartment. For security reasons, only he and Zoran knew where the hideout was.

'Okay, boys, everyone grab the weapons you need. There's forty-five minutes to go. We'll change now and go through it one last time once everyone has their gear on.'

They looked like a secret task force, he thought a moment later as they were crouching in a circle around Zoran, studying the map he had drawn in the sand with one index finger. All in black, masked, heavily armed.

'The truck will arrive just after ten. We'll get there fifteen minutes before then at the earliest, so we don't attract too much attention. The truck's most recent stop will have been Södertälje, so it's coming from the south, and it will drive in this way . . .' His finger marked a cross in the sand. 'The loading dock is here. The truck will drive into the area behind the security door, where it will be under camera surveillance, so we have to lie really fucking low right then. Jorma and I will be here, thirty metres from the door, in the Audi. Lindros, you'll park across from us and come from the other direction on my signal. When the door opens, which ought to be within five minutes, you'll drive up here and block the exit. Jorma and I will move up behind it so they can't go anywhere.'

The scent of pitch and damp sand. Like in Finland when he was little, on the holidays Harri always managed to ruin.

The rain was falling harder. Zoran's voice had turned into background noise. He gave them further instructions: who should call whom . . . the exact moment they would strike . . . who would get the guard and the driver out of the front seat . . . who would keep them under control . . . when the plastic explosive should be applied . . .

'Questions?' he asked.

'Hell no, let's just get going! Everyone, come on now, dammit!'

'Good. We'll get in the cars in ten minutes.'

The commuter traffic had lessened. They went in a convoy, keeping fifty metres between each of the cars.

Gårdnäs exited at the Statoil station; Jorma could see him slowing down and stopping on a rise with a view of the traffic. He felt his arms grow numb as he leaned back. He slapped them lightly and realized that he was freezing.

The tail lights of Fredén's Saab vanished down onto the exit for northbound traffic. He turned at the intersection by Skärholmen city centre and stopped his car in front of a bus shelter. It was a no-stopping zone, but it was the best place to lay out the caltrops.

Two cars were left in the convoy. Lindros's Volvo and their own Audi. They were approaching the multi-storey carpark, passing the first entrance. There was a camera mounted on a pole, three metres up. But with its fake plates, the car was safe.

Then they were inside the multi-storey. Strange sounds were coming from the engine, sounds that shouldn't be there . . . A figment of his imagination, he thought as he fingered the pistol in his pocket.

Lindros turned off towards the loading dock. Zoran stopped across from it. He turned the key in the ignition. The engine went quiet with a sigh.

'Ten minutes until the truck is here. We'll hold off on the masks so people walking by don't wonder what's going on.'

It had happened too quickly, he thought; they ought to have worked out some attention-diverting tactics, set off a bomb a few kilometres away so any patrol cars would go that way. But there hadn't been time.

'Everything okay, Jorma?'

Those bad vibes were still in the background, like faint tinnitus.

'I don't know.'

'You sure as hell can't back out now.'

'I just have a really bad feeling about this . . .'

'It's like I don't know you, man . . . Here, have a drink!'

He took the mineral water Zoran handed him, drinking half the bottle and burping through his nose. Zoran's phone gave a faint buzz. Gårdnäs was reporting that everything was quiet on the police scanner.

At 10.15, Fredén let them know that the truck was turning off at the shopping centre. There were more people around by now, families on their way to the supermarket, regular shoppers, a dad on paternity leave with a new-born in a baby carrier, passing their car slowly on his way to the stairwell.

The surroundings crowded in on them. The odours of exhaust and warm car engines. The footsteps of a woman walking across concrete in high heels. The beeping of car locks. Shopping trolleys clattering as they were pushed across the floor.

His eyes danced this way and that over the parking level. The two cars over there by the shorter wall and the van over in the far corner . . . had those been there the whole time?

He fumbled for the handgun in his pocket, nudging the Uzi on the floor at his feet. Its barrel was aimed at his stomach.

A grey car drove in and took a right down the ramp. A few pigeons were picking at the filth in front of the loading dock. He could hear music from a car stereo.

Then he saw the armoured truck. It turned up ahead of them, passed at a distance and stopped at the steel door. No escort vehicle, which was a relief. Their insider had managed to prevent that.

The sliding door opened slowly. The brake lights flashed epileptically as the truck slowed down at a ramp. The door closed again, creaking sharply.

A few minutes passed. The roar of traffic on the E4. A strange silence until the door opened again.

'Put on your mask. It's time.'

The vehicle rolled out slowly, as if its driver had become suspicious. The lights of Lindros's car flashed on. *Zoran looks like an insect with his mask on*, Jorma thought as he fumbled for his own; he pulled it over his face and took out his pistol.

It was happening too fast; they weren't even up there yet and Lindros had already blocked the truck and was out of his car. The door was open and he fired five or six shots at the ceiling from his Uzi as he screamed like a madman. Jorma fumbled for the plastic bag of explosive and heard the tyres squeal as Zoran put the pedal to the metal.

The guards tumbled out of the cab with their hands up. One younger guy who seemed to be in shock. One middle-aged man with tears in his eyes. It felt like time stood still even as everything continued to happen, all at once, with no chronological order, with no rhyme or reason.

They had come to the truck. Zoran's jaws grinding in the rear-view mirror, the Rohypnol glaze of his eyes; it was like he was frothing at the mouth. More shots were fired. People were screaming, in full panic mode. Jorma saw a family with small children run for their lives towards the stairwell . . . He saw the headlights of a van flicker on in the distance, sirens blaring very close by, the blue lights on two unmarked cars.

'Go!' he screamed at Zoran. 'Get out of here!'

His neck snapped back with the sudden acceleration as Zoran drove against traffic, towards the entrance ramp, roaring as he leaned on the horn.

He managed to roll down his window and toss the dummy bomb out. Half-jacketed bullets struck the boot of the car.

In the rear-view mirror he could see Lindros being overpowered by cops, and he watched as the unmarked car following them slammed on the brakes in front of the dummy bomb and backed straight into a concrete pillar at high speed. Harri's voice in the back of his head: Finnish curses about how everything was about to go to hell.

It was raining harder. His mother's old neighbourhood flew past the car windows at one hundred and forty kilometres per hour. People stared after them in surprise. Sirens in the distance. It was total chaos at Kungens Kurva.

He grabbed his phone and tried to call Fredén as he vacillated between sweating and freezing. The call went through, but there was no answer. Same with Gårdnäs. Must have been caught.

His heart was pounding violently, as if a terrified animal were trying to kick its way out. He had been right from the start. Something wasn't quite right about this.

'Satan's goddamn fucking cunt!'

They passed a truck on the wrong side of a traffic island. An oncoming Volvo swerved straight into a ditch.

Zoran made another insane pass before turning left onto a smaller road. The ABS kicked in just before the car went into a skid.

Silence. Someone had turned off the volume. He could no longer hear Zoran, he could only see that he was saying something, his mouth moving like a fish behind the glass of an aquarium.

Jorma's window was still open and raindrops were lashing his face. Suddenly the volume returned. 'That fucking cunt ratted us out. That pencil pusher changed his mind and went to the cops. I'm going to fucking murder that arsehole.'

The sirens were getting louder. Jorma peered at the rear-view mirror: blue lights five hundred metres away.

A motorcycle was coming straight at them as Zoran cut another curve. He managed to swerve at the last second, slowing down as they approached the intersection in Vårby.

'Get out of the car, for God's sake!'

Zoran was holding a hand grenade in one fist and the Uzi in the other. He was waving them around like a madman. There was a strange noise in the distance; Jorma recognized it but couldn't place it and looked around in confusion as Zoran started pouring petrol from a plastic can all over the upholstery.

Suddenly the Audi was burning before him. It crackled as plastic and fabric melted. The wall of heat forced him to back up. He tossed the Tokarev through the open window. There were too many cops; they would never be able to shoot their way out.

That noise again – and this time he realized what it was. He raised his eyes and saw it, five hundred metres away: the hovering police helicopter.

Time was chopped up into tiny little pieces. He hadn't known it was happening, but they had run to the getaway car in the car park. Its tyres had been slashed.

'No fucking way! We have to get out of here!'

The odour of burning rubber. Flames from the intersection, where the car was burning. People in nearby buildings were throwing their windows open to see what was going on.

'Move, for Chrissake!'

Zoran tugged at him and made him run for the woods and the rocky hill. A police van had stopped at the intersection; he heard dogs barking, German shepherds, he thought. How the hell had they managed to dispatch a K9 unit so quickly?

They made it to the woods. He looked for a way around the hill but couldn't find one. Just a narrow path, straight over the rocks. He heard the sickly sound of his own lungs panting as he went uphill; he fought his way through the half overgrown path as branches and brush hit him in the face.

More barking. Cops calling through megaphones in the distance . . . They ought to split up; it would be better for one of them to get away than neither of them.

Twenty-five metres on there was a fork in the path. Zoran went to the right, towards a valley. He threw down his Uzi and the hand grenades before he vanished among the trees. Jorma was flooded with relief; they wouldn't shoot unarmed robbers.

He made it to the crest and continued along a ridge. This was a sparse beech forest. He found himself in something like a bower, where the light filtered down in thin columns. He could tell that the helicopter was above the treetops further off, but the pilot couldn't see him.

He sank to the ground to catch his breath. Lake Mälaren was about a kilometre to the west. A boat, he thought. If he could steal a boat . . .

He couldn't hear the dogs anymore, just the helicopter moving across the forested area.

Then he heard Zoran's voice in the distance – a sudden scream.

He jogged in the direction of the sound and found himself in a passage between some juniper bushes. He stopped short and took shelter. He was gasping for breath, suddenly terrified, though he didn't understand why.

He heard a faint mewling sound twenty metres off. He leaned forward.

He saw a tall man in a bulletproof vest.

A robber, he thought at first. The man was wearing a black cap and a mask with holes for the eyes; he adjusted it with the back of his hand as if it didn't quite fit. He was wearing gloves and dark clothing just like their own.

He was aiming a silenced handgun at Zoran. In his other hand was the Uzi Zoran had just ditched.

Zoran was on the ground, bleeding from his thigh. Shot.

The man in the mask ejected the magazine from the Uzi and calmly emptied the ammunition. He stuck the bullets in the pocket of his dark jacket and replaced the magazine. Then he aimed the weapon into the woods and fired the remaining bullets in quick succession before handing it back to Zoran.

The silence seemed unreal. The man nodded, almost politely, Jorma thought. He pulled off one glove and stretched his hand.

It was as if Jorma were living thirty seconds in the future, as if he were experiencing everything just before it happened. Something about the man's hand bothered him. Zoran looked in surprise at the unloaded Uzi the cop had given him.

The man shot him right in the forehead. The smacking sound as his skull crushed in, the halo of blood that spread out in an almost perfectly round pool, the greyish-red clumps of brain matter on his clothes.

Zoran's expression of surprise – the last he would see of him.

Gone. It was inconceivable.

The man placed one of the hand grenades in Zoran's lifeless hand and the other in Zoran's pocket. Then he walked calmly back towards the hill. Stopped. Turned around.

They were directly in one another's line of vision. They looked at each other for a split second before Jorma darted for cover and started running.

He rounded a pond and followed a path straight west. Cold sweat was running down his back. He felt a wave of nausea come over him and swallowed the sour liquid back down.

This is not happening, he thought. And yet it was happening.

Flowers grew along the path, and the autumn's last butterflies fluttered past. Birds were singing nearby; they sounded tinny, as if they were coming from a radio.

Zoran . . . He couldn't wrap his head around it.

He fell, hardly noticing as it happened. His foot caught on a protruding tree root and he landed chest-first on the ground. There was a stabbing pain in his leg, but he didn't realize he'd hurt his knee until he stood up.

The pain cut through the adrenaline. He bit his cheek. He limped another twenty metres down the path before stopping to remove his jacket. He tossed it in among the trees on the right side of the path, to confuse the dogs, and then he doubled back along his own trail. He stopped at a gap between two spruces on the left side and walked in between them. The branches closed behind him like a curtain.

He went on through what looked like an overgrown park, passed a few large houses in the distance, and found himself at the lake.

The trees grew all the way up to the shoreline, poplars and hazels. He looked out over the channel; it was too far to swim.

The cold penetrated his legs as he waded out, easing the pain in his knee and helping to clear his thoughts. Raindrops were sprinkling down, reproducing themselves as rings on the surface of the water. He could smell mud and damp sand.

He waded fifty metres in so the dogs would lose his scent before moving back towards the shore and continuing north.

Every time he took a step, it felt like someone was jabbing a screwdriver into the back of his knee and turning it full force.

Another bay came into view, with a caisson dock a bit further on. Right behind that was a rowboat. Homes perched on the slope above.

He approached the boat cautiously, as if it might go up in smoke if he moved too quickly. He swore under his breath. No oars. He looked around for a barge pole of some sort, hoping he could try to pole his way across the channel.

He could hear the helicopter again, but he was having a hard time judging its position. The barking was coming closer . . . men's voices, shouting. He was sorry he'd ditched his handgun; he wouldn't be able to defend himself if the masked cop showed up again.

He left the shore, limping up the slope towards the houses, rounded a thick boxwood bush, and stopped at a gravel path. A white Mercedes was backing out of a garage.

He spotted the helicopter through a gap in the trees, three hundred metres away, over the water. A gigantic, metal dragonfly. The wind from the rotors was so strong that it was whipping a crater into the water.

Barking in the distance, cop voices yelling hysterically on megaphones.

He hated dogs; he'd always been afraid of them.

He picked up a rock from the ground, walked over to the garage, stopped behind the car. A woman was looking at him in fright through the rear-view mirror.

'Get out, dammit!' he shouted. 'Do you hear me? Get out! Now, for fuck's sake!'

He yanked open the driver-side door before she could react, and he pulled her out and sat down at the wheel. The engine was still running. The barking was fainter. They had gone the wrong way, turning south when they lost his scent at the shore.

PART 2

The gang was standing further down Trondheimsgatan. They were up to something. They had formed a circle around a younger, dark-haired guy.

Suburb gangsters, Katz thought. Just like him, back in the day.

The one he assumed was the leader was a bit older than the others, maybe eighteen.

'Give me the phone!' he said to the kid in the ring.

The boy took a mobile phone from his trouser pocket and handed it to him.

'Do you have money?'

'No.'

'Breathe, man . . . look at your hands. Shit, man, they're shaking.'

The older boy turned to the others. 'This *shunne*'s pissed himself!'

The boy was crying heartbreakingly as he held his hand over his face, ashamed. Dirty fingers, black under the nails. His jeans were wet at the crotch. It seemed to be a robbery. Gangs stealing phones from little kids.

'You are our slave, got it? You've got more things to do for us.'

Katz put out his cigarette and walked over to them. The leader kid noticed him when he was five metres away.

'What do you want?'

'Just to have a little chat.'

'What the fuck you doing here?'

Looking for Ramón, he thought. An old junkie friend. The guy had saved his life after an overdose one time. Katz had run into him by chance in the city centre, surprised to learn that he was still alive. He'd got his address, and apparently that was all it took to trigger his craving.

'Who are you . . . *aina* or something? A cop? Get out of here or you'll have major problems.'

The guy had a tattoo on the knuckles of his right hand, three Gothic-style letters: FTL – Fuck The Law. He probably belonged to an older gang. This was just something he did on the side, training up little kids, steering them into a network of criminals.

'Does the boy owe you something?' Katz asked calmly.

'He's our *bossen*, our slave.'

'Okay. What do you want for him? A thousand?'

'Like we're gonna pawn off our slave? Fuck off. Final warning.'

The guy fumbled for something in his jacket pocket – in the worst case, a knife. Katz wondered if he should deck him before it was too late. *Not a kid*, he thought. *I can't hit a child.* Then he saw what the guy had been after: a pack of gum.

He felt the draw of heroin again. The longing for that warmth, that indescribable sense of homecoming as the drug entered his bloodstream. Like meeting God, he had thought thirty years earlier when he took his virgin hit, when he was even younger than the boy in front of him.

'Here.' He fished two five-hundred-kronor bills from his wallet. 'I'm buying him.'

The leader started to laugh, but stopped when he saw the Star of David around Katz's neck.

Bad plan. He might as well have been wearing a yarmulke and blowing a shofar for Rosh Hashanah, the Jewish New Year.

'Okay, Jew-man,' said the leader guy as he took a step forward and grabbed the bills. 'You can borrow him. Pound him in the arse. Sell him to the Israeli army if you want. They like that shit, you know . . . torturing kids. We'll take him back soon anyway.'

The gang vanished off towards the city centre. Cracking voices shouted something incomprehensible in immigrant Swedish. The boy was still standing there in front of him, hands over his eyes.

This was all just an evasive manoeuvre so he wouldn't feel the pull of heroin, Katz thought as he walked down towards Järvafältet with the boy. He had stopped crying and was just sniffling a bit, looking uncertainly at the grown man by his side.

'Are you from around here?' Katz asked. 'From Husby?'

'Nearby.'

'What about the others?'

'I don't know. I don't know them.'

'What's your name?'

'Alexandru.'

'Tell me, Alexandru, what was that all about?'

It was a type of kidnapping. The gang had bought the boy from a different gang a few weeks earlier, and had used him to buy goods on skimmed credit cards. They had promised him money, a certain percentage, but he hadn't received any so far. He lived with his mother and two younger siblings in a tent camp outside Akalla. They were Roma, and had come to Sweden from Romania one year earlier. The boy's mother had contacted a relative in Stockholm who'd said he could line up jobs. But there weren't any. She and a girlfriend supported the family by begging and collecting empty cans.

'What about your dad?' Katz asked.

'He took off to Italy when I was little. I hardly remember him.'

They turned onto a different street. Oslogatan – every street out here had a Norwegian name. Katz remembered that from the news reports about the uprisings last spring. This suburb had exploded into violence. Young people who had no great prospects for the future had burned cars and gone on the attack against riot police. Katz understood them better than he wanted to admit . . . the feeling of having been sentenced to a life on the fringe. And yet there was always someone further down the ladder.

'Don't you go to school?' he asked in Romany. *'Pirés ande e scoala?'*

Alexandru smiled at him. 'Where'd you learn that?'

'In the place where I grew up. There was a Roma boy there, and he taught me Romany. *Pen mange akaná.* Now answer me . . . do you go to school?'

'Sometimes. A couple of teachers hold lessons in an apartment on the weekends. Swedish Roma. They do it for free. But it's not a real school; you have to have a residency permit to be allowed to go there.'

'Well, you've learned Swedish quickly, anyway.'

'I had to. Mum only speaks Romanian and Romany . . . but she's sick. Something to do with her stomach. I have to help her and interpret when we visit the doctor. She's always afraid – that the police will tear down our camp again, or that they'll send us back.'

The boy was dirty; it had probably been a long time since he'd had a shower. Cheap trainers. A threadbare down jacket, ill-fitting jeans . . . charity clothes. His front teeth were crooked; he needed braces.

'Do you know the names of the guys in that gang?'

'Yeah, some of them.'

'The leader, for example, the one I gave the money to?'
'Miro.'

'Do you know how I can get hold of him?'

'I don't know where he lives. They took charge over me from some guys in Akalla, so he could be from there. Or from here. I've seen him on the square a few times, with older guys. Ones with tattoos.'

Career criminals, Katz thought. It had worked the same way in his day. Young guys from the suburbs ran errands for the older ones, handling stolen goods, holding on to weapons and drugs because they weren't of age and couldn't be convicted. They learned to skip school picture day so they would be harder to identify. He and Jorma Hedlund had done the very same thing once upon a time . . .

Jorma. He could have used his friend now, someone to tell him it was a bad idea to visit Ramón. But he hadn't answered his phone for the past week.

They had reached Järvafältet. The high-rises of Hjulsta looked like a mountain range far off to the west. To the south, Tensta and Rinkeby were visible. The old northern-suburb ghettoes.

'Have you seen your mother since they took you?' Katz asked.

'They let me go at night once I've collected their stuff. Then they pick me up in the morning, where we live. Usually someone is standing there waiting. I told Mum we were friends.'

He looked down at the ground, as if in shame.

'What else is it, besides telephones?'

'Clothes. Sunglasses . . . Sometimes they rent me out to other people. Once it was to a couple of junkies who wanted me to do something for them.'

'What was that?'

'It doesn't matter, because it never happened.'

The boy gave him a resigned look.

'Mum wants to go home again, it's not anything like we thought it would be here. But we can't. My older sister is gone. She ran away after they had a fight. It's been five months, and we have to find her first.'

Katz took a business card from his wallet and handed it to him.

'Call me if you need help. With those guys, for example. I get that you don't want to go to the police. But what would happen if you got caught?'

The boy nodded as if he hadn't realized what was on the line until just now: his family would unavoidably be dragged in, his mum, his sisters.

'So I can trust you?'

'I'll have a chat with that Miro, and after that he'll leave you alone.'

Katz stayed where he was as the boy vanished through a pedestrian tunnel. He seemed so fragile as he walked. His back was bent under his troubles; his steps were heavy and uncertain.

The blinds were pulled and the windows on one side were covered in cardboard. The apartment was on the ground floor of a five-storey building.

Katz punched in the door code and walked into the stairwell. Ten years since he had got clean. He didn't know what he was doing there.

I ought to be at home, he thought as he listened to the television sounds from inside the apartment, *immersing myself in my work*. For the past month he had been working as a security consultant for a Norwegian telecoms company that was expanding into Russia. They had their own sysops, but none had sufficient command of Slavic languages, so Katz had got the job. He had translated manuals that could now be read in Russian, Polish, and Czech. He had inspected the programs' source code and checked the servers for traces of unauthorized access, backdoors installed by hackers, or strange activity in the firewall log files. He had phished the employees to check out how easy it was to open a port. He had run into Ramón outside a lunch place in the city centre during a break from work and it had been like a trip back in time.

The volume on the TV was turned down when he rang the doorbell. Someone shuffled across the room and peered at him through the peephole.

'Who is it?'

It was a hoarse, drawling junkie voice.

'Katz . . . a friend of Ramón's.'

The rattle of a security chain being unlatched. The woman

who opened the door was in her mid-twenties. She had nicely chiselled facial features. Long brown hair. Blue almond-shaped eyes. She was beautiful, if you ignored her chalky junkie skin.

'Come in,' she said. 'Ramón said you would be coming by.'

He followed her into something resembling a living room. She plopped down on a stained sofa. Her paraphernalia was on the table in front of her: spoon, syringes, a bottle of water. A suitcase stood nearby. A can of pepper spray was poking out of its outer pocket.

'How do you know Ramón?' she asked.

'From before.'

'I've never seen you, so it must have been a long time ago.'

'We hung out in the same circles for a while. Over a decade ago. How do *you* know him?'

'We met at a shelter. I was streetwalking, and Ramón sold junk. Romantic, huh? He's somewhere nearby. You'll have to look around.'

There were no windows at all in the next room. Katz fumbled for a light switch and turned on the ceiling light. In one corner was a shopping trolley full of stolen car stereos. Spatters of blood on the wallpaper, diluted with water, left by people cleaning out their syringes.

The woman was cooking horse in a soup spoon when he returned to the living room. A couple of pencil drawings lay on the floor next to her: self-portraits, surprisingly naturalistic. One of them included Ramón.

'I went to art school for a while,' she said as she sucked the solution into a syringe. 'You can, like, see people better if you draw them – their posture, their facial expressions . . . their soul.'

She gently pressed down the plunger to get rid of the last few air bubbles, then inspected her arms for a good vein.

'Can you leave me alone?' she said. 'I hate it when people watch me shoot up.'

Katz continued his search in the kitchen. Piles of ad circulars lay on the floor. There were dirty dishes everywhere. The image of the cooking drugs lingered in his mind.

He opened the door to a bathroom. Something long and thin moved on the floor behind the toilet. It took a second for him to realize what it was: a snake. *Junkies and all their animals.*

When he returned to his starting point, the woman had rolled up her trousers and was using the cord of the TV as a tourniquet. Katz remembered his own shamelessness, how he had been transformed into a receptacle for the drug, just a vessel for heroin. He felt the craving again. Tried to resist it.

'Fucking A, I can't find a vein! I have to get this shit in me now.'

At last she got a flash, in her calf; she drew blood as a cold sweat dripped down her forehead, pressed the plunger all the way down, booting to get every last microgram. She had a butterfly tattoo right over the injection site. A yellow swallowtail. It looked like she had skewered it with the needle.

Then she put down the syringe and blinked at him sleepily. A thin rivulet of blood ran down her leg. He heard a sound from the other end of the hallway: someone was coughing. A door he hadn't noticed before was ajar.

This room was neater than the others. Two easy chairs and a small desk stood by the covered window. Paperback books in a bookcase. A plastic crucifix and a Chilean flag hung over the door. Ramón was sitting on a mattress on the floor, looking like he'd just woken up. Fifteen years earlier they had done burglaries together, apartments and suburban homes, stealing food from shops when they were desperate, beef fillets that they sold to restaurants staffed by Chilean friends of Ramón's. They had stayed in shelters or places like this one. Ramón, a Catholic, had worn a silver cross around his neck. Katz wore a Star of David. Ramón had jokingly called him 'Christ-killer'. The guy had been a bit of a pathological liar, Katz recalled. He would lie about anything, big or small – not unusual in junkie circles; people felt the need to embellish their life stories. Later he had prostituted himself, but that was after they'd lost contact in the endless chaos of the junkie lifestyle. Katz had heard rumours that he had sold himself to rich gay men.

'Sorry, I didn't hear you,' he said. 'Have you been here long?'

'A while. I chatted a bit with your girl out there.'

'Jenny . . . Nice, right?' He took a sip of water from a glass on the floor. 'And artistic. If she hadn't doped her life away, I think she could have been something. I really fucking like her . . . Did you meet Harry too?'

'Who?'

'The snake. Haven't seen him for a while. Shit, it was so great to run into you the other day. Didn't think you were still alive.'

There were a dozen packs of heroin on a piece of glass on the desk. Next to those was a digital scale for weighing the powder. And substances for diluting it. Phenazone powder, finely crushed paracetamol. It seemed that Ramón cut the drugs himself.

'Got some business going,' he said when he realized what Katz was looking at. 'I got lucky, for a change. None of that fucking brown shit you have to dissolve with citric acid. It's up to me to decide how strong to make it.'

He winked as he stood up. There was a mobile phone on the rug next to him. He poked it under the mattress with his foot.

'My girl and I came into some money a while ago. More or less by chance. And if you've got money, you should invest it, right? Try to start up a business. We've even got a stockpile. Don't want too much of it at home in case the cops show up. Maybe we could work together again?'

Katz remembered the incident in the bathroom at Burger King on Medborgarplatsen fifteen years earlier. The miserable state he'd found himself in. His filthy down jacket, baggy jeans, his body so emaciated he looked like a human skeleton. Ramón had loaned him the paraphernalia because he'd lost his own. He had cooked the junk over the sink, drawing the solution into the syringe through the filter of a cigarette. He had bought the stuff from a dealer he knew. Then he was suddenly hit by withdrawal. He had rushed himself, making the dose stronger than usual.

Ramón grew suspicious when he didn't come out after fifteen minutes. He had managed to talk the staff into opening the door. They found him unconscious on the floor, bleeding from a wound on his forehead. Ramón told him later that they had been paralyzed, terrified of a junkie's blood after years of propaganda about the risk of infection from HIV-positive drug addicts. Ramón had been the one to give him CPR until the ambulance finally showed up. Katz had been clinically dead for several minutes before they stuck him with a shot of adrenaline and his heart started beating again on the ambulance ride to Södra Hospital . . .

'You're a smart guy, Danny. Weren't you a military interpreter? You know a bunch of languages and all that. Seriously, you could get in on this, become a partner! Who knows how big it will become.'

Ramón walked over to the desk, grabbed a few packs and a plastic-sealed syringe, and handed them to Katz.

'See for yourself,' he said. 'But it's strong, so take it easy.'

Katz got another glimpse of Jenny through the door to the living room. She was lying on the sofa, numb. She looked like she was sleeping, though he knew she was wide awake behind her half-closed eyes, that the horse had transported her miles into her own body. She had changed into different clothes. An expensive-looking grey jumpsuit. He assumed she was going out to work.

He took the drugs and stuck them in his pocket.

'First time's free, Katz, you know the deal. We want satisfied customers.'

Ramón flashed him a businesslike smile, then bent down under the desk and fiddled with something. He stood up and gave him a few more packs.

'In case you want to share with friends,' he said. 'Test it out and see if you want in on this train. Anyone who uses this will definitely be back to buy more.'

The guy named Miro and two men were waiting for him in the walkway outside the house. The men appeared to be around thirty. Wearing hoodies and camouflage trousers. One of them had a dragon tattooed on his neck. The other was morbidly obese.

'Got a problem?' said the man with the tattoo.

'Sorry?'

'I said, do you got a problem?'

Katz took a step back.

'Have you been shopping at the Chilean's?' said the other. 'Or were you just doing the junkie slut?'

'I know Ramón. Why do you ask?'

'Tragic dude. Horse junkie. Thinks he's a drug kingpin.'

The man with the tattoo smiled.

'What about you? You went off with a young boy a little bit ago. Bought him for a thou. Are you a paedophile?'

Katz didn't respond. He looked around for an escape route but there was none. He felt the draw again, the easy way out, because you didn't give a shit about anything, could withstand anything.

'The old man's a Jew,' said Miro. 'And Alexandru is a gypsy.'

'Everyone's welcome here. Even Jews and gypsies . . . if they have cash. What did you want with that kid, Alexandru? Did you screw him?'

Katz looked at the man. He was carrying a gun. He just knew it. His years on the street had taught him all about that sort of crap.

'Give me your wallet.'

The man put out his hand, and Katz did as he was asked.

'Now go home. And next time you come around here, leave your Jew star in the city, at the Jew bank where you work. I don't give a shit about that sort of thing. But it bothers other people.'

They turned around and walked onto the street. They thought he was afraid, that he had shit his pants in fear. They slowly disappeared back towards the city centre. He heard Miro laughing at something. He heard the word 'Jew' again – *Jew fag . . . Jew druggie . . .*

Katz followed Edvard Griegsgången to the square. Sani Pizzeria, Riadh Gold & Watchmaker, Salam's Asian Food. He passed a barbershop and a sign that read 'Daytime care for Iranian elders'.

At the corner store, he bought a U-lock for a bike, using two crumpled hundred-kronor bills that were left in his pocket.

Then back to the street again. He looked over towards the doorway he'd seen Miro and the men disappear into. The pepper spray was still in his pocket; he had gone back to the apartment to get it. The door had been unlocked and Ramón had been asleep on the sofa next to Jenny.

A woman with a pram opened the door on her way out. Katz let her go by before he slipped inside.

He checked the list of occupants. Twenty names. Could be any one of them.

Fifteen minutes passed, and nothing happened. No movement in the house. He peered out at the corner shop across the street through the glass of the door. The billboards were all about the robbery of an armoured truck in Skärholmen. The woman with the pram came back carrying a bag of shopping. She nodded at him before vanishing into the lift.

One storey up, a door opened. Two boys of around ten came down the stairs, carrying a bike. They stopped when they saw him.

'Who are you waiting for?'

'Miro.'

'There's no Miro here.'

'His friend has a tattoo on his neck. Of a dragon.'

'I know who you mean. Ivan. He lives on four.'

The boys disappeared. Katz checked the names on the board again. Ivanović. Fourth floor.

This ought to be the one, he thought a few minutes later as he stood outside the door. He could hear loud hip-hop music coming through the letter box. The sweet smell of marijuana. Stickers of the Serbian double-headed eagle on the door. The apartment was at the end of the hall. It was dark. Katz had unscrewed the lightbulb in the stairwell.

He rang the bell. The door opened. The man with the tattoo didn't have time to react before Katz had yanked him into the hallway and sprayed him in the eyes. The man yowled like a cat and held his hands to his face as Katz closed the door with his foot and dragged him towards the stairs by the hair. He slammed the spray bottle into his skull, three quick jabs at his temple, and kneed him in the face.

Where did that come from? he thought as he watched the man lying on the floor, blood pumping from a deep gash in his head; that rage he had carried around for as long as he could remember, the fury he tried to keep under control, just as Benjamin had tried to do for all those years.

The man was groggy, almost unconscious. Katz hauled him over to the stairwell and closed the U-lock around his neck, fastening him to the railing. In the man's pockets he found a bunch of keys, his wallet, and a pistol – a Glock.

Heavy beats were coming from the apartment. The others

hadn't realized anything was up so far. So he opened the door and walked in.

Miro and the fat man were sitting on a leather sofa in the living room. They stared at him as if he were a ghost. Katz yanked the plug to the stereo out of the wall. The silence sounded like a rumble in reverse.

'Take it easy, mate! Just tell us what you want!'

He heard Miro's voice as if from a great distance. He noticed that Miro was staring at the gun in his bloody hand, his finger on the trigger. He had been a millimetre from firing it.

'Put your hand on your knee!' he said to the fat man.

'What the fuck for?'

'Just do it!'

The man did as he was told. Katz took the syringe from his pocket, peeling off the plastic with his teeth.

'Sit still!'

The man obeyed him like a robot. Maybe they thought their friend was dead. The guy's fresh blood was all over Katz's clothes. He drove the needle full-force through the back of the man's hand and into his thigh. He heard him squeal like a stuck pig.

'What the fuck are you doing? Are you insane?'

He shoved the barrel of the gun into his mouth and turned to Miro.

'I want you to leave that boy alone. Alexandru. You're not going to get anywhere near him. You don't recognize him if you see him on the street. Take a damn long detour if you catch sight of him. The same goes for your buddies. And no one gets close to Ramón.'

'Okay, okay . . . they can go.'

'Say it again!'

He pressed the gun deeper into the fat man's mouth and saw the gag reflex as the barrel reached his throat.

'We'll leave Alexandru alone, and Ramón too, I swear on my family!'

'Good. To be on the safe side, I'll be calling them to make sure. Or else I'll come out here myself to check. And that's not a threat; it's a promise.'

A little while later he was down in the metro station. He pulled up the sleeve of his jacket, looking at the scars left by old injection sites, running all the way from his wrist to his armpit. He thought of the fat man still sitting on the sofa as he left, his hand drilled through by a syringe needle that was lodged in his thigh muscles, like the toothpick in a club sandwich.

The train for Kungsträdgården rolled into the platform. Katz tossed the keys to the U-lock into a dustbin before he got on. He wondered how long that guy would have to sit there, stuck to the railing, before someone sawed him loose.

The Glock was chafing in his inner pocket. He would get rid of it as soon as possible.

He felt disgusted with himself, disgusted at the blood spatter on his jacket and hands. He thought about the New Year – it was the year 5774 according to the calendar – and he thought about how it was almost Yom Kippur, the festival when you were to ask your fellow humans for forgiveness.

The synagogue was on Sankt Paulsgatan. A couple of Hebrew letters in the window above the door were the only giveaway that this was an old Jewish shul.

Once upon a time this place had been a neighbourhood cinema. The women sat by themselves in the gallery; the men sat on the ground floor.

The service had just begun when Katz arrived. The cantor was singing from the *bimah*. Men in shawls, *tefillin* fastened to their foreheads and around their arms, were standing at their benches in prayer. A blue-painted Star of David shimmered near the ceiling. A golden menorah as tall as a man presided from the centre of the space.

Katz hung up his jacket, took a yarmulke from the box, and sat down at his father's old reserved seat in the very back of the temple.

Benjamin had kept his prayer books in the compartment in front of him: the *Siddur*, *Chumash*, and *Haftarah*. His prayer shawl had lain there too. Paradoxically, Benjamin had not been particularly religious in his everyday life. He didn't bother to keep kosher. He had a civil marriage, with a *shiksa*. And yet he had attended the Orthodox synagogue on Sankt Paulsgatan every Friday since the late thirties, when he came from Austria with his parents, Chaim and Sara. They disappeared shortly after the end of the war; they had emigrated to Israel and were never heard from again, at least not as far as Katz was aware.

Benjamin stayed behind. The son of a cobbler from

Vienna who spoke four languages fluently when he arrived in Sweden, just sixteen years old. He had studied philology at Uppsala University, earned a degree in classical languages, did a few years of research before he married Katz's Norrlandic mother, had a son in his late forties, and started teaching French and Latin in schools in the Stockholm area. But his positions never lasted very long. They changed addresses a dozen times before Katz even turned ten. Benjamin always managed to make enemies of people. In the last school he worked at, he was fired for beating up a caretaker so badly that he ended up in hospital.

Katz had been fourteen when his father died of lung cancer. Benjamin had smoked like a chimney his whole life; he even smoked on his deathbed. Katz remembered visiting him at the hospice centre at Ersta Hospital a few weeks before his death. The incredibly depressing grey weather outside the windows. Benjamin, who could only breathe with the aid of oxygen. A pack of red Commerce cigarettes had been on the nightstand. He was holding one in his hand; it had a long snake of ash at the tip. All that was left of him was skin and bones. And his temper: Katz remembered the way he bawled out the nurses.

He couldn't remember ever having been afraid of him, not even when he smashed up their home and then broke down, sobbing, in his wife's arms.

Anne, Katz's mother, was from a village in Jämtland, up north. She broke off contact with her family to marry Benjamin. Her father had been pro-German during the war. Katz had never met his relatives on his mother's side. He didn't even know their names.

Anne died shortly after his father. She stopped eating and wasted away at a nursing home, leaving Katz alone in the world because her sorrow at losing Benjamin was stronger than her love for her son. At least, that was what he had believed at the time.

Katz had been sent to a youth home in Hässelby. He met Jorma Hedlund and Eva Westin – or Dahlman, as she had been called then – and wound up involved with gang crime and addiction but was saved by his gift for languages and computers. He was hand-picked for military interpreter training, worked as an interpreter and eventually an intelligence officer, served as a data analyst in the National Defence Radio Establishment, and was stationed in St Petersburg and Berlin. He returned to Stockholm, but fell back into the mire of drugs. He spent nearly a decade homeless before managing to rise to the surface again. He had been clean for just over ten years. He ran a small IT and translation firm in Traneberg and lived in a one-bedroom apartment above the office. He didn't bring in all that much money, but it was enough for a simple life without luxuries.

Recently, he had been thinking more and more about his dark years. People had tried to help him. Jorma Hedlund had let him sleep at his apartment when he wanted to, and had overlooked it when Katz stole his money to buy drugs. Rickard Julin, his old boss from the military, who later betrayed him and died as a result of the Klingberg Affair, had also extended a helping hand. But Katz hadn't wanted help. He had wanted to sink away.

His thoughts hopped here and there throughout his memory as he sat on his father's old bench. His bar mitzvah had culminated in that pulpit as he read from the Torah, the year before Benjamin died. His father had stood next to him, beaming with pride. Anne had been with the women in the gallery, throwing sweets at Katz just as tradition dictated. Dumle lollies, he recalled. And raspberry fudge.

In another memory, his father was sitting at the kitchen

table and crying, in only his underwear. It was night, and the sound had awoken Katz. He heard his father saying that he had been forced to kill a man for the sake of a passport. Katz was only eight or nine at the time, and he didn't completely trust his memory. But he realized it had something to do with his family history, with their escape from Austria.

The rabbi took the Torah scroll from the cabinet and made a counter-clockwise round through the hall. The men kissed the case; Katz too. Since he'd started coming here six months earlier, he had been met by curiosity and questions about who he was. He had met people who remembered Benjamin. They were old now. Leo Silberstein. Abraham Josefsson. He had tried to angle for what had really happened to his paternal grandparents but hadn't got much in the way of answers.

A little while later, the service was over. The women came down the stairs from the gallery, and he heard people speaking Yiddish and Swedish in turns. Men in yarmulkes and prayer shawls sent friendly nods his way. Katz saw a few boys with sidelocks; they came from a deeply religious family. They looked like his father in the old black-and-white photographs, when he was attending yeshiva in Vienna.

He put on his jacket in the hallway, patting his pocket to check the packs of heroin. The craving had left him, as if it were tired of his hesitation and had decided to go and track down an easier target. He would return to Husby and give the drugs back to Ramón. Forget it all and move on. It was important. He wouldn't throw the drugs away, he would put them back where he found them. Prove to himself he was in control, that his drug abuse was history.

He was just about to leave when someone tapped him on the back.

'*Shana tova*, Danny! Happy New Year!'

It was an older man whom he didn't recognize.

'*L'shana tova tikatevu*,' he replied.

'Not bad. Your Hebrew is better than mine. I don't believe you remember me, but I remember you. David Frydman.'

The man put out his hand and Katz shook it.

'Silberstein told me you'd started coming here. We certainly are happy about that. Soon us old guys will be gone. And as you know, we need at least ten men to hold a service . . . It's important to have replacements, and not just in the big synagogue in the city centre. Last time I talked to you, you were thirteen, at your mitzvah.'

The man supported himself with a cane. Katz studied his wrinkled face. He was older than he'd first thought.

'Can you guess how old I am?' he asked, as if he had read Katz's mind.

'I wouldn't dare.'

'I was born in 1923, the year after your father.'

The man gave a sad smile.

'You knew my dad?'

'Benji Katz? Did I ever. Your father was an honourable man. He didn't take shit from anybody. He stood up for who he was.'

'I'm glad you remember him that way.'

The man had placed a hand on his forearm, squeezing it gently as if to reassure himself that Katz wasn't planning to slip away.

'Are you staying for coffee? We have *kreplach* and sandwiches. You like *kreplach*, don't you, Danny?'

'I don't know if I have time.'

'I can tell you about your father . . .'

A few moments later, Katz was sitting at a table in the big hall, drinking tea and eating chicken pierogies as Frydman told him about Benjamin.

'We came to Sweden the same year, Benji and I, 1938. He came from Vienna and I came from Salzburg. One year later, when the war broke out, the escape route was closed. We met here at the synagogue; our seats were next to each other. I looked up to him like a big brother.'

'Why was that?'

'He was like no one I'd ever met before. Charisma, I would call it today.' Frydman smiled sadly before he went on. 'Benji had everything the rest of us Jewish boys could only dream of: a good physique, self-confidence, no respect for *goyim*. He was fearless. He broke the noses of more Nazis in this city than you could count. By the way, did you know that he lived with his parents up in the Jewish house on Klippgatan those first few years?'

'I don't even know what that is.'

Frydman chuckled gently.

'It was a collective for people who had fled pogroms and other horrors. It was founded by Mr and Mrs Heckscher at the turn of the last century . . . they were Jewish patrons who had been established in Stockholm for generations. Not like us poor Jews who came to Sweden perfectly destitute with one suitcase in hand. It was like a little *shtetl* up there, with a view of Vitaberg Park. People spoke half a dozen different languages together, but mostly it was Yiddish. Jews from Germany, Poland, Romania, Austria, Czechoslovakia. You could get clothes, food, and a roof over your head. People would be placed out into society as they began to learn how it functioned. Today's politicians would have loved it, except maybe for the Sweden Democrats.'

The old man grew silent and looked at the air, as if something invisible were going on there.

'Benji learned Swedish as soon as he got here. And he caught up with and surpassed his Swedish schoolmates before anyone knew what was happening. He had a true gift for study, but he wasn't just some Jewish bookworm with Coke-bottle glasses and flat feet.'

'Sounds like stereotypes to my ears.'

'And they are. But I'm too old to get rid of them, even if I wanted to.' Frydman looked at him with a serious expression. 'The problem was that there weren't enough men like your father in those years, prepared to defend themselves and their people. Benji took boxing lessons at Narva, down on Frejgatan. He had a commanding presence. He flirted with *shiksas*. He smoked like a chimney, but you know that already. He defended us in fights. The Söder gangs liked to harass us. Hooligans from Katarina Real who supported the Germans. They didn't stand a chance against your father, he took them down in no time. And the *goyim* would run off, noses bleeding, to our delight. Benji took care of his parents, too, your grandparents. He helped them contact the authorities . . . It wasn't a given that they would be allowed to stay here.'

'Why not?'

'They had come here on fake exit permits. The documents your father arranged in Austria, all on his own, at sixteen. He didn't like to talk about that, and I didn't want to pressure him. But I understood enough to know that he was the one who organized the family's escape and that it cost him a great deal . . . which made me look up to him even more.'

Frydman chuckled again and placed a hand on Katz's shoulder.

'What happened with my grandparents? They went to Israel after the war.'

'Yes. Your father was angry with Chaim and Sara, but I don't know why. He claimed that Chaim was a typical ghetto Jew and a *shlimazl*.'

'Like a bad-luck magnet.'

'*Verter zol men vegn un nit tseyln*, as we say in Yiddish. Words should be weighed, not counted. And Benji always meant what he said.'

'But he didn't tell you any more than that?'

'No. Your grandparents emigrated right after the war and after that I didn't spend time with him anymore. We would only see each other very briefly, at *Shabbat* and around the holidays, here at Adat Jisrael. If you're curious, I think you should ask Boris Epstein.'

'Who?'

'Your father's best friend during those years. A staunch atheist. He would never set foot in temple, not even if the Messiah sent a personal invitation. He lives in a retirement home in Sumpan, in his own apartment. He's in the phone book.'

The old man stood up and picked up his cane, which was resting against the table.

'Sorry to have to leave you, Danny, but the van is waiting outside.'

'Nice to run into you, David.'

'Yes, it really was! *Shana tova* . . . and I hope to see you at Kippur.'

It was approaching midnight, but the day's warmth still hung in the air. It was unbelievable, Katz thought as he stood outside the door to Ramón's building: his heroin craving was gone, as if it had never even been there.

He entered the stairwell. He heard the sound of a TV a few floors up. The door to the apartment was ajar.

It was dark in the hallway. He fumbled for the switch and turned on the lights. He called out, but there was no answer.

The coffee table in the living room had been cleaned up. The woman's tools were gone, and so was the suitcase of her clothes and the drawings that had been on the floor. Katz just wanted to give the drugs back, as a symbolic gesture. Wish Ramón good luck and then vanish again, back to his life of sobriety, without extravagances, guided by routines – his only method of survival as a sober drug addict. But no one seemed to be home.

He heard laughter from the back courtyard. Teenagers, joking around about something. The kitchen fan was rattling in the distance.

'Ramón!' he called again, without receiving a response.

The door to Ramón's room was closed; Katz opened it and turned on the light. He could barely take in the scene before him.

The body seemed relaxed, lying there on the mattress. One foot rested on the floor as if he had been trying to get up but suddenly changed his mind. He had used a nylon stocking as a tourniquet on his arm. The needle was still stuck in a vein, just above the crease of his left elbow. Katz noticed the burn marks between his index and middle fingers, the same kind he'd had once upon a time when he would fall asleep with a lit cigarette in hand, too high to even notice. Pink foam at the corners of his lips. His face was blue.

Katz absorbed the scene as if in small, unedited clips. The packs of heroin and the Pesola scale were missing, as was the stuff Ramón had been using to dilute the drugs. The snake was lying under the radiator by the window. Its body was crushed in three or four places.

Suicide? he thought as his eyes roved about the room. But Ramón had seemed normal when he'd been there earlier in the day.

Had he accidentally overdosed? From stress, as Katz himself had that time at Medborgarplatsen? Katz knew how it felt when withdrawal hit you suddenly, how the world seemed to narrow, your thoughts, your field of vision. Your whole existence became focused on one thing: getting the junk in your veins as quickly as possible. But Ramón had had plenty of time; he'd had everything he needed within reach.

He crouched beside him. He couldn't look at the face; its bluish-purple hue made him feel sick. He felt the forehead. The body had only cooled a few degrees. He had died only a few hours ago at the most.

The cooking vessel was at the foot of the bed: half a Coke can. There was still solution in the bottom of it.

Jenny must have been in the apartment when it happened. Had she panicked? Grabbed all the drugs and her things, and taken off? Happened to trample the snake to death in the chaos?

Katz went out to the living room and dialled 112 on his mobile phone. He waited, listening to the dial tone, but hung up again. If he stayed, he would be dragged into this, and he had no desire to get involved. None of this had anything to do with him; this was part of his former life. He had returned by mistake.

He realized that there was a terrarium next to the wall. Jenny's suitcase had been standing right in front of it, which was why he hadn't noticed it before. Old rubbish was sticking up among the rocks on the bottom: receipts, tissues, one of her pencil drawings that might have fallen in by mistake as she was gathering her things.

Katz picked it up. It was a portrait of Ramón and Jenny in profile, arms around each other, smiling happily. The drawing had the precision of a photograph; she had probably based it on a photo, one that had been taken a few years earlier, before the drugs turned her face into a plaster mask.

He called the emergency number from a playground two blocks away and told them that there was a dead junkie in an apartment in Husby. He gave the address and explained that they could walk right in; the door was unlocked. When the woman at the dispatch centre asked if he could stay there until the ambulance arrived, he hung up.

It took half an hour for them to arrive. Two men in yellow reflective vests carried the body out on a stretcher, covered by a county medical blanket. A cop car showed up, and the driver had a short talk with the ambulance guys through his window before the vehicle moved on. No fuss, no bevy of police. Just a suburb druggie who died of an overdose.

Once the ambulance was gone, he went back to the city centre. The square was deserted. The apartment where he'd hunted Miro down was dark.

He took out the drawing and studied their loving smiles.

His subconscious was searching for something, but whatever it was slid out of reach. Something about the atmosphere in the apartment, he thought. And the fact that Ramón had too much experience to overdose.

He had to get hold of Jenny. Hear her version of what had happened. This wasn't just the regular old death of a tragic junkie. It didn't add up.

Ritorno, a cafe on Odengatan, had been there for as long as Katz could remember. He had gone there with his parents as a child and almost nothing had changed. It was like spending time in an old relative's living room.

He paid for a cup of coffee and walked to a room at the very back.

Eva Westin was sitting at a corner table, flicking through a newspaper. Her hair was up in a messy bun. He observed her from a distance. Her eyes always seemed surprised, as if she was constantly discovering the world anew. She seemed restless as she flipped through the newspaper. They had been together when Katz was sixteen, back when her last name was Dahlman, but they broke up under dramatic circumstances and hadn't seen each other again until the year before, in connection with the Klingberg Affair. They had embarked upon something like a relationship, but it had all fizzled out. Unmatched, he thought. That was the word that best described them.

She stood up and embraced him.

'Have you been standing there watching me for long, Katz?'

'A few seconds at the most. I'm glad you could come.'

'Well, I had nothing better to do. The kids are with Ola; it's his week.'

'How are things on that front?'

'We have a truce for the time being. The fact is, we're communicating better than we have for a long time. How about you?'

'Better than I deserve.'

They reminded each other of the past, Katz thought as he sat down on the chair across from her. Survivors, both of them. Eva had grown up with an addict mother and a father who spent most of her childhood years in institutions. It was incredible that she'd made it so far in life, getting a law degree and a job as a prosecutor with the Economic Crime Authority – and becoming one of the best ones, besides.

'You needed help?' she asked. 'Shoot.'

He told her about Ramón and Jenny and what he had seen and heard in their apartment.

'So you're bothered by the fact that he died of an overdose. Come on, Katz, that's the kind of thing junkies die of. If you want, I can make a few calls and obtain a copy of the autopsy report. And if that's not enough, maybe you should look up his girlfriend and ask her some questions about what happened.'

'That's part of my plan. But the problem is, I don't know her name, just that her first name is Jenny.'

Her handbag was open; its contents appeared subject to the laws of entropy. Katz saw a box of condoms sticking up in the mess. He felt a sting of pain, though he had no right to.

'If you could check the databases for me,' he said, 'to see what Ramón's been up to recently . . . there's bound to be something there. Apparently he was bringing in money by selling horse. He was homeless until a year or so ago, until they finally came into some money to buy drugs. Ramón claimed that they were sitting on so much that he didn't dare to keep it at home.'

'A full-blown junkie who suddenly becomes a heroin dealer?'

'I know, it sounds weird, and that's only one of the things that's bothering me. So if you could check and see if he's in the crime information database. And see if his girlfriend is mentioned anywhere. In the best case scenario you would find a last name so I have something to go on.'

She looked at him intently. With a prosecutor's eyes, Katz thought.

'Be honest. Why are you digging into this? Because he saved your life once? That's not enough of a reason; there's something else too.'

'Out of a junkie's nine lives, Ramón had at least three left. I can't explain it, but I don't think his death was an accident.'

She looked at the clock on her phone and sighed.

'I'll see what I can do. Do you have any idea where you'll start your search for the girlfriend?'

'Shelters. Or else on the street. She's a prostitute . . . or at least, she was until recently.'

The evening traffic rumbled in the distance. The contours of Vasaparken were visible through the door onto Odenga-tan. Eva lived just a few blocks away on Sankt Eriksplan.

She had kept the apartment after her divorce. It was only a twenty-minute ride by car to the suburb where they'd grown up, but the addresses might as well have been in two different universes.

'Are you on your way home?' he asked as she reached for her coat.

'To the office. We're drowning in work. I'm doing over-time while I can, since Ola has the children.'

He didn't know whether she was lying; maybe she actually did want him to come along. Sort out something physical between them, try to heal something she didn't even know the name of, something that was probably best healed some other way.

As he remained at the cafe table and watched her move towards the exit, he happened to think of his father's old friend, Epstein. He would look him up, try to fish around a little more in Benjamin's life history, but that would have to wait until later.

The receptionist at the homelessness resource centre on Östgötagatan gave him a list of current shelters that were known for having low expectations. Considering how deeply submerged Jenny was in her drug abuse, he imagined that this was the sort of place she would have lived, or in places that only accepted women. Or couples – after all, she had drifted around with Ramón for a while before they managed to get an apartment in Husby.

As Katz wrote down the addresses, his phone clamped between his ear and shoulder and the surprisingly friendly voice of the receptionist in the background, his memories came flooding back. The short-term shelter called Hvilan in Vanadislunden. Grimman, on Maria Prästgårdsgata. Hammarbybacken, where he had occasionally stayed after being kicked out of the military due to his drug use. Carema Care in Skarpnäck, the shelter in Västberga, and Supportive Living in Råcksta. Beyond these, there were the church-run institutions. Ersta Diakoni in Söder, Filadelfiakyrkan in Vasastan. And the City Mission in Kungsholmen.

He numbered them in geographical order, with the City Mission first because it was the closest to Husby on the Blue Line.

The City Mission's day shelter was on the corner of Mariebergsgatan and Fleminggatan, in a drab building from the late 1800s with a clock tower on its roof. Its interior was fairly new. It had been remodelled since Katz's time.

He rang the bell and was let in by a young male volunteer

with a hipster beard who asked if he wanted to sign in. There were still beds available if he needed to sleep for a while. And the washing machines were free; a change of clothes was provided while waiting for the laundry.

It was plain to see on him, Katz thought as he explained his errand; his history was carved into his being. A leopard can't change its spots.

'I apologize,' said the man, looking genuinely ashamed. 'But all sorts of people find their way here, some in suits, others in rags. Come in! My name is Magnus.'

They walked up the half set of stairs to a common room. Colourful sofas lined the walls. Past that room was a kitchen. The odours transported Katz fifteen years back in time: the smell of industrial-scale cooking and dirty clothes, cleaning solution, detoxing bodies, when all sorts of shit removed itself from your metabolism . . . the faint odour of vomit and urine.

'So you're looking for a woman you think might have sought help here,' the man said as they sat down at a table further inside the building. 'Are you a police officer?'

'Do I look like one?'

'I thought it would be best to ask.'

'It's a private matter. It's about a friend of mine.' Katz took the drawing from his inner pocket, unfolded it, and handed it to the man.

'Do you recognize her? This is a self-portrait done a year or so ago. She calls herself Jenny.'

The man looked at the picture for a long time, then looked at Katz again and shook his head.

'Sorry,' he said. 'Doesn't mean anything to me.'

'How about the guy?'

'Unfortunately I can't help you there either.'

The door to the day-sleeping room was open. A thin man in his fifties was sitting on a camp bed, rocking back and forth, obviously high. Katz could hear some people bickering about money in an adjacent room. Someone shouted the word 'whore'.

The man with the hipster beard gave a guilty shrug.

'We're not here to teach manners,' he said. 'We're here to support people. In the best case, we convince them to enter rehab, arrange supportive living, get them back into the system . . . If you'll excuse me for just one second.'

He stopped a young black man who had just come through the door. He took a pharmacy bag from his pocket and handed it to him.

'For your scabies,' he said in English. 'Apply twice a day where it itches, especially between your fingers. And I will see that you get some new clothes today.'

The man gave him a grateful smile before disappearing with the bag.

'A refugee from the Ivory Coast,' said the guy with the hipster beard. 'Some people's fates are extra painful. Abou is here illegally. He had just managed to turn eighteen before he came to Sweden, so he's not protected by the Convention on the Rights of the Child. He knows he'll be deported if the police catch him. The poor guy has been sleeping in parks all summer. And now he's got scabies. We're not technically allowed to hand out medication here. I had to buy the ointment myself at Apoteket.'

He looked sadly at Katz.

'Katja will be available soon. She might know who you're looking for.'

'Katja?'

'A colleague. She's the one who's been here the longest. Her shift starts in a little bit. I'll go knock on her door. Wait here.'

There were more people around now. Volunteers with name tags on their chests. Shadowy figures who'd come in from the street. Another couple of men with African backgrounds – Katz assumed they were also in Sweden illegally – were playing cards at one of the tables. Haggard people from the city's junkie zones, from the outskirts of the city on the Blue Line, people who had fallen through every safety net, if they'd ever had any to start with. New recruits were scattered among survivors from his own generation, a time when people had dropped like flies because of the city's restrictions on methadone and refusal to hand out free needles. Katz wondered if he would recognize anyone, or if anyone would recognize him. But his memory from those days was like a sieve – they were years of darkness with no chronology to hold them together – and anyway, most of those people were dead.

A young blond guy with odd red spots on his face was walking around and begging for money. Dirty hoodie, unwashed hair. His eyes flickered here and there around the room as if his gaze couldn't stick to any one object. He was detoxing, Katz thought, and was absolutely desperate.

A couple of older alcoholics were standing in a queue for food. A redheaded, rail-thin woman was sitting on a sofa outside the dormitory and talking to herself as she held a compact mirror up to her face and tried to put on an earring. The fight in the next room was still underway; someone gave an outright scream, a roar of undiluted despair from the very bottom of a life.

A little while later, he was let into a storeroom. A round middle-aged woman was standing at a work table and unpacking cans of food. Katz explained his errand once more.

'I can't give out information about the people who find their way here,' she said as she looked at the drawing. 'Unless they're a suspect in a crime and the police are looking for them. People have to be able to trust us.'

She opened the perforated edge of another box, took out a few cans, and inspected their use-by dates before putting them down.

'So what is this all about, anyway?'

'The guy in the picture just died of an overdose. I knew him, and I thought I could help with the funeral costs. But I can't get hold of his girlfriend, Jenny.'

The woman broke down the empty box and placed it in a plastic recycling bin.

'It must be six months since I last saw them. They used to come here sometimes. For a shower and some food. To do some laundry. Sometimes they picked up new clothes when the old ones were worn out. But I don't know where they went after that; they just stopped showing up.'

Sounds from the cafeteria reached the room: the clatter of cutlery and plates, a forced laugh.

'Jenny?' said the woman. 'Was that her name? I really don't remember. And we only keep the check-in lists for three months.'

'Do you know anyone who could give me more information?'

'Ask one of the girls out there. They know each other from the street. It's a hard life, not the kind of thing you'd wish even on your worst enemy. I think Jenny knows Mona. A skinny girl with lots of red hair. But be careful with her; she has a tendency to become aggressive if people get too close to her.'

Katz found the redhead on the street outside the shelter. It was the same woman he'd seen talking to herself in the common room. She was standing on the steps and smoking. She seemed calmer now, but appearances could be deceiving.

'What do you want?' she asked when Katz stopped next to her.

'I'm looking for Jenny.'

'So?'

'She's dating a friend of mine. I need to get hold of her.'

The woman stubbed out her cigarette against the wall and rubbed off the ash spot with her elbow. She glared furiously at him.

'Why would I even talk to you in the first place?'

'Maybe it would be worth it?'

'Go to hell!'

She took out another cigarette, lit it, and blew a smoke ring, then another that passed right through the first one. She seemed pleased with her achievement.

'What would you say if I gave you five hundred kronor if you help me?'

'Stick it up your arse. I'm not going to tell you shit. I don't even know who that chick is. Hel-*lo*, who the fuck are you even talking about? Jenny-fucking-who? Go away before I die of boredom.'

She sank down, her back against the door, hugging herself. She looked at Katz, fixing her eyes on his face and then his hands, and his wrists with the pale scars left by old needle sticks.

'Old junkie, huh? Jesus, my radar is shit. I thought you were a cop at first. Or a trick. Or both . . . that's not unusual these days. Do you have anything? I'm starting to feel bad . . .'

'Tell me a little about Jenny first. How do you know her?'

The woman gave him a sceptical look. She took a dirty cotton bud from her pocket and frantically dug it into one ear, which was covered in a rash; the earring fell out but she left it on the ground.

'What do you want to know? We worked Malmskillnads-gatan together for a while. We shot the shit while we waited for customers. We took turns buying coffee and bumming cigarettes off each other. But it must have been a year since I saw her. And I don't even know if Jenny is her real name. She calls herself something different every time. Amanda, Jessica, Jennifer, Therese . . . like she can't decide who the fuck she is, or she really doesn't know. I met her for the first time on Vasagatan, about two years ago. Outside the hotels. Tons of tricks there. I talked to her a little because she was so young . . . asked why she was doing it, wouldn't it be better for her to go home to mummy and daddy. But it was like talking to a wall.'

The woman gave Katz a reproachful look.

'You don't have anything, do you? Forget it, I'm not telling you any more.'

Katz dug in his inner pocket and took out one of the packs Ramón had given him.

'It's yours,' he said. 'Now keep talking.'

'What can I say? We each kept an eye on the cars the other got into. You have no idea the kinds of things that can happen if you're not careful. But then we lost touch. She and her guy came into a ton of drugs, and why would she have to work the streets after that? If she's whoring now, she's doing it in nicer places.'

The woman stopped talking, picked something up off the ground – the earring she'd dropped – and put it in her pocket. She scratched her ear with the cotton bud again.

'Lucky enough for her, I guess. She'd started doing some sick shit for drug money. Pervy stuff. And she wanted me to join her, but I still have some honour left, dammit. Better to hang out on Malmis and meet up with plain old square johns. Fuck you very much!'

'Her boyfriend is dead,' Katz said. 'Ramón. I have to get hold of her and ask her how it happened. It's personal.'

He offered her the drugs.

'Try checking at the porn place around the corner,' she said. 'They might know something. The last time I saw her she was hanging around there. Trying to get customers outside the booths . . . following dudes in if they wanted company. The supervisor usually looks the other way. But like I said, that must have been a year ago.'

She grabbed the drugs and stuffed them into her underwear, then disappeared back into the shelter.

Blue Dreams was on Alströmergatan, not far from the City Mission, between a musical instrument shop and a chess club. Katz heard lift music mixed with exaggerated moans as he came through the door, turned a corner, and found himself in a dark corridor with video booths on either side.

A broken emergency exit sign blinked a dull green light. The walls were painted black; water pipes and electric cables ran along the ceiling.

He peered into the closest booth. A television screen, a vinyl-clad chair, a roll of paper towel on a holder, and a waste-paper basket on the floor. Coin slot and credit card machine next to the screen. The booth smelled faintly of air freshener.

A man slid past him and disappeared down an adjacent corridor – the guy with spots on his face. The same one who'd been begging for money at the shelter.

Katz rounded a corner and came to an unmanned cash register in front of a set of double doors; the doors were open. On the other side of them was a cinema. He didn't see any people, but he did see a couple of smaller rooms at the back of the stage. A cramped opening seemed to lead to a narrow passage behind them.

He peered into one of the spaces. A big-screen TV, a sofa, and an easy chair. There were holes drilled in one wall; they opened out onto the corridor beyond the rooms. Glory holes. For men to stick their cocks in so that someone on the other side could suck them off.

On the movie screen, a haggard woman with silicone breasts was taking a faceless man into her mouth. She gagged as he shoved his cock too far down her throat. Katz closed his eyes, feeling disgusted and slightly turned on at the same time. When he looked up again, he realized that the guy with the spots was in the passage behind the theatre. The man stared at him in fear and then disappeared further into the darkness.

At the back of the building was a sex shop. A young girl in a tracksuit was sitting behind the register and reading a gossip rag; she took no notice of Katz.

Various types of sex toys were arranged on a sale table: whips, dildos, ball gags. Lacy underclothes hung from a rack.

One whole wall was covered in DVDs, sorted by category. One cover, in the bondage section, depicted an Asian woman on all fours with a muzzle covering her face. A young man had her on a lead. Another few movies were facing out on a shelf marked '*bukkake*'. One of them caught Katz's eye: a group of masked men formed a half-circle around a bound, naked woman. It was impossible to see what she looked like, because her face was covered in semen. It took a moment for him to realize what his attention had been drawn to: the tattoo on her calf, a swallowtail butterfly . . .

He took the DVD to the till.

'Rent or buy?' the woman asked without looking up from her magazine.

'Buy.'

'Two hundred.'

Katz paid cash but didn't walk away.

'Will there be anything else?'

'Are you in charge here?'

'No. And unfortunately my supervisor is busy right now.'

'Tell him I'll wait here until he shows up.'

The woman looked at him uncertainly. Then she got up and vanished behind a curtain. She was back less than thirty seconds later.

'My boss will be out soon,' she said. 'Who can I say is here?'

'That's not important. Say that it's about a mutual acquaintance.'

A woman of around thirty-five came out of the back room. She was wearing jeans and a T-shirt, with her hair up in a ponytail. *Attractive*, Katz thought, *if it weren't for her chilly gaze*.

'What can I do for you?' she said in a businesslike manner.

'I'm looking for a girl who hangs out here. Jenny.'

She looked at him indifferently.

'That name doesn't mean anything to me.'

'She sells sex. Or at least she did, a while ago. In the video booths or the private rooms.'

The woman laughed.

'We don't allow prostitution on the premises, and if we see signs of it, we ask people to leave.'

Katz nodded, making an effort to keep up a friendly tone of voice.

'I'm not here to create problems for you. I just want to talk to her. It's about a private matter.'

He took out the pencil drawing and showed it to her.

'Nice portrait,' said the woman. 'But unfortunately I've never seen that person. If you'll excuse me, I have work to do.'

'She's in the movies you sell.' Katz moved the DVD so she could see its cover.

'We sell hundreds of movies here. Are you saying I'm supposed to keep track of everyone in them?'

The girl at the register had moved away from them. She was paging through a binder beside the coffee maker. She peered nervously at her boss.

'It's important that I get hold of her.'

'You don't seem to understand what I'm saying. I want you to get out of here. As I see it, you're disrupting my place of business. You have one minute to leave before I call the police. They're usually quite helpful when we have trouble with a customer.'

Katz took the movie and stuck it in his jacket pocket, giving a short nod before he headed for the exit. He ran into someone in the dark outside the wanking booths; it was the guy with the spots. He heard him mumble something that might have been an apology. But it was impossible to make out the words among all the moans from the porn videos.

There were no pre-credits on the DVD – no title or production information. The action began abruptly. About fifteen naked men standing in a room – the parlour of a luxury turn-of-the-century flat.

The men were looking at a door that was ajar. Some of them were grey-haired, with flabby bodies; others were younger and fit. All of them were wearing black masks on their faces.

Judging by the light falling in from the bay window, it seemed to be early evening. A crystal chandelier with prisms the size of hen's eggs hung from the ceiling.

The door opened. Through it Katz could see the back of a person who was speaking to someone; the person bent down, took something from the floor, and stepped aside, out of the frame. The camera continued to film the door. A few seconds passed before a woman revealed herself.

Jenny.

She was naked. She kept her hands behind her back, or perhaps they were bound. Her gaze was perfectly vacant. She slowly walked to the centre of the room. She stopped under the chandelier and looked around. She seemed aware of the camera by this point. She looked over at the men who were standing with their backs to the wall, some with erect cocks.

There was the sound of a camera shutter – someone was taking still shots in the background. The room was bare; the only piece of furniture was the easy chair that stood on the parquet floor in the middle of the room. She sat down in it, turning her face upwards. Katz looked into her eyes again as he sat there before the computer in his office. She was high . . . in another world.

He heard heavy breathing, perhaps from the person holding the camera. The image zoomed out. The group of masked men formed a circle around her and began to masturbate. Katz didn't know how long this went on, maybe five minutes, maybe less. They weren't doing anything else, just masturbating, and they seemed to be waiting for each other. Then they moved closer to her face, still with their cocks in their hands. Someone cried out in excitement, and then they suddenly came, almost on command, all over her face and upper body.

Four variations on the same theme followed. Joint ejaculation. But it was more painful to watch each time. At one point she was bound with zip ties and had a dildo driven up inside her as the men formed a ring around her – this was the photo on the cover. At another point, they collected their ejaculate in a drinking glass, which she drained, gagging. Once she had a noose around her neck.

He stopped the disc when he couldn't stand to watch any more. There was no information about where it had been filmed. Homemade, he thought – the cover seemed to have been made on a plain old copy machine.

He went to Wikipedia and found an article on 'bukkake': 'Japanese for "splash", a sexual act commonly found in pornography. The act involves several men simultaneously ejaculating on the face or in the mouth of a woman.'

Then he googled Blue Dreams. The company had a website to advertise their space; it showed images of the interior of the booths and the cinema. There were private rooms and a common sauna. They also sold porn films and sex toys online.

There was a search field on the menu. Katz entered the word 'bukkake'. A hundred titles popped up, but all of them were foreign. Then he searched 'gangbang' and 'group sex', but found nothing of interest there either.

Then he rewound the film and paused just after the French doors into the parlour opened, shortly before Jenny appeared in the frame.

The bay windows with their hand-painted glass. The chandelier, the decorative stucco on the ceiling, the dark grey door that stood ajar. The masked men waiting in the background . . . He studied the back of the person who seemed to be speaking to Jenny just before she approached the men. The person who had bound her hands behind her back. It was difficult to make out details.

He enlarged the picture. The resolution became worse, but now he was certain he knew who he was looking at.

He pressed play again and noticed how she bent down, took something from the floor, and moved off camera.

Katz pressed 'eject' and put the DVD back in its case. He pictured the sequence in his mind. The same movements as two days earlier. The dirty cotton bud. The earring that had fallen off and landed on the ground.

A whole new part of the city had emerged between Bällsta-viken and Sundbyberg city centre. Since the last time Katz had visited the area, on an errand he could no longer recall, the industrial buildings from the previous century had been renovated and turned into flats. Fancy apartments with private docks had been built at the water's edge. The old Signal factory had been turned into a shopping centre.

He parked his car on a street close to the Grand Garbo nightclub and walked to the building he was looking for. The window in the stairwell offered a view of the train tracks and Esplanaden. An armada of graphite-coloured clouds had sailed in from Lake Mälaren.

A solidly built man in a wheelchair answered his knock at the door. His steel-grey hair was in a crew cut; his eyes were nut brown and his face was lined with deep furrows. He had cauliflower ears, and his nose was flattened like an old box-er's. He resembled Benjamin, but this was more thanks to his aura than his appearance.

'Come in,' he said brusquely. 'I just put in my hearing aid. If you'd shown up fifteen minutes ago, I wouldn't have heard you.'

Katz had called the night before, so he was expected. The old man rolled into the apartment ahead of him. Katz looked around as they passed a kitchen and a spartan living room. A bottle of whisky stood on a table next to a chessboard that was ready for play. A collection of sports trophies shone down from a bookcase.

They made their way to a glassed-in balcony, where Epstein parked his chair with a certain amount of difficulty.

'Benji's boy,' he said with a small smile. 'I have to admit, I was surprised to hear from you. I lost touch with your father when you were a little boy. My job took me to Skåne and my whole family came along. I saw the obituary when he died, but I didn't make it up in time. You and Anne were the only people mentioned. Do you have any siblings?'

'No, unfortunately I don't.'

Epstein took an asthma inhaler from his pocket and placed it on the table.

'I don't smoke anymore,' he said with a grimace. 'My doctor has forbidden it. This is the closest I get.'

He poured a glass of mineral water and handed it to Katz. An IV port was taped to the back of his wrinkled hand.

'Drink up,' he said. 'It's as hot as the Negev desert on my balcony . . . and don't worry about my port-a-cath. It's for the chemo. A tumour the size of a peanut in my left lung.'

The old man eyed him intently, as if he were looking for traces of Benjamin.

'Where in Skåne did you live?' Katz asked, for lack of anything better to say.

'Malmö. I liked living there for twenty-five years, until the anti-Semites started making too much noise. Young Muslim guys on the outskirts of town have got the idea that Jews are the root of all evil. Some fanatics even believe in *The Protocols of the Elders of Zion*. Most of them have never met a Jew in their whole life, and yet they know everything about us. It's like with Shakespeare. Three hundred years had gone by since the Jews were driven out of England when he wrote about Shylock, and yet that guy knew exactly how greedy and shameless they were . . . I'm not a religious sort. I haven't worn a yarmulke since I was a child. But in my opinion, everyone has the right to dress as they like without suffering threats or abuse. That goes for Jews as much as it does for Christians and Muslims.'

'I didn't know things were that bad.'

'They're worse. The former government commissioner down there, whose name I refuse to utter, really stirred the pot. He claimed that the congregation had been infiltrated by Sweden Democrats and suggested boycotting Sweden's match against Israel in the Davis Cup for political reasons. This same person had no problem receiving business delegations from one-party state China, occupier of Tibet for sixty years. And when the extremists tried to vandalize the synagogue, he encouraged the congregation to distance itself from Israel's occupation of Palestinian lands in order to put a stop to the persecution. Have you ever heard the like? People whose families have been Swedish citizens for generations are supposed to apologize for what is going on in a country three thousand kilometres away to make their persecutors leave them alone?!'

Epstein picked up his inhaler and took three deep puffs to calm himself down.

'There are anti-Semites everywhere, and they don't have to be wearing brown for me to know who they are. What's the best way to downplay the Holocaust? To insinuate that Jews haven't learned anything from history, so they behave like their own old tormentors and oppressors in the West Bank. How best to demonize them? By plastering them with fantasies of complete power, claiming that their lobbying groups are so influential that they control American foreign policy, that they have such a grip on the media that they control the news, that they are greedy, that they own the banks and live by the Old Testament morality of an eye for an eye and a tooth for a tooth, which Jesus distanced himself from two thousand years ago. I thought I wouldn't have to listen to this sort of shit anymore after the war . . .'

Epstein stopped talking and gave Katz a look of rage as he fingered the hearing aid behind his ear.

'But that's not why you're here,' he said. 'You're not here to listen to an old man's fears about the direction the world is heading in. I understand you have questions about your father and grandparents?'

Katz nodded.

'Your father and grandfather didn't get along particularly well. They had different views of the world. And of what resistance was. Chaim was one of the people who were forced to scrub the streets with a toothbrush when the Nazis took power in Austria. I'm sure you've seen the pictures . . . It happened everywhere, and worse things too. But Benji, as young as he was, realized that this was just a taste of things to come.'

'He was the one who convinced the family to flee?'

Epstein gazed emptily at the air.

'He more or less forced the decision by putting himself in danger. He distributed anti-Nazi flyers, risking his own life at only fifteen. He resisted the Brownshirts, along with some other brave boys. He was a fighter even then, a large boy, almost like me, and he looked older than he actually was. Chaim and Sara realized that the situation was untenable, that they had to leave the country. But it was difficult to get an exit permit. The noose was starting to tighten. In the end, Benji managed to obtain the correct papers. He had a chokehold on someone. I don't know what happened – he never said – but someone helped them with false visas. People said that your father was forced to kill a man so they could escape.'

So that memory of his was accurate after all. That his father had killed someone for a passport.

'But Dad never told you about it himself?'

'Only by way of insinuation. A formal request for extradition to Das Reich was issued, but by then they had taken control of the situation and had been granted asylum, as it would be called today, for political and humanitarian reasons. They made it through the eye of the needle, and, as you know, there weren't all that many circumcised men who managed that. This country sided with the Germans much longer than anyone cares to admit.'

Epstein closed his eyes and gave a heavy sigh. Katz peered down at the street. More mysteries, he thought, just like his whole childhood, the reason for their constant moves and his father's irrational sorrow and rage.

'Terrible things happened in their lives,' Epstein continued. 'I knew your grandfather too, you know. He treated me almost like a son. We would play chess on Saturday evenings after Havdalah . . . before Benji and I took off for Narva to go to boxing lessons. Their memories caused them to leave this country as soon as the war was over, to move to Israel and start a new life. But loss caught up with them, and they died young . . .'

'What kind of loss?'

'They had a daughter, too, didn't you know that? A little older than your father. Hannah. They couldn't get her out of the country.'

Epstein shrugged in resignation. '"She rests in a grave in the sky, where it's roomy to lie," as Celan famously wrote. No one knows what happened to her. She was four years older than your father, and she was the apple of her parents' eyes.'

Epstein poured a glass of mineral water for himself and drained it in three loud gulps. He gave a start when the front door opened and a male voice called, 'Hello.'

'Age takes its toll,' he said as he watched Katz with an endlessly distant gaze. 'Or maybe it's the weight of memories. My doctor is here. I'll have to ask you to leave. But it would be great to see you again. Promise you'll visit me again sometime.'

Katz spent the next few days finishing up his job for the tele-coms firm. He checked the results of the phishing program, tightened the firewalls in the servers, and collated his observa-tions in a new document. *Kaspersky Lab couldn't have done a better job*, he thought as he emailed it off. He received a quick answer from the security division and sent an invoice right back.

When he was done, he pulled up the info for his next assign-ment. A dozen articles from Russian military magazines that he was to translate into Swedish for the Ministry of Defence. He gave them a quick glance and realized that the job would be easier than expected. It would only take a few days, and the deadline was almost a month away.

He called Eva Westin instead and was surprised when she picked up.

'Sorry I haven't called, Katz,' she said. 'I've been busy, but I haven't forgotten you. In any case, it's just as I suspected with your friend. Respiratory arrest with resultant heart fail-ure due to an overdose. Plus pulmonary oedema. I suspect you saw pink foam around his mouth . . . In short, a natural death for a junkie.'

Katz stared emptily into the air.

'It seems unlikely that he would overdose on stuff he was cutting himself.'

'But he did. They checked for traces of the typical by-products of heroin breakdown. Monoacetylmorphine, for example . . . and it was there. So were traces of ampheta-mines and alcohol.'

'What happened to the syringe itself . . . or, more accurately, its contents?'

'There's nothing about a syringe in the report. It was probably thrown out at intake. The pathologist made a formal report to the police, as is customary, and it was accepted just as formally – that is, with no follow-up. The official cause of death is cardiac arrest.'

Whether it was sloppiness or disinterest, this bothered him.

'Maybe if the police had actually been in the apartment,' she went on, 'the contents of the syringe would have been collected for testing. But the ambulance crew took him straight to the morgue, not the medical examiner.'

Katz took a pen from his desk and started to bite it, but put it back down again.

'Is there anything else in the report . . . what was he wearing when he was brought in?'

'The clothes you found him in. And there was a wallet in his pocket, with an ID and six thousand in cash.'

'No mobile phone?'

'No. Is that significant?'

'Maybe.'

'Like I said, there has to be a suspicion of crime for the police to investigate further, and in this case there isn't. I think you can rest easy when it comes to the reason he died. Nothing strange, just awfully sad.'

'What about the woman, Jenny; have you found anything on her?'

'I checked for missing and wanted persons, and there are plenty in the database, but no one named Jenny. I would need more information to go any further. A last name, for example.'

'Has anyone contacted the police to ask about Ramón?'

'I checked on that too, but no one has as yet. His mother

died within the last year or so. Juana Suárez, on disability, lived in Kärrtorp. His parents were divorced and his father returned to Chile once the military dictatorship fell, but there's no address listed for him.'

Katz heard children's laughter in the background, and then Eva mumbled something that wasn't meant for him.

'Are you still there?' he asked.

'I'm picking Lisa up from school. It's my week now.'

'I can call back later if that's better for you.'

'No, it's fine, go on.'

'What does it say about Ramón in the police database?'

'I can't find anything on him. Just ten-year-old cases for possession and petty theft. Nothing in the general crime information database. It seems he managed to stay under the radar in recent years.'

This surprised him. Ramón had been dealing; there should have been something on him fairly recently. A report of the police taking him into the interrogation room at Plattan, or something along those lines. But apparently there was nothing like that.

'The lease for the Husby apartment was in his name, at least; he got it through the housing authority. Ramón was the only one listed as living there, so there was no information about his girlfriend. And I also got hold of my contact in the drugs unit. No new or purer heroin in circulation as far as he was aware. But then again, the organized crime gangs are usually a step ahead.'

'Was that all?'

'I can keep digging if you want me to,' she said. 'If you choose not to let this go.'

'Maybe you're right,' Katz said. 'Maybe I ought to focus on my own life instead. Get it under control, become happy.'

He heard her breathing close to the mouthpiece, about to say something, but then she changed her mind.

'Got to go now,' she said. 'Lisa wants to stop by a cafe before we pick up her little brother. Mother–daughter time, you know. Sit around and gossip a little. Bond. Talk to you later . . . Take care of yourself in the meantime.'

The neighbourhood somehow seemed to float all on its own, high up on Brunkebergsåsen. The area below it, Hamngatan and all its gallerias and fancy boutiques, was completely separate from the world up here.

Katz parked the car on Herkulesgatan and walked towards the rough-hewn granite palace that was Riksbanken. Ugly seventies buildings flanked this red-light district: banks and office buildings with dark windows. A Russian-looking woman in fake fur gave him a long look from where she was standing near Brunkebergsparken. In the distance there was a dry cleaner's, a shoe-and-key shop, and the entrance to a multi-storey carpark.

It was nine o'clock at night. He stopped along the bridge railing above Hamngatan. The 'no loitering' signs hadn't put a stop to prostitution any more than the sex-purchase laws had done fifteen years earlier. There had been just a short break, then everything returned to normal. Cars carrying johns cruised slowly by; a few young, high girls stood on the pavement and tried to look sexy.

It took fifteen minutes for him to catch sight of Mona. She was climbing out of a beat-up Toyota by the NK garage, and she immediately took up her post again to pick up another client. She took a compact mirror out of her bag, touched up her make-up, and then washed her hands with a wet wipe. Her jeans were dirty and one leg was ripped. He had just decided to approach her when another car stopped: a white SUV. The window rolled down, she bent forward and said something to the driver before climbing in, and then the door closed and the vehicle vanished in the direction of Gustav Adolfs Torg.

Half an hour later, she was back. She came up the stairs from Hamngatan by herself. She stopped by the shop window of the dry cleaner's and gave her reflection a critical look. She went to stand at the edge of the pavement again.

'What do you want this time?' she said when she saw Katz.

'Just to talk a little.'

'Can't you see I'm working?'

'You're not going to get any customers in that condition.'

She glared at him, irritated. Her lip was split; it was bleeding again. She took the handkerchief from her bag and pressed it to her mouth. She followed him as he began to walk.

'Fucking psycho,' she said as they drove through the diplomat district out towards Djurgårdsbrunn. 'I said I wouldn't stand for any violent stuff and the first thing that guy does is punch me right in the face. The more worn down you are, the more the perverts are drawn to you; they take advantage of desperation.'

Katz didn't say anything. He understood that she needed time to collect herself.

'He tried to rape me. That's how I look at it, anyway . . . and it doesn't make any difference that he paid in advance. Five hundred kronor. What a fucking cheap-arse pig. The dude obviously had money – he had a big SUV and a huge Rolex. He tried to stick things up inside me, stuff he had in a bag . . . I was fucking terrified, so I screamed as loud as I could. Then he suddenly let me go and it was a damn good thing I managed to get a taxi.'

She cautiously touched her split lip with a nicotine-stained finger.

'Have you heard anything from Jenny?' Katz asked.

'Why would I have? Maybe she moved in with some old john. What do I know? She could be sitting around chilling somewhere with a new dude. Why is it so important for you to get hold of her?'

Katz didn't answer. They had driven past Berwaldhallen and the National Museum of Science and Technology. The illuminated top of the Kaknäs Tower hovered in the air above them.

'Tell me about that movie.'

'What movie?'

'The bukkake movie. I saw you in it. You tied her hands behind her back before she joined a bunch of masked men in a ritzy apartment somewhere.'

She whipped around to face him, then looked away again, staring into the darkness, disgusted.

'How did you end up seeing that?'

'I bought it. And something tells me that it wasn't actually for sale. That it ended up on a shelf of other pornos by mistake.'

She lit a cigarette but held it in her hand without smoking it.

'What is it you actually want from me? Are you a pervert?'

'I want to find out how her boyfriend died, because he saved my life once. And I'm pulling at what few threads I can find.'

She took a drag of her cigarette before tossing it out the cracked window.

'Okay. I went along to a get-together full of pervs because Jenny asked me to. She didn't even want to go, but she needed the money. That was before she and Ramón got on the gravy train. The kind of people who do that stuff are such fucking sickos. They pay money to come all over women's faces as a group.'

'Who organizes it?'

'I don't know his name. A pretty young guy. He mostly does normal sex films; he's a regular old porn producer. That's how Jenny knew him. But he does that other stuff, too . . . more perverted things. I saw him in a magazine once, in a picture from some celebrity party. Jenny said he has a list of people he can contact.'

She snorted back some mucus, then coughed it up and swallowed it again.

'I was only there once, like I said, and I was high as a god-damn kite too. We were taken to a luxury apartment somewhere in Östermalm. They blindfolded us like it was some sort of fucking state secret. I was actually supposed to join in, but I couldn't handle it. So all I did was tie her up and let her into the room of ten waiting perverts.'

Katz had turned the car around and was slowly driving back into the city.

'How can I find that porn producer?'

'Check out Kontiki Self Storage. That's the best thing I can think of.'

'Kontiki?'

'It's an old warehouse where they shoot movies. It's in the business park in Johannelund, near Vällingby. It's like an assembly line. The equipment is already there. The crew arrives in the morning, and that evening they leave with a finished product. Jenny told me about it once.'

'How do I get in?'

'Spectators are welcome for a fee.'

Katz nodded and made a note of the name and address in his memory.

'Just one last question. Do you know if Jenny was afraid of snakes?'

'That would be a weird fucking question if I didn't happen

to know the answer. She loves snakes; she raised them for a while. Corn snakes, I think they're called, from Mexico. One time she had a baby snake with her while she was working Malmskillnadsgatan. In her bag.'

They passed Norrmalmstorg. The shapes of waiting women were visible on the bridge over Hamngatan.

'I should quit,' she said as she stared into the dark night. 'Get out of this shit before something happens. Two girls have disappeared in the past few months. Just vanished without a trace. And not a single person cares. There's nothing in the papers, the cops don't give a shit. Magnus, the guy from the City Mission, says he can help me; he knows a place outside the city where they take hopeless cases. I have a son – he's seven now. He lives with a foster family in Dalarna. I love that little guy . . . He would be crushed if anything happened to me.'

She took paper and a pen from her bag and scribbled down her mobile phone number.

'In case you have any more questions,' she said. 'And this way you won't have to bother me at work. Can I get yours too, in case I run into Jenny?'

Katz gave her a business card. She flashed him a quick smile before she opened the car door and got out. He had no idea how old she might be – anywhere between twenty-five and forty. Her eyes were empty, and yet he could see the child deep down inside her. Just a little girl, a prisoner at rock bottom, and she had no idea how to get out.

The windows of the apartment were dark, aside from a bluish light filtering through the blinds. Katz guessed it was from the terrarium. It was two in the morning. This residential neighbourhood was asleep.

He wondered where the boy was, Alexandru, and how things were going for him. He ought to make sure everything was working as it should, he thought, that the boy had escaped his tormentors. But he would have called if there had been any problems, Katz was sure of it.

He took out his torch and walked up to the front door of the building. He opened it and walked in. He tried the door to the apartment. Locked. The landlord had been there.

The light in the stairwell was broken. Katz fished a feeler gauge out of his pocket and flipped out the one he thought would fit, then bent the top in two spots and inserted it into the gap. He had done this a few times a week during his dark years. It wasn't something he was proud of; it had just been a necessary evil, to finance his drug abuse.

He carefully moved the feeler gauge upwards, two or three turns until he found the right spot. Then he took out the needle-nose pliers and used them to increase the force. He heard the bolt tumble back in the lock . . .

A faint scent of rot struck him as he opened the door. He closed it behind him as he turned on the torch. He twisted the regulator to narrow the beam of light.

He checked the kitchen and the smaller, unfurnished room. Untouched. The same went for the hall and the living room.

He hesitated for a moment outside the door to Ramón's room before he went in.

He looked at the mattress where Ramón had lain. He recalled the bluish-purple face with pink foam at the corners of the mouth. A dirty sock remained on the floor, but there was no syringe. A couple of tissues littered the head of the bed.

Katz lifted the mattress. The phone was gone. Had Jenny taken it?

Katz had only been given Ramón's address; he didn't know his phone number. *Wouldn't be traceable anyway*, he thought. It would definitely have a pay-as-you-go card.

He walked over to the window, bent down, and peered under the radiator. He breathed through his mouth. The snake was still there, partially rotted. He illuminated it, looking at its crushed head and the four points on its body where someone had stomped it to death in panic or rage.

The snake had been a pet. Neither Ramón nor Jenny would have stomped it to death.

A drug deal gone wrong. Was that what this was all about?

He walked over to the wardrobe. Only Ramón's clothes were in it. No trace of Jenny.

He went back to the desk. He looked at the outlet above the baseboard, and at the lamp cord that was hanging loose next to it. The screws of the plastic cover were gone. Ramón had been fiddling with something right there when Katz visited, and then he had stood up to give him more packs.

Katz wiggled the cover until it came loose. He saw a cylindrical hole in the wall, and severed electrical wires. A bag of pure heroin lay in the hiding spot, maybe ten grams of it. Next to it was a folded piece of paper.

Speed Services 0021. At first he thought it was a queue number, until he discovered the row of numbers further down.

He stuck it in his back pocket and got up. He thought of the moment Ramón handed him the drugs. And then of Ramón's corpse lying on the mattress, and the syringe stuck in his left arm. He didn't understand, at first, what was bothering him, and he fought with his memory until the image became clear, the way he had held out the packs with his left hand . . . If Ramón was left-handed, the syringe had been in the wrong arm.

PART 3

Arvid was playing on the trampolines. He had bonded with a boy his own age who seemed much braver. Her gentle little six-year-old, the furthest thing from macho you could imagine, who had just started school and wasn't doing well. He had a hard time concentrating and complained of headaches. Ola, as usual, had been the first to react; he took Arvid to a paediatrician who diagnosed him with migraines. They were thinking of placing him in a Montessori school in the spring, but that was Ola's project – he was the organized one.

Lisa was sitting on the bench next to her, playing *Super Mario* on her Nintendo. She would be nine soon, and she thought she was too old for playgrounds.

Her grown-up little girl. She wanted to be a fashion designer when she was older. Eva had no idea where that interest came from. She herself was totally uninterested in fashion, if not flat out bad at it. She hated shopping; when she needed new clothes, she just walked up to the first sale rack she saw and picked up whatever was closest. It was easier at work. There she just dressed as a prosecutor.

Arvid had left the trampolines for the time being. His playmate had gone to play with some other boys who seemed cooler. They were using the climbing wall. And Arvid was no tough guy; he was afraid of heights.

'Can I have some sweets, Mummy?' he asked, sliding his hand into hers.

'It's only Thursday; sweets are a Saturday treat. You can ask Dad when he gets here.'

'But the boy I was playing with, Ossian, he was gonna get some sweets.'

'No buts, please.'

'You're so owned, Mummy, you know that? *Owned.*'

He glared angrily at her before trudging off to the sand-box, where a few younger boys were playing. He often played with smaller children so that he could be in charge for a change. Be the brave one, the one the others looked up to.

Fifteen minutes until the start of a lonesome week. She took out her phone and pulled up her new app. It was as discreet as the guaranteed anonymity it offered. No one could see your name or where you lived; it didn't ask for an email or a phone number. It was designed for people who liked no-strings-attached sex. Preferably in odd places, if she understood correctly: nightclubs, restaurants, parks, multi-storeys, public toilets . . . anywhere people could find an outlet for their urges. She had downloaded it a few weeks earlier after reading about it in a 'scandal' report in an evening tabloid, and in one day she had created a profile and received more outrageous propositions than she would normally get in a year at the seedy bars along Sveavägen. Back in the day, she would have gone to Lion Bar when desire started pecking at her. There she would hit on the first man who didn't look like he'd make things difficult afterwards. Have a few shots of tequila, go home with him, or take him home with her if he happened to be married. Fuck. Make sure to get rid of him as quickly as possible after. But this seemed more rational. Sex without even the need for introductions.

Maybe tonight, she thought. She hadn't had sex in a long time.

She gave a start as she saw a familiar figure strolling by on the other side of the park cafe. Hoffman. Or someone who looked just like him.

'Wait here,' she said to Lisa. 'I'll be back in a minute.'

I'm acting like a stalker, she thought as she crossed the asphalt and walked past the swings to the path where the man was sauntering along.

She was twenty metres behind him now, and she watched him focus his gaze on a young blonde woman waiting on a park bench. He bent down and kissed her on the lips. She felt something heat up inside her. *Jealousy?* she wondered. It just couldn't be possible.

She stayed put, half hidden by the swing set. Hoffman was her new boss. He had come from a position on the vice squad, and his task now was to build up the new international division of the Economic Crime Authority.

Her heart pounded as she saw his hand curl around the back of the woman's neck. But then he turned around and looked in her direction.

It was a totally different man. The feeling that flooded her body was a strange cocktail of relief and disappointment all in one.

When she returned to the playground, she discovered that Lisa and Arvid had wandered over to the climbing frame. She thought about opening her app now that they were playing together for a change, but she managed to restrain herself.

A sex addict on top of everything else. But there was no longer anything that would surprise her about herself. She liked it, didn't she? She liked casual relationships. She had abused heroin in her teens, with Katz, and she hadn't *really* quit when she quit; she just filled the empty spot with other things. An addiction to studying in law school. A workaholic at the job that followed. So why not this too?

She looked at the time again. Ola might arrive at any moment.

'Come on, kids, let's go look for Dad.'

She herded them down to Odengatan. She felt a pang of guilt at the thought of Katz and the fact that she hadn't been more help with his old friend who'd died of an overdose. But she had enough on her plate already. Six months earlier, she had changed jobs and moved to the new international division under Hoffman's leadership. They worked with cross-border economic crime. At the moment, she was helping some Bosnian colleagues with a particular project. Mafia money from the Balkans that they suspected was being laundered in Sweden. She had just started sniffing around, trying to pin down amounts that had moved from one virtual wallet to another. Her colleagues in Sarajevo were in the process of compiling a list of what they believed were front organizations.

The organization they were trying to get at had its roots in Albania. According to a memo from Interpol, they dominated the narcotics and human trafficking trade in the Balkans. And they were well on their way to taking pole position when it came to weapons trading and sophisticated money laundering.

Katz, she thought again. It was like she couldn't decide what sort of feelings she had for him, mixing up the way she'd felt about him when they were young. And then there was Hoffman, muddling the situation even further.

Suddenly the children started running. They had spotted Ola further down the hill. He had come straight from his job at the law firm; he was still wearing his suit. Arvid threw himself at his father.

'Hello there,' he said as she approached. 'Did everything go okay?'

'Sure did.'

'Did they go to bed on time, like we talked about? It's important, especially for Arvid . . . If he doesn't get enough sleep it can bring on a migraine.'

'Don't worry.'

'Did you bring Lisa's weekly letter from the school? Her football boots and piano homework?'

'It's all in their backpacks.'

Her phone dinged. Her match, 'Marlon', had entered new coordinates for their encounter. She stuck her phone in her purse with a feeling of bottomless shame. The children were her biggest priority – plus appearing to be in control as she handed them over to Ola. Things had improved between them since the Klingberg Affair the year before, but she knew he was keeping an eye on her. Checking to see if she was hungover, interrogating the children about how she had behaved while they were with her after they arrived home. He could cancel her weeks with them anytime he liked since, on paper, he had sole custody.

'Dad, I saw one of those jean jackets with sequins again; a big girl in the park had one . . . You promised I could get one.'

'And I want a new Skylander – Swap Force. You can change their heads so they turn into totally different guys. They're mad awesome, Dad!'

The kids were talking over each other by now. They'd already forgotten about her, on their way into the world of their beloved dad. They would go home to their adorable little brother, whose name she had never learned, and to Erika, her ex-husband's ten-years-younger wife.

'Okay, kids, say bye to your mum, then let's go.'

They hugged her – a bit dutifully, she thought. Though Arvid had a hard time tearing himself away.

'I'll see you soon,' she said. 'I already can't wait.'

She waved as they walked over to the car. They didn't even glance in her direction, they were so busy talking to Ola, each holding one of his hands, clinging to him lovingly, laughing together in a way they would never do with her.

She waited until they were out of sight before she fished her phone out of her bag. She clicked on the app. Sure enough, there was a short message: 'Marlon' wanted to meet her at a restaurant before they moved on to the real reason for their encounter.

The safe house was an apartment on the seventh floor of a neighbourhood of high-rises near Hallundavägen. It had once been a stash for stolen goods; the name on the lease belonged to a guy who was sitting in the clink in Denmark. Two rooms, a kitchenette, and a balcony. A large hole in the wall between the hallway and the bedroom, left over from a former renter who had flipped out.

The neighbours weren't the sort to ask questions, if they even spoke Swedish.

Jorma heard cop cars in the area sometimes, but that didn't worry him. They wouldn't find him here. It wasn't even a given that they knew who they were looking for.

At least his knee had got better; it was only a sprain and the swelling was going down. Against all odds, he had survived. He had driven the stolen Mercedes down the back streets through Bredäng and Mälarhöjden as they searched for him further south. He returned to the E4 and saw the blue lights of the emergency vehicles that were still at the shopping centre. He slowly began to grasp the enormity of what had happened. That the robbery had gone to shit. That Zoran had been shot.

On a forest road outside Salem, he dumped the extra can of petrol he'd found in the boot all over the seats. He set the car on fire before he took off. One hour later he was in Fittja.

The hideout was paid up for another month. There was a TV and a laptop, and wireless internet. Sheets and blankets, food in the fridge and larder. They had left an extra revolver in the nightstand. A Colt and four boxes of bullets. There was a roll of zip ties and two foreign licence plates in one wardrobe. Things he might have use for.

The images from the execution came back to him again and again, like a film on repeat in his head. The smacking sound when the man in the mask pulled the trigger and the bullet went through Zoran's skull. That surreal feeling, as if it were all happening in a parallel universe.

He didn't understand how he could have got himself into this situation. Why the hell had he accepted the job? He had already made up his mind, no more crime . . .

He followed the news reports on the TV and online. The robbery was the top story. He saw images from the multi-storey: the armoured car and the terrified guards.

One photo showed Lindros being escorted to a waiting police van with his face covered by a jacket. 'Former boun-cer from the Uppsala area,' according to the caption in one of the evening tabloids.

The armoured car had been stopped by three men, but they hadn't had time to open the vehicle before the police arrived. Another two had managed to flee in a stolen car. One person, with origins in the former Yugoslavia, had been shot and killed in a firefight with the chasing police. One dead, three in custody. The fifth robber was still at large.

There was speculation that it was an inside job. A former employee of an armoured-car company said in a television interview that the drivers didn't receive their schedules before the morning of their delivery. Yet the robbers had known where and when the truck would show up.

And so had the police, Jorma thought.

He laid low for a week until the robbery was no longer front-page material. The cops were still looking for him, he presumed, but the cameras must not have captured him during the job. They'd had a hard time linking the fifth robber to the crime scene, and because he had been wearing a mask they had no description of him. He was sure there weren't any fingerprints or DNA on the fake bomb; he'd worn gloves and a hairnet as he put it together. The getaway cars had burned up, so there was nothing to be found there. And the others seemed to be keeping mum in interrogations.

His self-hatred had started to let up a bit. But his mind was churning at high speed. The insider was the only one who'd known when the armoured vehicle would be on the move. Had he got cold feet and contacted the police?

That night when they met him in the forest on Ekerö, the sound they'd heard, which he'd thought was from a deer . . . Had they been under surveillance even then?

And what about the vandalized getaway car, the slashed tyres?

The insider had been in contact with Hillerström, the middleman. But how had they met? Out of the fucking blue? The police must have discovered their trail at some point.

He had to be patient. Wait until people felt safe, lie low for a little bit longer.

He stole a car from a car park in Alby, changed its plates, and drove out to Bromma two mornings in a row. He sat a hundred metres down the road, keeping watch with binoculars, moving around the neighbourhood to get an overview.

An honest-to-goodness villa: a two-storey detached home in Stora Mossen. On paper, Hillerström ran a construction company. Two kids, girls, eleven and fourteen years old, and a wife who worked at a shoe shop in the city.

He seemed to stay at home during the day, working on office

tasks, sticking to a room in one wing of the house. The man was a career criminal, so there were probably guns in the house.

Morning was best. People felt safer in daylight; they relaxed, let down their guard.

Jorma had checked the map and the aerial images on Google Earth. The best way would be to park on a parallel street, come in via the neighbours' garden, and climb over the fence into Hillerström's place.

One more day, he thought, two at the most. After all, the guy must have worked out that Jorma was at large. It was possible that he was prepared for an encounter.

He called the security firm from a cafe in Fittja. A female receptionist answered.

'Trans Security. How may I help you?'

'I'm looking for a guy who works at your office.'

'I'll transfer your call if you can give me a name.'

'I'm really sorry, but my brain is on the fritz . . . Logistics. Skinny guy. About twenty-five. Shit, I know him. We're usually in frequent contact, but it's been a while now. I'm calling about cash deposits for our firm in Södertälje.'

The woman's voice lowered half a notch.

'You're thinking of Jocke.'

'Yes, is he there?'

'Unfortunately he no longer works for us.'

'Did he quit?'

A short silence before she went on. 'I'm terribly sorry to have to be the one to tell you this, but Jocke is dead.'

He hadn't expected this; he realized his heart was beating faster.

'Oh my God.'

'I know, it's horrible. Is there anyone else here I could put you in touch with instead?'

'I have to digest this first. What happened?'

'It was a week ago now. He didn't show up to work. We were recently the target of an attempted robbery, and Jocke took it hard. A colleague went over to his apartment and found him. He had hanged himself.'

'Shit, I just can't wrap my head around this.'

'I know, it's so sad . . .'

A pair of chavvy girls snickered at the table next to him. He remembered boxing the guy's ear back in the forest, degrading him. He was almost ashamed of it now.

So the insider hadn't been able to handle the pressure. If he had allied himself with the cops, it was too late to talk to him now. And there was no guarantee that he had anything to do with it. Maybe he owed a debt to the wrong sort of people, as Hillerström had claimed, and had tried to solve the problem by contacting people in the underworld. And when the robbery went to hell he thought that suspicions would be directed at him. Thought it was all over. Took his own life rather than squeal.

'Hello, are you still there?'

'Yes, I'm sorry . . . I think I'm a little bit in shock, actually.'

'That's okay. Shall I transfer you to someone else?'

He pictured the guy again. He thought too highly of himself to be a candidate for suicide, Jorma thought. Someone had offed him.

'No. I'll call back a little later once I've recovered.'

Teatergrillen was more Ola's type of place than her own. Or maybe Hoffman's . . . though she knew nothing about him. She never set foot in this sort of restaurant. She didn't fit in. She always got the feeling that people could smell her working-class background.

She walked down the stairs to a hall with a built-in sofa on one side and a hardwood bar on the other. A waiter glided by with a servile smile. She tried to see herself through his eyes: a woman in the throes of a midlife crisis, all dolled up in a baggy black trouser suit and sandals with heels that were too high. She felt like she was at a masquerade. As if she had picked her clothes out of someone else's wardrobe.

To the right, a set of stairs led to the ladies' room. Terry-cloth towels lay in neat piles on a rack next to the fancy sink. She checked her handbag, making sure that the pack of condoms was still there.

She looked younger in the mirror, thirty-five rather than forty-three. Blue-grey eyes, thick, medium-blonde hair, full lips with a noticeable Cupid's bow. High cheekbones that made her look vaguely Asian. The scars on her neck, the ones Klingberg had given her once upon forever ago, were hardly visible anymore.

She thought about calling it all off, turning on her heel and going home instead, starting up her computer and getting back to work on the Bosnia project in the company of a bottle of JD. The man who was waiting for her had no idea what she looked like, much less what her name was.

*

You can't escape your nature, she thought a minute later, as she stood in the dining room and looked around at all the upper-class patrons. The paintings on the walls depicted the rooftops of some city, maybe Paris. The wall-to-wall carpet was so thick that her feet sank a centimetre into it. Next to each table was a bucket of ice on a stand. Booths with red benches. Bordello atmosphere, she thought. A fitting place to meet.

She peered to the left, towards one of the smaller booths with a table set for two. A lone man, a few years younger than she was, was sitting there with a glass of champagne and a menu. He gave her a questioning look.

'Rita?' he said.

She had no idea why she'd gone with that name. It belonged to her mother, the woman she hadn't seen in twenty-five years.

'Yes. And you're Marlon?'

'Please, have a seat. Would you like a glass of bubbly?'

She sat down on the bench across from him as he poured from the bottle. She took in the person she might sleep with before the night was over. A black T-shirt under a black jacket. Fit. A handsome face. Tanned. A bit young for her taste, but maybe that was what she needed – a boy toy.

'Or would you like something to eat?'

'Thanks, I'm fine.'

'Let's get right to the point instead. Feel free to tell me how you want it in greater detail.'

He had lowered his voice, even though it wasn't necessary. It was very loud in the restaurant.

'How do *you* want it?' she said.

'Like I said in my preferences: I like it rough . . . not violent, but rough. I like to dominate . . . and be dominated.'

His gentle voice clashed with his words.

'I have a suggestion,' he said. 'Let's finish our glasses and then get out of here. Do what we came here to do.'

The scent of aftershave in the car – the same brand Ola had used once upon a time; she couldn't remember what it was called.

'Where are we going?' she asked as he drove towards Valhallavägen in a discreetly luxurious Audi.

'To my place.'

'Do you live nearby?'

'Yes.'

There was a porn magazine in the compartment between the seats. She picked it up and looked at the cover. A man was doing something to a tied-up woman.

'For inspiration?' she asked.

'Maybe . . . it's up to you.'

She remembered a film she'd seen with a girlfriend at Rigoletto in the late nineties. The people in it had worn blindfolds and masks as they had orgies in a palace-like building out in the countryside. Tom Cruise had a troubled relationship and suspected his wife was unfaithful, and somehow he ended up in this house where a sex sect had their meetings. Her friend had thought that the movie was degrading to women. She had pretended to agree, but the fact was, it turned her on.

I've always been like that, she thought as she watched Humlegården sweep by outside the windows, *I've never understood the codes that dictate what I'm supposed to think and feel as a woman.*

Marlon kept driving south, towards Gärdet. This part of the city was a blank spot on her mental map. He turned left onto a smaller street, in a neighbourhood she didn't recognize. He stopped in front of a door that slid aside and continued down into a garage.

'Are we there?'

'Having trouble containing yourself? I got the sense that you're used to this . . . that you do this kind of thing more often than I do.'

There was a joking tone to his voice. Or was it . . . did he take her for a professional? It occurred to her that the app might be used by prostitutes.

He turned off the car, breathing close to her. Then he got out, walked around, and opened the door on her side. He took her gently by the shoulders and led her over to a lift.

The *funkis*-style apartment was decorated in a minimalist fashion. Modern art adorned the walls. There were glossy lifestyle magazines on a concrete table. A dress and a pair of tights hung across the back of a futon.

'Your girlfriend's?' she asked as he dimmed the lights by remote control.

'Something like that.'

'Out of town?'

'Just for a little while.'

'How old are you?'

'Thirty-four. Why?'

The faint scent of incense lingered in the air.

'No reason. What do you do? I'm sorry, I'm just curious . . . what do you do professionally?'

'Does it matter?' His tone was playful but she knew he was irritated by her questions. 'I'm in advertising.'

'What kind of advertising?'

'All sorts. TV ads, mostly.'

They walked through a kitchen. There was post on the counter, brown office envelopes with windows. She tried to find a name and address, but it was too dark in the room. He didn't have any kids, though. The flat was far too neat.

'What about your girlfriend . . . does she have other lovers too?'

It was like she couldn't help it. Tourette's syndrome, she'd thought when she was younger. The compulsion to say the wrong thing at the wrong time.

'Don't know. I've never asked.'

He had opened a sliding door into a bedroom. A plastic bin full of various sex toys stood on the floor. Objects that looked like they would hurt.

'Is there a bathroom nearby?'

He pointed towards the hallway.

'Out there.'

'Thanks. Gotta pee.'

As soon as she was inside, she locked the door behind her and stood with her back to it. She remembered the times she had come home in the middle of the night, aged fourteen, after hanging out with Katz and Jorma Hedlund in Hässelby Gård, and heard sounds from the bedroom. Rita had been with a different man every night. Her father had been in prison at the time. Those fake moans, the realization that she wasn't enjoying it in the least, that it was all an act. It had never occurred to her before, but maybe her mother had fucked for money.

Who am I? she thought as she looked at her reflection in the mirror. *Who have I become?*

An image of Katz flickered through her mind. And then one of Hoffman. Why not him instead? Why not pursue a normal affair, like sleeping with your boss?

When she returned to the bedroom, the TV was on, showing a muted porno. She meant to say something, but she knew she would stutter; she could already feel them in the back of her head, the knots of words that always popped up at inopportune times, words that got jammed between the speech area of her brain and her mouth.

'Do you want to watch this while we do it?' he asked.

'Mmm.'

He pulled her close; he was stronger than she'd expected. He kissed her, gently at first, then more passionately. His erection pressed against her thigh. She smelled his deodorant again. She saw the flicker of the movie, three men tying up a woman, putting a muzzle on her, like a dog.

'I want to try something. When I come . . . I want you to squeeze my throat. Hard.'

Something about a lack of oxygen, she thought. It made your orgasm more intense. There was even a name for it, but she couldn't remember what it was. She had read about it somewhere, maybe in a sex column in a regular old evening tabloid.

It had been three days since his last recce, and he felt ready. He would find out who was behind the execution; he owed Zoran that much. And he owed it to himself, too.

He lifted his binoculars and looked at the house. Hillerström was in the office wing. He took a binder from a shelf and removed a document from a plastic sleeve. He returned to the desk, took a hole punch from a drawer, and began to punch holes in some papers.

Jorma focused on the back of the room. Bookcases, a built-in safe. Framed portraits of his daughters on the wall. The man lived an average bourgeois life. The neighbours had no inkling that he was a criminal.

He took out the prepaid phone he kept in reserve in the glovebox. It wasn't too late to call for reinforcements. Katz, he thought. Or Emir. But he hesitated. No one knew what he was caught up in, not even his sister, who was probably starting to worry about him by now.

Something told him that he had to run this race on his own and avoid putting anyone else in danger.

He drove over to the parallel street and parked. He opened the gate to the neighbour's property. No one was home; he had already checked.

He followed the gravel path to the back of the house. There was a trampoline on the lawn. He climbed onto it and peered over. Everything seemed fine.

He went over the fence where it was shielded from view by the garage. The critical part was just ahead.

Hunching over, he ran to the cellar entrance. He looked around the corner and checked on the office wing. Hillerström was still sitting with his back to the window. He hadn't noticed a damn thing.

The door was unlocked. He didn't even need to use the picklocks. He cautiously pulled it open. No alarms.

He found himself in a wine cellar. Dusty bottles lay on shelves along the walls. Further on there was a small spa area with a hot tub and sauna.

He passed a laundry room where clothes were hung to dry. A pile of white boxer shorts lay on a work surface. Neatly ironed shirts hung from a clothes rack.

The stairs up to the ground floor creaked softly. He entered a living room. A display cabinet of expensive whisky stood in one corner. Hillerström seemed to be into seventies retro, or else he just had bad taste: next to the window was a bar with beer taps, and one contrast wall was covered in wallpaper that depicted a tropical beach.

He heard the sound of a radio in the distance. It sounded like Gershwin.

He passed a narrow servants' passage and a room with an aquarium and a piano.

It was inconceivable. He had just been sitting in the apartment in Kransen, playing, and now he was here.

He entered the kitchen. Floral wallpaper and matching curtains. A brick stove hood. On the other side of a narrow door was the office.

Hillerström was talking to someone on the phone in there, giving a forced laugh.

He took up position beside the door. He held the revolver

in one hand and the zip ties in the other. He just had to walk in. He was looking forward to it.

'Jorma . . . what the hell are you doing here?'

He aimed the revolver at Hillerström's face as he slowly approached the man.

'Shut up! Get down on the floor, hands behind your back!'

'Okay, okay, I hear you . . .'

Hillerström sank to the floor. Jorma put the ties on him, pulling them as tight as he could.

Then he yanked him up into a sitting position. He struck him in the face, two hard punches. The man's right eyebrow swelled up within a few seconds.

'Take it easy, for God's sake! What do you want with me?'

'Shut up, I said!'

'Come on now, Jorma, let's discuss this. My daughter is on her way home from school. She just called and said she forgot one of her books . . .'

The guy suffered from some kind of verbal diarrhoea that apparently got worse when he was scared. Jorma pressed the barrel of the gun to his eye. He searched his pockets and found car keys, a tin of *snus*, and a wallet.

'Where's the car . . . in the garage?'

He received a nod in response.

'Is the garage door locked?'

The swollen face twisted into a grimace as someone came in through the front door. There was a dull crash as it slammed shut.

'Hello . . . Dad . . . I'm home.'

The cheerful voice of a young girl. Unaware of what was going on in her father's office.

'Dad . . . are you there? I'm just going to grab my maths book.'

'If she enters this room, I'll shoot you first, and then her.'

'Okay . . . take it easy.'

Hillerström cleared his throat to collect himself.

'I hear you, sweetie . . . I just don't want to be disturbed in here. I'm working on some important papers. We'll talk on the phone later, okay?'

'Okay, Dad . . . I found it. It was on the kitchen table.'

The front door slammed again, and they could hear steps on the gravel path as the girl vanished.

Two minutes later, he took Hillerström out through the door that faced the garden. A black Lexus gleamed in the dark light of the garage. Jorma opened the boot. It was empty aside from a bag of newspapers. He pointed the barrel of the revolver inside. Hillerström climbed over the edge and whimpered as the boot closed on him.

The garage door opened by way of a button on the wall. Jorma took a pack of wet wipes from the glovebox and dried the blood off his hands. He fished a cigarette out of a pack and lit it. His fingers trembled as he stuck the key in the ignition.

A patrol car was waiting at a red light on Drottning-sholmsvägen as he approached the intersection next to the Stora Mossen metro stop. Hillerström had gathered his courage again, or maybe he was suddenly panicking. He was kicking wildly in the boot. A cyclist who had stopped alongside the car looked around in surprise.

Green light. The cop rolled by without paying him any attention.

He took a left on Ulvsundavägen and continued northwards through the sparse traffic.

It was eleven a.m. when Katz arrived at his destination, a yellow-brick building from the late eighties, squeezed between rentable office space and a catering firm. The old tenant's sign was still mounted on the facade: 'Kontiki Self Storage'. He loitered for a few minutes. A taxi stopped to drop off two young men who quickly vanished into the building. A couple walked by from the other direction: a guy with cornrows and an Asian girl. The guy glanced at the buildings, found the street number, took the girl by the arm, and pulled her through the front door.

A little while later, Katz found himself in the same building. A man with the arms of a bodybuilder was leaning nonchalantly against the wall just inside. A depressed-looking Rottweiler was tied to the radiator.

'Looking for someone?' asked the bodybuilder.

'A friend told me you could pay to watch.'

'It costs five hundred kronor.'

Katz handed over a bill, and the man stuck it in the back pocket of his jeans.

'You're the last one in,' he said. 'Follow the hallway to the end.'

The room was a sort of atrium, with a glass ceiling. An old loading dock ran along one wall. There were no windows and thus no one could see inside. There were about fifteen people there, mostly men. Two half-naked women sat on a sofa, sharing a joint.

Film equipment was set up: cameras and spotlights. There was an Oriental rug on the cement floor. Plastic palm trees were scattered about the room.

The guy with the cornrows was standing at the coffee machine and trying to choose a Nespresso pod. His girl was nowhere to be seen. Katz went to stand next to him.

'Excuse me, but do you know how this thing works?'

Katz took the pod from him and inserted it into the slot.

'Thanks. These machines are more complicated than a fucking spaceship. Are you here to watch?'

'Maybe. You?'

'My girl's gonna work. She's getting ready right now.' The man gave him a nicotine-stained smile as the coffee began to trickle into the paper cup. 'Two thousand kronor for three scenes. And tonight I'm giving her a ride to an apartment in Huddinge where she'll bring in another five thousand – seven grand in less than a day.'

The coffee was ready. The man blew on it before taking a sip and nodding towards a door at the other end of the room.

'My fourth one. From Pattaya. I exchange them when their tourist visas run out. There are any number of girls down there who want to come up here and earn some money.'

Katz struggled to sound friendly.

'Do you know who's in charge here? Who rents this place out?'

'That musclehead at the door. Ronny . . . Oh, hey, there she is.'

The door had opened. The Thai woman came out, wearing a G-string and a transparent bra, the bruise on her cheek passably covered in make-up.

It took a while for filming to start. A younger girl whom Katz hadn't noticed before was sitting on a stool, cleaning her genitals with wet wipes.

Someone had turned on house music in the background. The Thai woman removed her last few articles of clothing. Katz couldn't help staring at her. Her pointed breasts with their nearly black nipples. Her pubic hair, which was trimmed in a heart shape; one of her labia was larger than the other and hung down pathetically.

'Are you interested?' said the man with the cornrows. 'You can have my number. You just have to call. I deliver straight to your doorstep, all over town.'

'I don't think so.'

'You won't regret it. That girl'll ride your cock like a porn star. Or else you can get a massage with a happy ending. Here . . . take my number.'

He shoved a crumpled business card into Katz's jacket pocket.

'Look! They're starting.'

A short man whose upper body was covered in tattoos came out of a door across the room. He approached an older man who was standing at the nearest camera, and they had a discussion.

Katz's eyes roved here and there, looking for the bodybuilder, but he couldn't find him.

The spotlights came on. Someone signalled for him to go and stand by the wall. The scent of lube and sweat. Laughter and heavy breathing from excited men who stood along the wall, watching.

Katz had seen enough. He left the room, walking into the corridor.

He heard faint music from another room in the distance. He headed towards it.

The bodybuilder was sitting in an office chair at a desk; he looked up as he discovered Katz. The dog lay on the floor between his legs.

'Are you lost, man?'

'I'm looking for someone . . . a porn producer.' Katz dug in his jacket pocket and placed the DVD on the desk, face up. 'Someone told me he sometimes rents this place for filming. I need to get hold of him. Or, actually, the girl on the cover.'

The man cast a hasty look at the DVD before he shoved it back to Katz with a grunt.

'Sorry, but we don't do work with that sort of product here.'

'I know. But this guy does straight porn too. Does it mean anything to you?'

The musclehead sighed.

'What are you really after? Are you a journalist? An anti-porn activist? We have problems with that type sometimes. Last week our front door was graffitied.'

'I'm just looking for this girl. That's all.'

The man looked out the window, where a truck was reversing into a tarmacked area behind the building. The Rottweiler had stood up and was tentatively nosing Katz's trouser leg.

'She's a junkie chick, right? They knock on our door some-times to ask if there's any work. Mostly people say no. They're too unreliable; not the kind of girls you can hire long term.'

'But do you know who she is?'

'I don't know her name or how to get hold of her. And I don't remember which production she was part of. Don't take it personally, man, but people appreciate me for my lousy memory, and I've already said too much. Go back out and watch instead; after all, you've paid for it. And a piece of advice, with best intentions: it's a bad idea to ask after people in this branch. Some of them can be awfully touchy.'

The door of the filming room was ajar as Katz walked

towards the exit. The music was louder now. The Thai woman was on all fours on the carpet, under a plastic palm tree. The cameraman had placed his foot on her back and was filming her from above. She looked at Katz as he went by. She seemed to be trying to communicate something with her gaze, but he didn't understand what it was.

Katz got off at T-Centralen, went through the turnstiles, and followed the stream of people through the pedestrian tunnel to Central Station. A woman was selling *Situation Sthlm*, the homeless paper, next to one of the pillars. Further on, a man was begging for money from his electric wheelchair. Katz had the feeling that someone was watching him. He looked around but didn't see anyone.

He found the locker in the storage area in the upper hall of the station. *Speed Services 0021*. He punched in the six-digit code at the bottom of the receipt and heard the lock spring open.

There was a brown envelope on the bottom of the locker.

It contained a pocket calendar. There were no entries, except in the address section in the back. Twenty or so mobile phone numbers were written in sprawling penmanship, each followed by a letter. Initials of names, he presumed. First or last.

A folded sheet of A4 paper was tucked inside the plastic pocket on the inside cover. An ink drawing of a woman crouching in what he first thought was a cramped prison cell; he realized after a moment what it was: a cage. In the background of the drawing was a dock on a lake. Three letters were scribbled in the margin. *Jenny's signature?* he wondered in the instant before his brain deciphered them: 'H.o.P'.

A movement caused him to turn his head. A school group was passing by and a person in a grey hoodie vanished behind them. Katz recognized the gait. The guy with the spots on his face, the guy he'd seen at the shelter and the porno cinema.

He stayed put for a moment and pretended to be reading the billboards outside Pressbyrån. The man was watching him from a distance. Katz walked to the escalators and went down to the lower hall. He peered in the window of Pocketshop as he went by. The person was following him.

He increased his speed as he walked through the pedestrian tunnel, pushing his way through the stream of commuters, taking a sudden right turn behind one of the pillars and sinking down into a crouch. The man with the spots hurried past him.

Thirty metres on, the man stopped short and looked around. He took out a phone and made a very brief call, then hung up and kept moving towards the metro platforms.

The man got off the train at Alvik. Katz followed him, always hidden by other passengers. He followed him down the stairs to the ticket hall and then to the exit onto the square.

A tram bound for Solna was waiting on the Tvärbana platform; it was scheduled to depart in two minutes.

The man got on, took a seat, and began to page through a newspaper someone had left behind. The other passengers seemed alarmed by his junkie appearance.

Katz moved to the last carriage, stood in a disabled spot, and kept an eye on the man through the window between the carriages. A sleepy conductor walked around, checking tickets.

The tram started to move, passing through the kilometre-long rock tunnel and coming out into daylight at Margretelundsvarvet. An airplane was thundering in to land at Bromma in the distance, licking the roofs of the old factory buildings as the tram made its way through the industrial area.

The man got off at Norra Ulvsunda and followed the tracks. Katz slid in behind a tram shelter to hide, pretending to read the timetable and letting thirty seconds pass . . . The man had reached the warehouses on the other side of the railway. Katz waited until he was out of sight.

He caught his trail again on Ranhammarsvägen. The streets were lined by neo-Gothic brick buildings from the last century. Further on there were asbestos-sided buildings from the fifties, a period in which this area had undergone lots of renewal. Heavy industry was gone now. The neighbourhood was dominated by car repair shops, tyre warehouses, and food wholesalers.

The man passed the bunker-like headquarters of the Hell's Angels with its no-trespassing signs. Katz had been there once with Jorma Hedlund, back when he had been a member; they'd attended a surprisingly tranquil party where the juiciest incident was a performance put on by a few strippers.

The man walked by a fireworks outlet and then through a back area that contained one surviving Aeronautical Research Institute wind tunnel: a giant L-shaped building made of copper and concrete reminiscent of the set of a dystopic science fiction movie. Then he squeezed through an opening in a wall and came out onto a deserted gravel plot with about ten scrapped cars parked in it.

He crouched down by one of the cars. He took a key from under the wheel rim, opened the door, and got in. A minute later he came back out. He was holding a can of beer in one hand, and he took a few sips. He had changed into a pair of clean trousers, but he had kept his hoodie on. He lived there, Katz realized; the junked car was his home.

The man was waiting for someone; he kept looking at the other end of the gravel plot, which was bordered by another street, narrower and darker. From Katz's spot along the wall, he could see a few warehouses and a dark yard where bushes grew between rusty oil drums.

Then a Vespa came from the opposite direction. The driver stopped, removed her helmet, and shook out her hair – a woman, but she was too far away for Katz to make out any details.

He took out his phone, selected the camera, and zoomed in on her. It was the woman from Blue Dreams. She asked the man a question and shook her head, irritated at his response.

A grey BMW approached from the warehouses in the distance; the door opened and a man stepped out. He was young, his hair slicked back, and he wore khaki shorts, a pair of white trainers, and no socks.

The woman seemed upset; she gesticulated at the man in the hoodie as the other man listened.

The faint smell of burned rubber drifted through the air. Another plane roared in, very low.

When Katz looked at the scrapped car again, the man and woman had climbed into the BMW. Half a minute later, they drove by him, just thirty metres away. Katz watched the woman lean up between the seats and teasingly kiss the man with the slicked-back hair on the neck.

The summer cottage belonged to an acquaintance who wouldn't mind if he borrowed it. Jorma had been to a mid-summer party there once. It was at the end of a forest road in northern Uppland. The nearest neighbours were several kilometres away. The key was in the outhouse. This place hadn't been used for ages.

A musty smell hit him as he unlocked the door. Mouse shit everywhere. The curtains were drawn. Three small rooms, one of which had no windows. There was a wood-stove with a brick chimney. Fishing rods on the walls. A pile of gun magazines lay on a table.

Hillerström gave him an enraged glare when he opened the boot. Jorma didn't say anything; he just tore up a T-shirt he'd found in the house. He used it to blindfold Hillerström.

He was in no rush. He took a little walk first, following a path around a lake before returning to the house. Hillerström was tied to the bed in the windowless room, alternately moaning and hyperventilating.

Jorma watched the news on TV. He drank a low-alcohol beer he found in the pantry. He chatted to himself, musing out loud about what he intended to do to the man.

It was dark when he dragged him outside, tore off the blindfold, and pressed the revolver to the back of his neck. Then he shoved him along in the moonlight, fifty metres into the woods, until they came to a clearing.

'Get on your knees, bend your head forward.'

He placed the barrel of the gun to his neck. Hillerström hung his head like a man condemned to death.

'Tell me everything, from start to finish: who came up with the idea, who you've been in contact with, and if I can tell you're lying, I swear you will never see your daughters again.'

Six months earlier, Hillerström had been brought in for questioning about a job he hadn't had anything to do with. It was just an excuse for the police to initiate contact with him. The interrogation had been held in a home outside the city, by an officer in civilian clothes, some sort of handler. After a while, the man played recordings of secret phone taps for Hillerström; Hillerström himself was on the tape. Work stuff, the sort of evidence that could put him away for a long time.

'I was terrified,' he said. 'That guy could have thrown me in prison for ten years if I hadn't cooperated . . .'

But there was one way to get out of his bind. He had to help the man arrange a robbery.

The man already knew that someone from a security company had contacted Hillerström. Now he wanted Zoran to hear about it. Hillerström was surprised he'd even heard of Zoran. But it wasn't just that: the cop knew that Zoran needed money, and it was important to get him to do this particular job. He'd tried to ask questions about what was going on but wasn't given an answer. All he knew was that the cop was having a hard time getting to Zoran.

'So he was a police infiltrator, the guy who contacted you. You didn't get a name?'

'What the fuck do you think? This guy wasn't exactly dropping business cards all over the place.'

'What did he look like? About how old was he?'

'Thick blond hair . . . almost like wool. Just over thirty. Tall, about six foot five.'

'And you were the only two at this meeting?'

'No. There was an older cop there as well. His boss, I think. A fat old man in his sixties. I thought I recognized him from somewhere.'

'How do you know it was his boss?'

'That's just how it seemed. When he said something, it was like his word was law.'

'Keep going . . . Then what happened?'

'Things just moved forward. I kept in contact with the guy from the security firm. He had no idea the cops were keeping an eye on him. I called Zoran and asked if he was interested in doing an armoured car. No suspicion on his end, either. He saw it as a happy coincidence that I contacted him right when he needed cash. We met up, I gave him some info, he told me you were in, we arranged another meeting in Gärdet, and the ball was rolling.'

'And the handler was in contact with you the whole time?'

'Yeah. He wanted to know what was up, he said.'

'How many times did you meet with him?'

'Three. And you have to believe me, I had no idea they were going to shoot Zoran.'

'But you knew we would get caught.'

Hillerström didn't respond.

'Where did you meet him the other times?'

'At the Kungshallen market, in town. At an Indian restaurant on the ground floor.'

'Was he in contact with the security guy too?'

'I don't know . . . Why?'

'That guy is dead.'

Hillerström stared at him vacantly.

'Zoran was killed by a cop. And now the insider is dead too. Suicide. How likely is it that they're connected?'

Hillerström tried to open and close his swollen eye.

'I can give you something if you let me go, Jorma. There is a way to reach that cop. I happened to find out about it . . . by chance, you could say. After the robbery, when everything was going to shit.'

'Well?'

'Like I said, you have to let me go first. Let's defuse this whole situation. I want you to know I'm damn sorry for what happened to Zoran. I'll give you money, too; try to make up for all of this. We'll meet again in a few days, you can decide where. For God's sake, Jorma, we can fix this. I'm as pissed off as you are about what happened.'

Perhaps the address book was a backup for Ramón's phone, Katz thought as he sat in his office, gazing out the window at Tranebergsparken – phone numbers of clients, or maybe dealers? The first number was followed by the initial Å.

He looked up the first ten on the Swedish phone directory website, Eniro. No hits. He did a bit more digging around, trying to see if he could find matches for any of the other numbers, but got the same discouraging results. They all went to unregistered prepaid cards.

He took out the drawing instead. A woman, caged up in a house somewhere. *H.o.P.*

That abbreviation could mean anything. But the drawing had been in the address book, as if they belonged together.

He took out his mobile phone and dialled a random number from the book. No answer. He called another, but all he heard was the endless dial tone; no voicemail picked up.

He flipped to the last page. Two numbers. He called the top one, which was listed under the letter Å. Three rings, and then, to his surprise, an answer: a child, a boy.

'Hi . . . this is Linus.'

For a moment, Katz was at a loss for words.

'Hi, Linus. What are you doing?'

'Nothing. Are you a friend of Dad's?'

'Yes, I am.'

Silence on the line. The boy was rustling something; it sounded like a piece of paper.

'Are you looking for something?' Katz asked.

'Yeah, sweets.'

'Did you find any?'

'No, just this phone, it was buzzing in a drawer.'

'Where are you, Linus?'

'At home . . . in Dad's office.'

The boy pronounced the word as if he didn't quite understand the meaning of an office.

'Promise you won't tell Dad . . . that I'm looking in his stuff for sweets.'

'I promise, but only if you can answer a few questions.'

'Okay.'

He could tell the boy was nervous. Katz made an effort to sound calm.

'How old are you, Linus?'

'Five. Almost five and a half.'

'Do you know the name of the street you live on?'

'No . . .'

'Do you live in Stockholm?'

'Yes.'

'In the city?'

'Yes.'

The boy was breathing close to the receiver. He was stuffed up; Katz could hear him sniffling.

'What's the rest of your name, Linus?'

'That's it.'

'Don't you have a last name too?'

'Same as Dad's.'

'What is that?'

'Don't you know? You're his friend, right?'

'Yes, but I'm just wondering if you know it too.'

The boy laughed. He pressed a button on the phone and there was a beep.

'There are no games on this phone,' he said, disappointed.

'There are tons on Mum's phone, and I can play them as much as I want. Bamba Pizza and Toca Boca Hair Salon. And Minecraft, even though I'm not very good at it. My big sister is better, but she goes to school. You can't tell that I was looking for sweets in Dad's room, because if I don't eat sweets for a whole year I get a new bike.'

The line crackled; the boy seemed to have put down the phone. Katz heard his voice from a distance.

'I have to go,' he said. 'Dad came in the door and I'm not supposed to—'

The call ended in the middle of his sentence.

Katz put down the phone and stared at the last page of the address book. The boy's bright, childish voice was still echoing through his head.

When he called again a minute later, he heard a recorded voice telling him that the number was temporarily unavailable.

It was 10 p.m. and the person Katz was waiting for didn't seem to have any intention of showing up. Katz could sympathize. It had started to rain, a gentle, cold drizzle.

He left the spot where he'd been standing and walked over to the car. He fumbled underneath the rim until he found the key. He opened the driver-side door and peered in. There was a car battery on the floor, and it was connected to a light in the glovebox. A sleeping bag was unrolled across the back seat. There were a few letters from the Social Insurance Agency, addressed to a certain John Sjöholm at a P.O. box in the city.

Boxes of prescription drugs were sticking out of the side pocket of the door: Subutex, prescribed out of a clinic in Solna. Protease inhibitors. Fusion and enzyme inhibitors. The guy was HIV positive.

A dog-eared porn magazine lay on the passenger seat, open at the centrefold. The headline was in German: *Geile ficken im Klassenzimmer.* Katz saw nude images of the man, taken a few years earlier, when he was in better shape. His cock was erect. He was trying to look tough as he stared into the camera, but he didn't succeed. He was getting a blow job from Jenny, who was dressed as a little girl.

Katz put down the magazine and looked in the glovebox. Two syringes wrapped in a handkerchief. An electronic picklock and a crowbar.

He was startled by footsteps. A torch lit up the factory

wall in the distance. Katz locked the car door and put back the key.

Ten minutes later, when the man stepped out of the car, Katz was behind him and slightly off to the side, in the dark. The rain had stopped. The lights of the city were reflected against the thick clouds. He could hear rustling from a rubbish heap further off – rats, maybe.

Katz took two steps forward and the man didn't have time to react before he hit him in the chest with the crowbar. The man collapsed before him with a prolonged groan.

Katz followed him down to the ground, pressing the shaft of the crowbar to his neck, just under his larynx. He felt like he was looking at an enlargement of the spots on the man's face: the eruptions were yellow, filled with fluid. The man clawed at the air with his fingers, trying to scream, but all he could produce was a rattle.

A truck engine started somewhere nearby. Its headlights lit up the factory wall before it backed out and drove off through the industrial area. The man was still struggling, trying to tear at Katz's hair. Katz headbutted him in the face.

Katz removed the crowbar from the man's throat just one second before he would have slipped into unconsciousness and stood up, pressing his foot against the man's cheek. The man gave a violent cough; snot and blood ran from his nose.

'Don't do it,' he said. 'For God's sake, don't kill me . . .'

'Why were you following me?'

The man seemed to be processing the information, trying to nod as if he finally understood what was going on.

'Leona asked me to.'

'Who?'

'The girl from Blue Dreams. She asked me to find out who you are . . .' His voice was slowly returning. He remained on his back, grimacing with pain. 'You know, because you went there and asked a bunch of questions.'

A violent demon was running riot inside of Katz. He didn't trust it; didn't trust himself.

'What did you learn about me?'

'Nothing. I lost you. I don't even know your name.'

The man was peering nervously at a point just behind him. And then at the crowbar in Katz's hand. He touched his nose cautiously and seemed surprised to see blood on his fingertips.

'How do you know her . . . Leona?'

'She pays me to work the glory holes. Most people know it's a guy on the other side, but they pretend it's not; they fantasize about a chick instead . . . they don't care if their cocks happen to rub up against a little stubble.'

'What about Jenny?'

'The two of us worked there. But she quit.'

Katz took a step back. The man crawled to his knees, massaging his chest and neck.

'I want you to tell me what you know about Jenny.'

They had known each other for a few years, the man explained. She was from Stockholm, but she had spent a couple of years living abroad. Her real name was Jennifer, but she went by all sorts of pseudonyms.

'She claims it's because her mum is looking for her, and she doesn't want to be found. But that girl lies so much she believes herself.'

'What's her last name?'

'Roslund. Why do you want to know?'

'When did you last see her?'

'It's been a few months. I ran into her in town by chance. We got coffee, but she was stressed as shit and left after five minutes. She had clients waiting, she said.'

'How can I get hold of her?'

'No idea. I had her number in my old phone, but it got stolen.'

Katz stared intently at him, unsure whether he was lying.

'You did porn shoots together,' he said. 'You have a magazine in the car.'

'So what? I needed the money . . . Shit, I'm a whore anyway; what the fuck does it matter? I don't even like it. Have to use pills to get it up.'

The man looked at him with a mixture of shame and defiance.

'Tell me more. About what happened the other day. When you were following me.'

He had seen Katz for the first time when he was asking about Jenny at the shelter. He'd overheard the conversation Katz had had with the man on duty, Magnus, and had become curious; he'd followed him to the porn club and slipped into the background while he was talking to Leona.

When Katz left, she'd asked him to follow him and find out who he was. He had lost sight of him. But a few days later, by chance, he saw him again at Central Station.

'You met Leona here afterwards,' Katz said. 'I saw you. A guy in a BMW showed up – who was that?'

'Her boyfriend. Wallin.'

'What's his first name?'

'No idea. That's just what people call him; I don't know him.'

'Did Jenny ever mention an address book to you?'

'What the fuck kind of address book?'

'For their drug deals, her and Ramón's. Or about something called H.o.P.?'

The guy was startled and gave him an odd look.

'No . . . and you ask really fucking weird questions.'

Katz realized that he was losing focus, almost as if he were falling inside himself. The craving was back, as inexplicable as the last time: a flicker of something like epilepsy. When he returned to his senses he saw that the guy was holding a knife in his hand. He was backing up and waving the blade at him.

Not dangerous, Katz thought. He didn't have it in him to kill anyone. So he let him go.

Where had Ramón got the money to buy drugs? Somehow he had come into a great deal of it, likely by criminal means.

A robbery?

But Ramón wouldn't make a good robber, Katz thought as he walked to the shelter on Flemingsgatan; he wasn't aggressive enough, wasn't ever wired enough.

Horse junkies were seldom robbers; they preferred burglary. The crackheads were the ones who would take an axe into a jewellery shop and grab the daily cash and as many gems as they could carry.

It didn't add up. He was on the wrong track.

He remembered how Ramón would make up lies about everything under the sun: about rich relatives who didn't exist, drugs he claimed he could get, places they could spend the night that turned out to be purely fantasy. Or how his mother had been forced to flee Chile for political reasons when in fact she had come to Sweden to work as a maid.

The young guy with the hipster beard was standing in the door of the shelter, waving at an older drunk who was walking over from the park across the street.

'A new volunteer, perhaps?' he said cheerfully as he noticed Katz. 'All jokes aside, have you found the girl you were looking for?'

He held the door for him.

'Not yet,' Katz said. 'Is Mona here?'

'I let her in early this morning. The poor thing couldn't

get a bed at any of the night shelters. She slept outside. Check the laundry room.'

'It's him,' she said when she looked at the video he'd taken on his phone in Ulvsunda. He stopped the video when the man with the slicked-back hair entered the frame.

'Are you sure?'

'Yep. Unless he has a doppelgänger. That's the guy I saw in the gossip mag. The dude who arranges the perv get-togethers. The organizer.'

'So, the same guy?'

'Yes. Without a doubt. *Peter.* That's what she called him. I just remembered.'

'What about the other guy, in the hoodie. Do you know him?'

'No.'

'John Sjöholm. Red spots on his face. That doesn't mean anything to you?'

'Should it?'

She snatched the five-hundred-kronor bill and made a kissy face.

'Thanks, darling. What would I do without you?'

Peter Wallin, Katz thought as she vanished into one of the dormitories. A name would lead somewhere.

Maybe the numbers in Ramón's address book didn't belong to clients or dealers, as he'd first thought. Maybe they were johns in Wallin's network. Men who gathered to degrade women.

Blackmail. Was that how they'd got the seed money to buy a whole lot of heroin?

PART 4

Jorma was waiting at a Japanese lunch restaurant on Ulvsun-davägen. The aroma of miso soup and fresh dumplings was making his mouth water. He hadn't eaten anything substantial in days.

He had spent his time finding a new hideout instead. In the end, an old friend had let him borrow a studio apartment in Högdalen, and had even arranged a car for him. Emir. He'd known him since his Hell's Angels days. A dependable guy.

He was starting to feel safer. He'd even toyed with the thought of heading out to Kransen to pick up some stuff. But it was still too soon.

Leena ought to be feeling relieved by now. He'd texted her to say that he was out of town, and that she shouldn't worry. He'd asked her to take some money out of the safe deposit box in Huddinge and keep it at home in case he needed it on short notice.

He looked at the clock that hung above the sashimi counter. Hillerström didn't seem to have any intention of showing up.

He would give him another five minutes, ten at the most, before he drove out to the house. The guy was as good as dead already.

The handler's hands, he thought . . . He'd forgotten to ask Hillerström if there was anything special about the man's hands. He couldn't quite put his finger on the memory; he'd been in shock in the forest and the whole scene had been too chaotic.

There were other things that bothered him, like the fact

that Zoran had moved around, staying with different friends in the weeks leading up to the robbery. And the tone of his voice when he told Jorma about it in the car at the shopping centre, as if the two things were connected.

He looked at the clock. Ten minutes had passed. It was time for Hillerström to eat shit.

He stopped the car in the same spot as he had four days earlier, but this time he walked right up to the house. The front door was unlocked. This ought to have raised his suspicions, he realized later. But it didn't at the time. He was full of adrenaline; he would start by shooting the pig in the kneecaps. It was two in the afternoon. The man might have prepared himself for a visit and called in backup. His wife and kids might arrive home at any moment, but either way, Jorma didn't give a rat's arse.

To his surprise, they were already there. They were sitting at a table in the room with the ugly contrast wallpaper, staring at him expressionlessly. Two girls, surprisingly like their father . . . and their mum was there, too.

Their faces were red from crying. Vases of flowers, condolence cards attached, lined the bar counter.

'Who are you looking for?'

The woman had spoken to him, Hillerström's wife.

'I'm trying to get hold of . . .'

That was as far as he got before he stopped. He suspected he knew what was going on.

'Don't you read the papers?' said the girl closest to him, in the same voice he'd heard a couple of days earlier when she returned home to get her schoolbook. 'Dad has been murdered.'

The office was nearly deserted. People had found excuses to go home early. The lights were on in Hoffman's office. A few days ago, she definitely would have made sure he knew that she was there. But not this time. She snuck past his door as discreetly as she could.

She took off her shoes as she entered her office, and she closed the door cautiously. She aired out her feet as she peered out the window at Kungsholm Church. The autumn leaves had started to fall on the cemetery surrounding it.

A pile of folders she didn't recognize lay on her desk. Other divisions of the Economic Crime Authority trying to saddle her with projects. She ought to have been on hand during the day, looking out for her own best interests. But she'd been anxious about events of the previous day and had chosen to work from home instead.

As she sat down at her desk and turned on her computer she could hear Hoffman talking on the phone, his office door open. Something about the unacceptable flow rate in the petty-crime unit. His friendly but firm voice made people feel secure and motivated all at once. The man was popular, and not just with her. In under six months he had managed to raise morale throughout the whole department.

She opened an email from her contact at the investigative unit; he had sent the survey results. According to the law governing electronic communication, an individual's telephone records cannot be accessed unless the individual in question is under suspicion of a crime punishable by at least two years in prison, but the guy owed her a favour, and, furthermore, she could always refer to the rules of confidentiality governing international matters.

The log files were in order of date: all the traffic that had travelled to and from the prepaid phone numbers in the last six months. The last number called was the one Katz had told her about, his conversation with the little boy named Linus; its closest base station was in Liljeholm.

Accordingly, the only number that could be traced was Katz's. The rest of them had only been called by other numbers on the list – not by traceable numbers or from contract phones where the owner could be identified. A closed circle, she thought: communication between corresponding vessels.

Traffic between the numbers increased at regular intervals – it happened about once a month, as if there were some important event.

She emailed the files to Katz with no comment of her own and logged into the Kobra intranet, through which she had access to the internal police databases. She entered the name he'd asked her to check: Peter Wallin.

The results were slim. There was just one note: the man had come up in a tax investigation during his time as manager of a now-defunct strip club called Wild Horses. According to the Companies Registration Office, he owned a video-rental service with an address at a P.O. box in Uppsala. He was twenty-nine years old. No known residential registration.

Could it really be true, as Katz thought, that Ramón had been running a blackmail scheme?

According to Katz's theory, Ramón's girlfriend had sold herself to a sex network organized by Wallin. She had participated in films where she was sexually degraded and somehow or other came across Wallin's address book, which contained a list of his clients' phone numbers. And she had potentially extorted money from the clients, which they then invested in drugs.

If it was true, as Katz maintained, then perhaps Ramón hadn't died of an accidental overdose after all; he may in fact have been murdered by the people he was blackmailing.

And what about his girlfriend . . . what had happened to her?

She sighed audibly. She didn't know why she was doing this. It was all too far-fetched.

She spent the next hour on her own business instead. She had received more emails from the financial police in Sarajevo. One of them contained a general question about whether there was corruption in the police authority in Sweden. Another contained data on transactions between suspicious accounts at Swedish business banks and less scrupulous ones in Luxembourg. A third contained a list of possible frontmen whom her Bosnian colleagues couldn't investigate because the people in question were outside their jurisdiction. There were about ten names, and their lowest common denominator was that they all had origins in the former Yugoslavia.

She ran them through the crime database but wasn't any the wiser for it. Some of them had been sentenced, but never in connection with running fronts. Others had a clean record but had been involved with companies that were under suspicion of running fronts . . . But that had taken place so long ago that they could not possibly still be of interest.

According to the information she found, three of the people on the list were the owners of relatively recently opened companies, but two of them actually seemed to be legitimate businesses and the third, whose type of enterprise wasn't listed, had only existed for a few months before being liquidated.

She realized that she was losing focus. She thought of the previous day instead, her aborted sex date. She had sobered up and told the man she'd changed her mind. Nothing strange there – it was all on a voluntary basis, of course. And yet, for an instant, she had been terror-stricken. She wondered if this was the way prostitutes felt when they were driven around to visit strange men in the middle of the night.

Marlon had seemed more resigned than disappointed. But he had driven her back into the city again and told her to be in touch if she changed her mind, which she did not intend to do. She had even deleted the app.

She didn't hear the knock at her door, so she didn't see him until he was standing in the doorway with a cup of coffee in hand.

'Don't you know the new rules, Eva? Twenty hours of overtime per month is the max.'

He looked at her with concern. And she tried to figure out if she felt anything for him. Maybe, she thought, or maybe she was just confused.

'Well, in case you were wondering, I'm doing flexitime; I had to take care of a few things this afternoon. And I'm trying to make up for lost time, see?'

'The Bosnians hassling you?'

'Yep.'

'Come knock on my door if you take a break and want some company.'

She knew next to nothing about his private life. Divorced, people said. But even that was an unsubstantiated rumour. Kids? She had never thought to ask.

She noticed that her heart was beating faster. It was not

possible, she thought. It was her imagination, autosuggestion; she wasn't a teenager anymore.

'I don't think I'll be that late,' she said in a neutral tone.

'It's almost the weekend. And there's a nice place around the corner. They have music trivia on Fridays . . . and happy hour prices. I was thinking of going there with some old colleagues from the police station. Friendly souls, all of them. You're more than welcome to come along.'

'I'll think about it,' she said, trying to sound as if she didn't mean it.

She wasn't getting anywhere on her project and didn't have anything better to do anyway. At least, that was her excuse for taking a seat among half a dozen men at a pub on Bergsgatan an hour later. Football on all the TV screens. On the other side of the pub was a separate room where music trivia had just ended. Sweaty waitresses were darting from table to table. Hoffman observed her over his Czech beer.

'How are things?' he asked. 'You look tired.'

'Thanks for the compliment. But working in a headwind takes its toll.'

He gave her a boyish smile.

'I only heard half the talk a few weeks ago. Had to leave in the middle of it. Can't you tell me a little more about it?'

She gave him the short version of her project.

'So money laundering and the Balkan mafia?'

'Yes. Profits from all sorts of criminal enterprises. But for now the Bosnians aren't investigating the serious crime, for tactical reasons. The organized-crime groups have contacts in administration down there. And the only department that isn't corrupt is the economic crime unit . . . at least, according to them.'

'So they're trying to get at the mob the back way?'

'They're following bank transactions, tracing their accounts.

Trying to nail them on crime-profiting grounds. That's new down there, and, as you know, we're at the forefront when it comes to seizing assets when their origins can't be accounted for. They're trying to do what the Americans did when they put Al Capone away for tax evasion because they couldn't convict him of murder.'

Hoffman nodded.

'Do you need more resources? I can bring in a free auditor if you like. This seems like the sort of project we should prioritize.'

'Maybe later. I have to find a thread to pull at first. There are a few new companies I need to check out.'

They sat in silence for a moment. A few patrons from a hen party were going nuts on the karaoke machine. Hoffman wasn't that different from Katz, she thought. She hadn't considered it earlier, but it was true: raven hair, brown eyes, but without that Keith Richards face that bore the traces of half a life on the streets. She could smell his scent, masculine and sweet at the same time. She had the sudden impulse to lean across the table and sniff him, and she almost started laughing at the thought.

One more glass, she thought, *and I might do something I regret.*

'Unfortunately I have to go,' she said. 'I promised myself I would clean the kids' room tomorrow. It looks like a battlefield in there.'

'That sounds smart . . . Where do you live?'

'In Vasastan, by Sankt Eriksplan.'

Hoffman seemed to be pondering something.

'How about a walk in your neighbourhood tomorrow?'

'You're going to have to state your reasons!'

Her response sounded more dismissive than she'd intended, but he just smiled at her, cheerfully immune to the possibility of being rejected.

'Just regular old concern, and a tiny bit of curiosity about a damn competent colleague. You don't have to take it so seriously, Eva. I like to take a walk in the city each weekend. A different neighbourhood every time. Last week it was Sjöstaden. But I don't mean to be forward.'

Katz, she thought, but she could no longer picture his face. As if he and all his complicated baggage were drifting out of her horizon, and her image of him was being replaced by one of Hoffman. Was that what this was all about . . . trying to forget Katz?

'Why not?' she said. 'The truth is, I need to get out and get some exercise. Breathe some fresh air. Talk about whatever. And who knows, maybe I'll make new inroads on my project.'

The apartment building was at the end of a dead-end street, not far from Tensta city centre. An abandoned scooter lay on the pavement. The cars in the car park, ten-year-old Mercedes, Audis, and BMWs, appeared to have been imported directly from shady dealers in Hamburg. Jorma was standing behind a bus shelter a hundred metres away, hesitating, unsure whether he had made the right decision . . .

He had called Leyla the night before to tell her they needed to have a chat. He realized he had to take the chance and ignore the risk that her phone might be tapped.

His situation had changed drastically. Hillerström had been executed when he was out for a jog in Judarskogen. Shot in the face at close range with a silenced weapon. According to the press, there were no witnesses. Would it be his turn next? If Hillerström had talked, it would.

He peered at the building again. He'd always had a sixth sense for plainclothes cops, but none of his warning bells were going off.

He took the long way round, through a grove of trees, and approached the back garden. If someone had been following him, he would have noticed.

The door to the basement was open. He stood next to the stairs, which led to the ground floor. He listened for any sounds – breathing, the gentle rustle of clothes against a body – but heard nothing.

*

The kids had hung drawings on the door. *Welcome to the Abramovičs'* it said in messy letters. Two adult figures, and two children, in crayon, meant to be a family portrait. He felt a stab of pain in his chest.

Leyla opened the door. She had dark circles under her eyes and short, greying hair. Ten years had passed since he'd last seen her. She had aged half a lifetime since then, or maybe it had all happened in the past few weeks.

He caught a glimpse of the playroom on the other side of the hallway. The kids were on the sofa, watching the Disney Channel. A framed photo of Zoran stood on a bureau, lit candles on either side.

The children came out to greet him. Jorma could barely look at the older boy, who had the same cautious expression as his father, the same shy demeanour. And he was so terribly vulnerable in this world he could no longer trust.

'Are you sure no one followed you?' Leyla asked a few minutes later as they sat alone at the kitchen table.

'Totally sure.'

'The police must be looking for you.'

'It doesn't seem that any of the cameras caught me. And the others aren't saying a word in interrogation.'

She moved her head in a gesture that might have meant anything. She peered out through a gap in the blinds. Jorma didn't know how much she knew, or how much she had managed to figure out on her own.

'You came here to ask me something?' she said.

'I have to know why he decided to get involved in a robbery.'

'Didn't he tell you?' She fingered her wedding ring nervously, twisting it around and around, counter-clockwise. 'I thought you knew . . .'

*

A few months earlier, Zoran had been contacted by a Bosnian man who asked if he was interested in being the frontman for a new company. He would receive fifty thousand kronor for his trouble. Leyla had suspected money laundering, but she hadn't wanted to ask. Zoran would only be listed as owner for a short time before the company was liquidated.

'So we went along with it. And after a while, this guy came back and said that the people he worked for needed help with something else. Zoran would pick up a truck by the harbour, in Nynäshamn. Workers from the ferry from Poland would drive it off the boat, park it in a particular spot, and then Zoran would take it to a certain place in Stockholm. And get another fifty thousand for his trouble.'

'Drugs?'

She shook her head.

'That's what we thought at first. But we were wrong.'

She started biting at a nail but stopped herself.

'To tell you the truth, I looked the other way; I didn't want one hand to know what the other was getting up to. And Zoran definitely knew something was fishy about this delivery. But we needed the money. I haven't been able to work since our daughter was born. The anaesthesiologist messed up my epidural . . . I have nerve damage. That was three years ago, and the pain still hasn't gone away. And we had no idea what was going to happen, of course.'

Her face was expressionless as she went on. 'Zoran took the commuter train down to Nynäshamn and walked to the harbour. It was the middle of the night, and they'd made sure it was deserted. He picked up the vehicle – a black delivery truck – and started driving towards Stockholm.'

She stopped talking and stared blankly at nothing.

'Then what? What happened?'

'He said he heard something . . . strange sounds. He stopped at a rest stop and opened the door, same key as the ignition. And there they were. Five terrified girls . . . He told me about it afterwards, once he got home. The girls thought they were going to be sold to brothels. In the worst case, they would be sent to something they called "the tunnel". It was very clear they weren't there voluntarily. They said that they had been accompanied by an armed man on the ferry, and he had returned to the boat after driving them off. Two of the girls spoke Serbian, so Zoran understood everything they said.'

She took a deep breath before continuing.

'So he let them go. There was nothing else he could do. He couldn't handle the situation. He called his contact and told it like it was. And when he got home, he explained to me what a mess we were in.'

'Who was his contact?'

'I don't know. I never met him. He lived in Sarajevo. Zoran had met him once in the nineties, when he lived in Sweden for a few months. He had come to get away from the war down there and went back again as soon as it was over, but back then he was just a small-time gangster. And afterwards, when Zoran went underground, I thought it would be best to know as little as possible.'

'But the police must have been here several times after the robbery. Didn't you say anything to them?'

She didn't have to respond. He could tell that she hadn't said a thing. That she was frightened to.

'So Zoran decided to rob an armoured truck to pay back what they claimed he owed them?'

'They threatened him. They threatened to do something to the kids, too. They said they wanted at least five million, one million per woman. That was their market value, they claimed. The kids had to go and live with my sister. And

Zoran was afraid to live at home. So he slept at friends' houses while he tried to figure out what to do.'

That added up with what Zoran had said before the robbery, that he had been staying with friends. And it matched Hillerström's story, that the handler couldn't find him. He had gone underground, just like Jorma was now.

'Did they come here looking for him?'

'I saw people sitting in a car outside the building several times. And they called and told me what they would do if he didn't pay. That was all it took.'

'After the robbery . . . after he was dead . . . did they stop showing up?'

'Yes. I guess they were even.'

She swallowed hard, avoiding eye contact.

'What is it?'

'I don't know if it's important.'

'Everything is important.'

'Zoran went to the police first. He called a tip line and was transferred to a detective.'

'I don't understand.'

'To get help. We thought if he informed against the people he owed money to, maybe a witness protection programme could help us. My sister knows another guy . . . an acquaintance who testified against a motorcycle gang. He was given a new identity.'

'Did Zoran get the detective's name?'

'No. He used a pseudonym. And Zoran didn't trust him. That was why he stopped trying and decided to go along with the robbery instead. The guy knew things he shouldn't have known. He happened to overhear him talking to his boss on the phone. They were saying the wrong things.'

'Did he meet the cop in person?'

'Twice, before he got cold feet.'

'Do you know where?'

'Yes, I do, actually. In Kungshallen, at an Indian restaurant. This guy was crazy about his food. He always ordered the same chicken dish.'

She grew quiet. Her son was calling for her from the playroom. She went over to him and said something in a low voice, in Serbo-Croatian, before returning with a pair of urine-soaked pants, which she placed in a plastic bag.

'This happens all the time. The school counsellor says it's not unusual in children who are dealing with grief.'

She sat down again. She rubbed her fingers over her forehead.

'The police said they shot him in self-defence. Do you think that's true?'

Jorma didn't respond. He wasn't sure how much she wanted to know, deep down.

'It's like I can't get it into my head that he's gone,' she continued. 'I got the news at night. Two policemen showed up and told me what had happened. They comforted me when I broke down. I don't know what happened after that. Time flattened out somehow. I remember people making food for me, taking care of the kids. They refused to believe that their dad was dead . . . they still *are* refusing to believe it in some ways. Every night when I put them to bed they ask when he's coming back.'

She looked at her hands. The nails were bitten to the quick. She placed them in her lap, as if they were strange objects she'd never seen before and she didn't know what to do with them.

'I have to put them to bed now,' she said. 'They need all the sleep they can get. Maybe it's best if you go.'

She stopped him as he headed for the door.

'You know . . . I'm proud of him. He freed those women. I just hope they made it home to wherever they came from.'

Two colleagues on a stroll through autumnal Stockholm. She wasn't going to sleep with him or try to start anything. She had made up her mind. She had nothing to worry about.

'How did you end up becoming a prosecutor?' Hoffman asked as they walked through the park below Karlberg Palace. 'Are there other lawyers in your family?'

'My advisor in *gymnasium* said it would be a good fit for me. I applied out of the blue, and when I got in I took it as a sign that I had made the right choice.'

'No moral compass to guide your way?'

'That showed up after a while. The desire to do the right thing. Or to strive to, in any case.'

The light of the pale autumn sun forced its way through the gaps in the clouds. A group of children in reflective vests was playing down by the canal.

'Plus I wanted to live a life as different from my parents' as possible.'

'That sounds so mysterious it demands an explanation.'

She explained her parents briefly, the tame version: Jonas and Rita had gone wrong in life, had children far too early, hadn't been able to leave their destructive lifestyle behind, and barely managed to retain custody of her. She said nothing about her disabled brother, who had been given away when he was ten, or about visiting her father at Österåker prison when she was seven, or cleaning up her mother's vomit when she was nine years old. And nothing about herself in her dark teenage years, about her abuse of heroin, her gang involvement, her time with Katz and Jorma Hedlund, the terrible things that had happened that she couldn't bear to think about, but which had at least brought her to the treatment facility in Vilhelmina where, against all odds, she got her life back on track.

'What about you?' she asked. 'How did you end up in law?'

'My story is less dramatic than yours. Dad is a judge. His dad, too. My other grandpa was a police officer. My mum and little sister are the only black sheep. They're child psychologists.'

Maybe that was why he behaved so calmly, she thought. He was a friend to himself and worked on self-awareness, a trait which was always in short supply in the male half of the population.

To her surprise, he had taken a plastic bag with pieces of bread from his jacket pocket. Like a retired person, she thought as he began to toss bits into the water, to feed a nearby flock of ducks. But she liked it.

'And why did you leave the vice squad?'

'It was so full of misery. And you get caught up in it, living day in and day out with a bunch of disgusting images in your head, listening to surveillance tapes where people talk about women like they're discussing livestock. Trafficking rings and child prostitution. Paedophile crackdowns where you find ten thousand child-porn images on a hard drive, and the youngest victims aren't even a year old. In the end you become numb. That's when I realized it was time to change jobs.'

He shook his head.

'I'm glad to be able to work on something else. Grateful . . . though maybe that's not the right word.'

They continued their walk, heading towards Hornsberg; they crossed the pedestrian bridge to Kungsholms Strand

and turned back towards the city. She realized that her current case had started buzzing in her mind again, the list of names of possible frontmen. It was the workaholic inside her, refusing to take time off. If she understood correctly, the names had come from tapped phones. She ought to take a closer look at anyone who was listed as an owner of a new company, she thought. The Swedish Companies Registration Office had a helpline.

'Like I said, if there's anything you need help with, just ask.'

Katz, she thought. She must not forget him, let him vanish. Hoffman was her boss and colleague, nothing more.

'Maybe you can help with something else. Does the name Ramón Suárez mean anything to you?'

'No. Does it have to do with your case?'

'An old friend needs help finding a missing person. It's more vice than financial crime. How about Peter Wallin?'

Hoffman's work instincts seemed to awaken.

'Oh yes, I know quite a bit about him. He ran a strip club in the city in the late 2000s. Wild Horses. He was under suspicion of cooking the books for a while, and being a pimp on top of that, but he managed to wiggle out of the trap just before they had him. Kind of a creep. He eventually ended up in the porn industry. But I don't know what he's up to these days.'

'Did you ever hear the name "Jenny" in connection with Wallin? A prostitute?'

'To be honest, I try to forget everything about my time in vice.'

She let the conversation die out. A little while later, they arrived at Sankt Eriks Bridge.

'Thanks for the company, Eva.'

He had placed a hand on her shoulder. That's just the sort of person he was, she thought. He touched people to show he appreciated them. She had seen it in the office; he didn't have the usual Nordic stiffness. He was physical, with both male and female colleagues. Sensual, but with no ulterior motives.

She felt the warmth streaming from his hand. She didn't want to like his touch . . . and yet she very much did.

'I'll get the bus from here,' he said. 'Next week it'll be Norra Djurgården. One of our chamber commissioners lives out there. I'm planning to ask him to show me around his neighbourhood.'

So this was just a plan he'd put in place, she thought; it had to do with the welfare of his staff, nothing more. She ought to have realized that.

The bus stopped five metres away from them. He gave her an awkward wave as he stepped on. She watched him for a long time, his outline through the back window, as he took out a paperback book and started reading it.

As soon as she got home, she called the Swedish Companies Registration Office and got hold of an on-duty administrator. She briefly explained her reason for calling. It only took a few minutes for him to bring up the data.

'Two of the companies are active,' he said. 'One of them imports perishables from Denmark. Meats and cheeses. Danish salami, and those cheeses that smell like sweaty feet. The other deals in clothing and has contracts with a number of Italian denim designers. The third, a real-estate company, was very recently liquidated by the minority shareholder, who lives in Split.'

'Why wasn't it the majority shareholder?'

'He recently passed away, a certain Zoran Abramović.'

At least there was one name she could cross off the list, she thought. A dead man wouldn't be of much help. But the real-estate branch was something her Bosnian colleagues had asked her to keep an eye out for.

'The company was registered with us in mid-July. The liquidation was finalized exactly two weeks ago. That's all I can give you right now.'

After she hung up, she took a turn through the children's room. She ought to spend the day cleaning, she thought when she saw the mess inside, or take a trip out to IKEA and buy the vanity table she'd promised Lisa over a year ago.

Become a better mother.

She went back to the living room. A half-full bottle of Jack Daniel's stood on the coffee table. She had the urge to pour a big glass, go numb, maybe for the rest of the weekend, because she couldn't stand the loneliness, but she managed to tamp down the impulse.

She turned on her computer instead. For lack of anything better to do, she googled the name 'Zoran Abramović' and was startled to see all the hits that popped up on her screen. The man had been shot by the police during an armoured-truck robbery a few weeks earlier.

She stood up and went to the kitchen for a glass of water. The name was ringing a bell in the back of her head, but it was so faint that she barely noticed it.

When she returned to the computer, she found that a digital copy of the preliminary investigation of the robbery was available on the Prosecution Authority's server. Three accomplices had been apprehended, and none of them had uttered a peep during interrogation. Abramović had been shot in a firefight with a task force team. An unidentified robber had managed to escape. The police had opened an investigation into the shooting death.

She wrote a quick email to the Internal Affairs unit in Kungsbron to ask if she could obtain a copy of their report. She knew she wouldn't get an answer until they opened again on Monday, but now she was out of excuses to put off cleaning.

She went back to the kids' room and tidied up the worst of the mess. She had just got out the vacuum cleaner when she heard a ding from her computer.

A woman from Internal Affairs had emailed back. *Yet another divorced workaholic*, she thought as she clicked on the attached file.

She read the report with a growing sense that something was wrong. The officer who had shot and killed Abramović was referred to simply as 'NN' in the report. On the surface, it appeared that everything had been done by the book, with debriefings and several lengthy interrogations. The officer had explained that he had been left with no choice because Abramović had threatened his life and fired a volley of shots from his automatic weapon. None of the others on the task force had been nearby to see what had happened. Case closed. And what's more, no chance of getting a name. The identity of the officer in question was protected.

She called up the woman who'd emailed her to ask a few follow-up questions, after which she took a taxi to the office.

She turned on the computer in her office, at the very end of the deserted hallway, and accessed Kobra again. She searched the intranet methodically in the echoing weekend silence of the deserted building, but it wasn't long before she came across an interesting coincidence.

According to one investigative report, which had been carried out for an unrelated reason and compiled by the criminal police a few months previously, a certain Lars-Göran Hillerström, a suspected middleman, had met sporadically with an employee of the security firm that had been the target of the robbery. Joakim Åslund, from the firm's logistics division, had committed suicide two weeks ago.

And Hillerström, she found in a recent report from the murder squad, had recently been shot while out jogging in Judarskogen. A gang-related crime, according to a memo. The case was lowest on the priority list, which included a dozen murder and manslaughter cases that were currently under investigation in the county.

Furthermore, as the log noted, Abramović had called the police tip line one month before his death.

Little India was on the lower level of Kungshallen, a three-storey food court at Hötorget. Jorma went there at lunchtime three days in a row and sat at the table closest to the self-service counter, his hood drawn up over his head. He sneaked glances at the counter, looking for men who fit the description. He fingered his beard, which he'd let grow out. It would have to suffice as a disguise for the time being. He read newspapers people had left behind. No one was writing about the robbery anymore. There was hardly anything about Hillerström either. The underworld was self-cleaning. The police didn't seem to expend much effort when dealing with gang murders.

On the third day, he gave up. At the counter, he waved over a teenage Indian kid with a downy moustache whom he'd seen working every day. He asked if they had a regular client of around thirty, tall with thick blond hair, who always ordered the same chicken meal.

'Yeah, we do. We call him the chicken tikka man. Why do you ask?'

'I need to get hold of him. It's private.'

'Should I ask him to contact you if he shows up?'

'No. In fact, I was planning to surprise him.'

He scribbled his mobile number on a receipt that lay on the counter and handed it over along with a five-hundred-kronor bill.

'Call me next time he shows up here, as fast as you can. I'll give you another five hundred when you do.'

'There won't be any trouble, I hope?'

'No, no, it'll be a happy reunion.'

The guy's eyes roved about the hall; he looked over at the escalators and back at Jorma.

'You're not going to believe it . . . but there he comes.'

Jorma turned around slowly and saw two men coming down the escalator; one of them had white-blond hair and was a head taller than the other. He placed another bill on the counter.

'Thanks. Just act normal. Don't even look in my direction.'

The food court was almost full by now. Office drones from the city. Tourists and shopaholics who had taken a break from shopping at PUB and on Drottninggatan to eat food from a dozen international kitchens.

The men had taken a seat at the table closest to the escalators. They ate lunch as they conversed. Jorma took an empty tray and moved closer. He pulled his hood closer around his face. He tried to figure out what they were talking about, but it was impossible.

The shorter man was powerfully built, around twenty-five. He was average-looking. The blond man was a bit older. He had prominent cheekbones and pale eyebrows. Thick, nearly white hair. Jorma tried to picture him with a balaclava covering his face, but his brain couldn't form the image.

At one point he took an earbud from his jacket pocket and showed it to the other man. Surveillance gear. Jorma was absolutely positive now: these guys were cops.

'Excuse me, is it okay if I take a seat here?'

The voice came from behind him. He turned around to discover a skinny junkie type holding a tray of food. Unnaturally large pupils. Currently high.

'Where the hell did all these people come from? This is worse than the Christmas rush. If you just shove over a little, I'll have enough room.'

The shorter cop was looking their way; Jorma turned so his back was to the cop.

'Sorry, I'm waiting for someone,' he said. 'Did you check to see if there are tables one floor up?'

'No. It's fucking full up everywhere.'

His mind was working in high gear. They would land on the cops' radar any second now.

'I'll eat fast, I promise. And if a spot opens up anywhere else, I'll move right away.'

The man gestured towards the busy tables behind them.

'The police are here,' Jorma said quietly. 'If I were you, I'd get out of here damn quick.'

The guy looked at him in surprise and gulped, then nodded gratefully and vanished into the crowd with his tray.

Jorma's heart was pounding. He was prepared to get up and run at the slightest odd movement. But nothing happened. When he turned around, he discovered that the shorter man had left the table. But the blond man was still there. Jorma tried to catch a glimpse of his hands, his right hand, but the man was searching his pockets for something.

Then he took it out – a mobile phone. He looked at the screen.

Half his little finger was missing. The image came back to Jorma, the one that had been blocked by his shock – the man in the woods, removing his glove and flexing his hand, one finger of which was too short. It was the same guy.

He followed him through the drizzle, heading west on Kungsgatan. The man was walking fast; he turned left on Drottninggatan, passed all the knick-knack shops and tourist traps disguised as restaurants, and crossed Apelbergs-gatan before stopping at a traffic light.

Twenty metres behind him, Jorma slowed down, allowing others to walk by him, keeping an eye on the man through the gaps between umbrellas. The man walked up Drottning-gatsbacken and took a left onto Tegnérlunden.

It was less crowded here. Just a group of schoolkids on their way to classes at Adolf Fredrik's Music School. Jorma let the distance between them increase. Once the man was out of sight, he walked up the little hill next to the Strind-berg statue. He caught sight of him again. He was walking down towards the Barnhus Bridge.

The man was walking purposefully, block after block through Kungsholmen; he passed the Sankt Erik Eye Hos-pital, then he crossed the street and turned onto Celsiusgatan. Then he suddenly stopped short, bent down, and tied his shoe. A door to Jorma's left swung open and a young girl on crutches came out. He gave her a friendly nod and slid inside. Out of the corner of his eye he saw the cop turn around and cast a long glance in his direction.

A minute later, when he dared to come out again, the man was gone. Jorma jogged down towards Kungsholmsgatan. He rounded the corner and stopped in a different doorway. He saw the outline of the gangly figure taking something from a car in one of the parking spots in the police car park and then passing through the glassed-in entryway. He made an internal call from a wall phone inside, waving at a uni-formed colleague with the receiver pressed to his ear. He walked through the automatic doors, vanishing from sight.

Jennifer Roslund. Once he had a name, it was easy to find out about her. Born in 1987 in Stockholm. Raised in Vallentuna by her mother, Beata Roslund, a nurse at Danderyd Hospital. Her father's name was Carl-Adam Tell. He was a former chief doctor at Karolinska Hospital and before that had owned a small pharmaceutical company that held patents on allergy medications; he had been dead for a year.

After *gymnasium*, Jennifer applied to a folk high school in Skåne. That was how Katz had found his first lead on her. During her studies at Österlen – life drawing, oil painting, sculpture, all in the 'picturesque surroundings and creative environment' that the school's kitschy website advertised – she had started using her mother's name and Jenny instead of Jennifer.

For someone from her generation, she had left few digital traces behind; she wasn't on social media, didn't show up on Instagram or Facebook. And there were only two photos of her online, at least under her real name. One was with her folk high school class, taken on a field trip to the Louisiana Museum of Modern Art in 2006, and the other was from the same year, when she had participated in a poll in a Skåne daily paper and responded 'yes' to the question of whether she would ever consider becoming vegan.

Starting in 2008, she was missing from every Swedish registry. According to the national registration database, she had emigrated. Her last known address – the one the Tax

Authority demanded before releasing their grip on her – was a P.O. box in Zurich.

Katz stepped out of the car when he noticed the woman who had stopped her Land Rover outside the clubhouse. He watched her remove a checked golf bag from the boot, place it on a trolley, and scan the car park for the person who had called her an hour earlier to find out if he could meet her and ask a few questions about her daughter.

She knew who he was even before he had time to introduce himself.

'Beata Roslund,' she said, with a surprisingly firm handshake. 'I don't mean to be rude, but I'm supposed to meet someone by the short course. It might be best if you follow me over to the driving range. We can talk on the way.'

She was a slender woman in her late fifties who looked like a slightly faded model. Lanky legs, flat-chested. Her face would have been beautifully sculpted it if weren't for the scar tissue on her left cheek and the black patch over one eye. She had described her appearance to Katz over the phone, joking that he should be on the lookout for a woman who looked like she could scare the daylights out of small children.

'So you think something bad might have happened to Jennifer,' she said as they followed a path to the greens of Täby Golf Club. 'That she and her boyfriend might have been involved in blackmail. Isn't this a job for the police?'

'Maybe. But someone would have to report her missing first.'

She looked at him out of the corner of her eye.

'And you say her boyfriend is dead. Murdered.'

'Yes. I'm afraid so.'

'Don't be alarmed if I seem blunt. But my daughter has spent her entire adult life placing herself and others in catastrophic situations. Whatever it is that's happened to her, I no longer care.'

She turned onto a new path and Katz followed her.

'How long has it been since you last saw her?' he asked.

'Face to face? Almost six years.' She lifted her eye patch, flipping it up onto her forehead. 'Since she did this . . .'

Her cornea was milky; the blind eye stared at nothing. There was more scar tissue on her cheek; her skin looked like melted plastic.

'I answered the door and noticed that she had some sort of container in her hand, that she was aiming for my eyes. I would have gone completely blind if I hadn't managed to turn my head a bit. She threw acid in my face. Because I wouldn't give her money for drugs.'

Heroin muted every life-sustaining feeling, Katz thought as he looked away from the disfigured eye. Every shred of empathy. Hadn't he been just the same? Capable of almost anything?

'Jennifer is an evil person,' she said. 'I know it sounds horrible to say that about your own child, but it's true. She wasn't born evil . . . I don't believe in original sin. The accident turned her evil.'

They had reached the driving range behind the clubhouse. Beata Roslund removed a club from the golf bag, weighing it in her hand as she looked over at Lake Vallentuna, which was visible through the trees. And then she told him about the happy little girl who had once given her life meaning, the girl she had raised alone after her husband left her, the girl who'd had a normal childhood, playing normal games with normal kids her own age, the girl who had been gifted, charming, beloved. The girl who had learned to read when she was only five, who had been the brightest in her class for her nine years of compulsory school, and who had suddenly, overnight, transformed into someone Beata didn't recognize, a wildly foreign person.

'So what happened?'

'The summer she turned eighteen she was on the way to Frankfurt with her father. Carl-Adam was an absent father, always working, totally absorbed in his company. Jennifer only saw him sporadically, on school breaks and her birthday . . . and a few weeks every summer when he would take her on road trips to the continent or go sailing in the archipelago. They were in a head-on collision with a so-called *Geisterfahrer* just south of Frankfurt. Have you heard of those? Young German guys who make bets on how long they can drive the wrong way on the *Autobahn* without chickening out. The guy in the other car was killed instantly, but my daughter and ex-husband had a guardian angel. Calle made it through with a broken shoulder. Jennifer had a crushed spleen and a few scrapes. But *something* must have happened to my daughter. Something the doctors could never pinpoint no matter how many CAT scans they took of her brain. The sort of injury you can't locate . . . She was never the same again.'

After the accident, Jennifer became emotionally isolated. She lost interest in school. She skipped class, instead spending her days drawing – fantasy motifs, other worlds, often frightening ones. She started dressing differently, provocatively. She got pet snakes, like a protest against her environment; there was something deeply symbolic about her interest in herpetology, Beata Roslund explained, as if she wanted to frighten other people away.

'It was like she was no longer in touch with herself. There was some sort of disconnect between her body and her soul. And maybe that was why she started taking drugs, to fill the emptiness between them, try to bridge that gap. And it happened fast – it only took a few months for her to develop a full-blown addiction. I tried to get her help. From child psychologists, drug clinics, the Maria Youth Centre. But Jennifer was impervious to care; instead my interventions caused her to become even more destructive.'

She sighed, replacing the golf club in the bag. She stuck her hands in her armpits as if she were freezing.

'What about her dad?' Katz asked.

'Calle died just over a year ago. An accidental drowning. He fell off his boat near Norr Mälarstrand while heavily intoxicated. I found out about it from the newspapers. And like I said, he never had much contact with her. Even less after the car accident. My ex was from an upper-class family, all of whom were experts in repressing problematic emotions. I suppose he couldn't handle not recognizing his own little girl, the one who used to worship him, possibly because he was so inaccessible, because they so seldom saw each other.'

She looked at Katz defiantly, as if he suspected her of something even though she was innocent.

'I want you to know I didn't have many warm feelings for my ex. He left me in the lurch with a small child. Sure, he gave me the house in Vallentuna, and he paid child support so we wouldn't have to live on my nurse's income. But he was never a dad in the true sense of the word.'

She gazed sadly at Katz with her good eye.

'Anyway, when she turned eighteen, there was nothing more I could do. She was of age, free to do whatever she liked with her life. First she took off for Skåne; somehow she got into art school down there. She studied painting and drawing. Her only passion, besides drugs. She went to Copenhagen and bought drugs off the street dealers in the Vesterbro district. She was kicked out of school after stealing a computer from her boyfriend at the time. She frequently came to Stockholm to beg for money. And when I finally refused, she threw acid in my face.'

She stopped talking and touched the scars on her cheek as if she still couldn't grasp what had happened.

'She moved abroad,' Katz said.

'Yes, to Switzerland. She wrote me a letter while I was in hospital, where the doctors were trying to save my sight, to tell me that she was going to Zurich with some guy. I don't know what happened there, except that she became a prostitute and started doing porn. Later I heard that she lived and worked at an escort company that advertised sex services by way of a website.'

She looked at Katz with disgust, as if he were one of her daughter's johns.

'And then suddenly she showed up in Sweden again. At that point I hadn't heard from her in several years. I was convinced she was dead. Of an overdose . . . or just from the life she was living, killed in the line of duty, so to speak. She stayed at shelters in the city, as far as I could tell, avoiding the authorities, living with another man. That Ramón, I suppose, the one you mentioned on the phone. Yet another pimp.'

'Did you see her?'

'No. I refused. But she called to tell me she was working at a sex club. I don't know if she's alive or has killed herself with drugs, nor do I care. I'm done crying, you know? I'm out of tears.'

She turned away from him, adjusting her eyepatch, which had slid down. A man in his forties was approaching from the clubhouse, his arm extended in a greeting. Her lover, Katz thought. Fit, tanned, looked like a model; they resembled each other somehow.

'That brings us to the end of this audience,' she said drily. 'And there's just one thing I want to ask of you.'

'What's that?'

'If you find her . . . don't tell her the two of us met. I don't want anything to do with Jennifer. I don't want her to know I was talking about her. I don't want to be part of her life, even as a thought.'

Hiding spots were holy places for heroin addicts. It was an art to find secure areas for your junk so it wouldn't be found by the cops. Or other junkies.

But where was Jennifer's?

Katz merged onto the E18 and drove past the racetrack and Näsby Park. The sound of the car engine was soothing. He rolled down the window to get some air.

His thoughts swam through his head like small schools of fish as he approached the city centre. Where had he kept his goods during his dark years? The small doses he sold on the street, zip lock bags full of heroin capsules? In electrical boxes in the city. Inside the service panels on streetlights. The few times he'd handled larger amounts? In a forest outside the city. And during the short time he'd hung around with Ramón? A secret place in Årsta; they had managed to move a manhole cover, and one metre below ground there was a niche where they had been able to hide a small lot that they were planning to sell on commission.

If you could just find the hiding spot, you would find the owner. That was how he would locate her.

He went right at the Bergshamra exit, crossed the E4, and continued west on the old Enköping road.

Why hadn't he thought of it until now? Ramón had screwed him over that time. Stolen the goods. And he hadn't confessed where it was until Katz tracked him down at a dope den in Söder and put a knife to his throat: the junk was in an old banger parked in a long-stay car park.

Katz drove faster. He remembered his encounter at the junkie's car. The way John Sjöholm had looked back over his shoulder as Katz was bent over him, against the boot. Nervous at the thought that Katz might have suspected something.

He parked outside a removals company and walked the last little bit to the empty car park.

He was thinking that he had misjudged everything, that this was all much simpler than he'd first thought. Jennifer was out there somewhere. She was the one who had killed Ramón; it was the most plausible explanation. Together they had blackmailed people and invested the money in drugs. But she had become greedy and wanted to keep it all for herself. Perhaps along with Sjöholm.

She wasn't the person he thought she was. She was the one who'd fixed the rig for Ramón, full of a dose she knew he couldn't handle. She'd injected it in his left arm, in a vein he couldn't get at, because he asked her to. She watched calmly as his heart stopped . . .

The car door was unlocked; the crowbar was on the floor next to the prescription medication and the porn magazine.

Katz stuck the fork end into the gap and broke into the boot. At first he didn't see anything, just a tarp covering the space. He pulled it aside. Swallowed hard.

Sjöholm was in a foetal position. His face was bluish-black. A nylon rope was wound around his neck several times.

Nearly a week passed. Eva learned more about the robbery. She pored over reports and newspaper articles, conspiring with her old contact at the National Intelligence Bureau, Wernström, who had better insights into confidential material than she did – not to mention the nose of a bloodhound when it came to strange coincidences. She wondered if she should contact the robbers who had been apprehended, but she decided not to bother; none of them would talk to her anyway.

For the time being, she was letting the matter of the tip line rest. Instead she emailed her colleagues in Sarajevo, wondering about their question regarding corruption, but they were taking their time getting back to her.

And all the while, that little bell was ringing in the back of her head.

She needed help from above, but Hoffman was on a business trip and didn't answer his phone until late Wednesday evening. He was at a conference in Östersund. She skipped the small talk and got straight to the point, telling him what she was after.

'So you want to get hold of a higher-up to find out why they closed an investigation into the shooting of a robber. What is your reason, if I may ask?'

'This guy was the most interesting person on my list of suspected frontmen.'

'You'll have to give me something juicier than that.'

She knew it was a long shot. And she wondered how much

more she could reveal at this point without giving away her source. According to Wernström, who had definitely exceeded his authority by helping her, there seemed to have been a lengthy investigation before the police action, possibly going as far as entrapment.

'I know I'm coming out of left field with this,' she said, 'but something tells me that this robbery is connected to my case.'

'How so?'

'I don't know yet, but I intend to find out. And isn't it odd that one of the suspects died suddenly during a manhunt for the robbers?'

'I'm not seeing the direct connection.'

She studied the photos of her children on her office walls. She hadn't even called them since handing them over to Ola. She felt a pang of guilt, which she managed to stuff in that special compartment for feelings that must be immediately repressed.

'For one thing, Abramović left the criminal life behind ten years ago and hadn't had so much as a parking ticket since. He was happily married with small children. He had a steady job as a massage therapist at a clinic near Hötorget. And then, out of the blue, he robbed an armoured truck! For another, why was an internal investigation closed after less than twenty-four hours? Isn't that a bit too speedy? They're usually careful to get to the bottom of fatal shootings – to avoid a civil-rights mess. And out of sheer self-preservation. If criminals think the police are cold-blooded executioners, it gives them reason to become quicker on the draw . . . Abramović, my suspected frontman, was holding an automatic weapon with an empty magazine when he was shot. But it seems that the robbers had tried to ditch their weapons earlier in the chase. An empty revolver was found in the car, and another pistol and three hand grenades were in the bushes along the path they fled.'

'Perhaps the robbers were just trying to drop ballast? Maybe they didn't want to be carrying so much weight – just enough to force the task force to be cautious?'

'Or else the automatic weapon was placed in Abramović's hands once he was already dead.'

'An execution?'

'Well, he was shot at close range . . . right in the forehead. No witnesses.'

'And a cover-up on top of it all?'

She couldn't tell whether he was being sarcastic.

'It's not out of the question. The police in Sarajevo were asking strange questions about how corrupt the Swedish police truly are. And Abramović had called the police tip line about a month before he died. About what, one might ask.'

Hoffman gave a loud sigh.

'Okay,' he said. 'I know a few people in the upper echelons. I'll check and see if anyone is prepared to talk to you. Karl Mattson, for example; my old boss. He works for the county police these days. But not until I'm back in town. And I want you to take time off from this case until then, Eva. That is a direct order to a colleague who has apparently never heard the term "burned out". Call me on Friday when I'm back home.'

Katz took off his outerwear and went to the kitchen. He drank a glass of water while listening to his messages. A slurred voice said the name 'Mona', and then there were sirens and the call cut off. He dialled her number but there was no answer.

The rain was tapping at the window. He took an apple from the fruit bowl to cut it into slices, but his hand was shaking so much that he had to put down the paring knife. He was startled by a sound but couldn't tell where it was coming from. He looked out the window at the dark street.

H.o.P., he thought. Something about missing women. But the thought slipped out of his grasp.

Sjöholm's body flickered through his mind, the rope around his neck, his black and blue face. Katz had flashbacks to the Klingberg Affair the year before; all the events he had experienced still gave him nightmares sometimes.

Jenny was likely dead, just as he'd suspected from the start. And if she was alive, she had nothing to do with the murder of John Sjöholm. It took raw strength to strangle a person.

He thought about calling the police but realized that he would have a difficult time explaining his own involvement.

Had anyone seen him at the deserted industrial area? He didn't think so.

He pulled out the porn magazine he'd taken from the car. According to the information on the editorial page, it was produced in Zurich. The price of the single copy was given in Swiss francs. Had she moved there with Sjöholm? Was he her boyfriend at the time?

The craving was back again and almost irresistible. He had four packs of heroin left, and all he needed to escape everything was a syringe.

Battling the growing emptiness that screamed out to be filled, he went to the hall and picked up the pile of post that had collected over the last week, pulling out the advertising fliers and bringing the rest back to the kitchen. He noticed a draft of air coming from somewhere.

Katz stood still. Listening, concentrating . . . He thought he heard something.

The handgun he'd brought from Husby was in the safe in his office, along with the bukkake DVD and Ramón's address book. He took the paring knife and walked into the living room.

The balcony door was open; the windowpane was broken. *The address book*, he thought. *That's what they were after. Or the DVD. Or both.*

The room was dark. He walked over to close the door. A faint scent of autumn on the breeze, from rotting leaves and asphalt wet with rain. Earthy smells that blended with something else he couldn't identify at first; *the scent of adrenaline*, he had time to think before a movement out of the corner of his eye startled him and a painful blow to the back of the head made everything go black.

Darkness . . . He didn't know how long he was out; probably only a few seconds. He was lying on his stomach across the glass table – must have landed on it; blood was flowing from a wound on his forehead. Someone had an arm around his neck in an iron grip, squeezing his larynx so hard it creaked. Weird little gnomes moved across his field of vision and were projected into the room. The walls seemed to be flowing with colour.

The table gave way under the weight of two bodies; they fell onto the Tabriz carpet and it soaked up the blood.

Sounds seemed to reach him from a distance, the animal-istic panting of the man on top of him, music suddenly coming through the balcony door from one of the neigh-bouring buildings. The growl rising from his own throat.

The grip loosened for a split second and he managed to suck in more air. The pain sent a shot of adrenaline through his body. He fumbled among the shards of glass in front of him and caught hold of something. The ashtray. He whacked it backwards as best he could, but all he hit was empty air.

As the oxygen slowly drained from his brain, he groped with his other hand and found the knife he'd dropped. He swung to the side this time, downwards and diagonally, and hit something soft. The denim fabric absorbed the blow. Katz struck again, but he was losing strength . . . He could feel his hate, the old hatred of his life streaming out of him like a geyser, that genuine desire to do harm to another per-son. His rage erased the pain; he struck again and felt the tip of the knife pierce the other man's thigh.

The man screamed and let go of his throat. Katz sucked in air and managed to turn halfway around. He lost his grip on the knife but got hold of the man's hair, pulling him closer, embracing him, gnashing his teeth in the air, biting until he caught the man's cheek; he felt his front teeth break the skin, felt its rubbery resistance before they cut through. He bit onto the man's cheek as hard as he could, like a human tick, just below his eye.

The man's grip loosened when his skin broke. Blood rushed into Katz's mouth. The man roared in pain.

Katz was so dazed he couldn't manage to stand up. The man staggered backwards through the room. He couldn't see his face in the darkness, couldn't make out his features – just his limping figure as he moved towards the open balcony door. The way he came in was also the way he got out.

PART 5

Hoffman lived in a cosy apartment near Hornstull. A man who lived for his children, she thought as she followed him through the rooms and back to the kitchen. The apartment was like a miniature play land, with a small trampoline in the living room, gymnastic rings suspended from the hall ceiling, and mattresses on the floor so small people could tumble around without hurting themselves.

She was sitting on a kitchen chair as he made mojitos at the counter. Jazz came from the stereo. Coltrane, he informed her. She could smell the faint odour of foot sweat from her own socks. She'd gone straight to his place from the office at 8 p.m. after having tried to digest all the new information.

'Strong or half-strength?' he asked as he muddled the mint leaves in the glasses.

'Strong.'

There were activity books on the kitchen table. Crayons and watercolour paints. A couple of playdough figures were drying beside the dishwasher.

'How old are your kids?' she asked.

'Five and seven.' He smiled discreetly over the blender. 'And yours?'

'About the same age – six and nine.'

She had the urge to show him pictures from her phone, present herself as a normal mother, even though she knew she wasn't – she had embarrassingly few photos of them; she would never measure up to people like Hoffman, who had their lives in order.

'But this week is your off week?' she said instead.

'Yes. Emelie, my ex, only lives a few blocks away. Very practical. In a couple of years, the kids can come and go freely between our two apartments. The only downside is that it will be the end of this kind of spontaneous date.'

Her smelly feet – she ought to do something about them.

'Or am I reading too much into this? I was a little surprised when you rang my doorbell. I just expected we would chat on the phone and then see each other at work next week.'

She had gone to his house on a whim because she needed someone to talk to . . . or did she have an ulterior motive?

She snuck a look at the handbag at her feet and the black plastic folder sticking out of it. In under twenty-four hours the situation had changed drastically. Her Bosnian colleagues had faxed over new material. Transcripts of phone taps, conversations between members of organized crime syndicates. Several calls were between Sweden and Bosnia, and it seemed as if that part of the investigation had been done without authorization. She hadn't had them translated yet, but her contact had given a description of the contents in English in a separate document. Abramović was mentioned a number of times. Apparently he had owed money to the mob and had somehow sabotaged some sort of transport, possibly containing narcotics. But there was something else that made this matter a potential bombshell: they had emailed over some pictures taken last summer in a tourist resort near Split. Albanian and Bosnian criminals having a meeting with a high-up Swedish police commissioner inside a brothel.

It was Hoffman's old superior at the criminal police and the vice squad: Karl Mattson, currently assistant head of the county police – the man who was in charge of the task force in the hunt for the robbers – plus a man with blond, woolly hair.

And what's more, while she was sitting in her office, staring at the photos, which had been taken in secret – pictures from a meeting that, according to her colleagues in Bosnia, dealt with human trafficking – she had finally realized what she'd missed, what that bell ringing in her head was trying to tell her: Jorma.

He had known Abramović for over twenty years. She would bet a thousand kronor that he was the unknown robber who had managed to escape. He was somewhere out there, and it was not up to her to report him. *Loyalty,* she thought. Apparently being loyal to Jorma was more important to her than the ethics of her job; she had grown up with him. And that was stopping her from moving forward on the case. At least for the time being.

'Did you talk to anyone higher up about what I told you?' she asked.

'Haven't had time. I tried to get hold of Mattson, but he's out of town. Has anything new come up?'

New things were coming up all the time. But what concrete evidence did she have? Just a couple of phone taps in Serbo-Croatian and a few photos of Balkan mafiosos in the company of Mattson and his white-blond underling. And two phone numbers from Katz's list that kept showing up in the material from Bosnia. The ones listed under 'M' and 'Å' in the address book. M as in Mattson, she thought. And Å for the phone answered by the little boy.

'Earth to Eva! Are you with me?'

'Of course . . . I was just thinking you might as well not bother for now.'

'Talking to people higher up?'

'Abramović is a dead end. I'm planning to cross him off

the list. The guy is dead, so he's not much use. I have to find another way in.'

He gave her a brief smile.

'Just say the word if there's anything else I can help you with.'

She hesitated. Should she say it after all, just pour it all out? No, it was better to wait, at least until the phone tap logs were translated.

'It's fine,' she said. 'By the way, where's your bathroom?'

'Straight ahead and to the right.'

She walked through a hallway where the children had been allowed to draw on the walls with crayon. There was a bulletin board with a collage of holiday photos in which Hoffman was posing along with his ex-wife and kids. *Rational people*, she thought. They took trips together even though they were divorced. They met for coffee and responsible conversations about their kids' futures.

She walked by the boy's room. The door was open. It was cosily furnished. Posters of Ronaldo and Messi on the walls. Chima Lego figures in a glass cabinet. A Kapla construction reminiscent of the Leaning Tower of Pisa. A lone Skylander stood on the desk, a figure she thought was called Crusher; he was the hero of an adventure Wii game that Arvid loved, a being who could kill everything in his path with a magic hammer. She felt another pang of guilt; she hadn't talked to the kids all week and had gone so far as to reject their calls when they'd tried to reach her on her mobile . . .

The next room belonged to the girl. She had her own TV and computer, and a pink canopy on her bed. Dress-up clothes on a coatrack. An easel, and real oil paints. A vanity table, of course, full of Body Shop products.

She realized she had taken a wrong turn, because she

suddenly found herself in Hoffman's little home office. She walked in the opposite direction instead, until she found the toilet. She peed, and as she wiped she saw a little bit of blood on the paper. She had noticed she had been in a mood the past few days; she was about to get her period.

'Eva . . . did you get lost?'

Her boss's voice was far away. She took off her socks and flushed them away with her urine.

By the time she returned, he had moved into the living room. He had pulled out a beanbag for each of them. Two drinks stood on a Marimekko tray on the floor.

'Here,' he said, handing one to her. 'What are we toasting to?'

'Success – what else? Putting away all the bad guys.'

He had dimmed the lights. She could glimpse the lights of the southern suburbs through the window.

'What did you really come over here for? Excuse me for asking, but this certainly seems to be turning into a date.'

'I don't really know. I just needed company.'

Her drink was almost gone. She must have drained half of it in one gulp. They were sitting so close their knees touched . . . *What if I start a relationship with him,* she thought, *what would happen?*

She pictured them together, in a house outside the city, a big old house they had renovated, Hoffman with flecks of paint on his face, the children playing in the yard, all four of them. But she would manage to bring everything crashing down before they even had time to blink.

'It's getting late,' she said in a half-hearted attempt to avoid whatever was about to happen, what she had promised herself must not happen. 'Maybe we can see each other some other evening . . . tomorrow, maybe?'

'Tomorrow won't work. And you have to tell me why

you're *really* here. To tell me that you're planning to reprioritize your cases? You could have waited until Monday for that.'

To sleep with you, she thought. *To cut the cord to Katz.*

He took her hand, massaging it gently, and looked her straight in the eye without blinking.

Not with your boss, she thought, *don't do it.*

One second later, she leaned forward and kissed him, experiencing the taste of his tongue, the taste of saliva mixed with rum and mint, finding that he tasted nice, that he was a good kisser.

She unbuttoned his fly, hesitantly circling his cock with her hand. Then she took him deep into her mouth, milking him with her cheeks and tongue. She was wet herself, she noticed as she pulled off her trousers and pants. The music from the radio faded as she straddled him, letting him slide back and forth between her labia, without entering her, as the pebbles of Styrofoam in the beanbag squeaked. She observed him as if through a magnifying glass. He was in a whole different world; his eyes were glassy, happy, as he stroked her clitoris with one finger he'd somehow worked in between their bodies.

'I've wanted this so bad,' he whispered. 'Eva, you have no idea how much I've wanted to do this . . .'

According to the Swedish Companies Registration Office, the owner of Blue Dreams AB was Maria Leonora Alsén, born in Solna in 1979. Katz guessed that Peter Wallin lived at the same address in lower Kungsholmen. The grey BMW parked on Pontonjärgatan indicated that he did. He had clicked his way to the Swedish Transport Agency's website on his phone to search for its licence plate. The vehicle was owned by Wallin's video distribution company, Sin City.

Katz checked the tools that lay beside him on the car seat one last time. The adjustable spanner, the Glock, the full plastic bottle . . .

The lights were on in the windows when he walked to the pavement across the street and climbed up on an electrical box so he could look straight into the apartment.

The lower floor was made up of three rooms and the kitchen in a line. A person was walking between two of the rooms, a wine glass in hand. Wallin. The flickering light of a TV in the background. It was 11 p.m. There was no one else on the street.

Katz walked over to the BMW, stopped near the front of it, took out the spanner he'd concealed under his jacket, and used it to break the window. The car alarm sounded immediately. He calmly kept walking until he reached the blind spot next to the front door of the building.

Not thirty seconds had passed before Wallin rushed onto the street, swearing, wearing a pair of flip-flops. Katz slid through the front door. The door to the apartment was wide open.

*

He quickly glanced through the room. Leona didn't seem to be home. There was a credit card and a few untouched lines of cocaine on the coffee table in the den. An open bottle of champagne stood next to them, but there was only one glass.

Katz turned off the TV. When Wallin came back, he was sitting in an easy chair, aiming the handgun at him. He watched the man go pale. No bite marks on his face. Nor had Katz expected there to be.

'What the fuck is going on?'

Katz didn't respond, he just pointed the barrel of the gun at the leather sofa on the other side of the table. Wallin took the hint and sat down.

'I don't want to look at you. Turn around . . . hands on your head!'

Wallin did as he was told. He kneeled on the sofa cushion, his back to Katz.

Katz didn't speak for a long time, letting the seconds tick away. He studied the wall with its signed posters of American porn stars.

'Tell me about Ramón and Jennifer,' he said at last.

'Tell you what?'

'You had them killed, didn't you? And John Sjöholm, too.'

'Are you totally nuts?'

'Because they knew too much about your network . . . because they tried to blackmail your clients.'

'My girlfriend will be here in a little while. This is her apartment and I don't want to scare her. If you take the wallet from my back pocket, you'll find five thousand in cash . . . and there's another ten thousand in the inner pocket of my coat, in an envelope . . . Take it and let's forget about all this.'

Katz stood up, walked over to the man, and bent towards his ear.

'You sent someone to my home. To get hold of a couple of things. An address book . . . and a DVD. You know I have them. Sjöholm told you.'

'What the fuck kind of address book? I don't even know who you are, I've never seen you before.'

Katz placed the barrel of the gun to his temple with one hand, used the other to take out the plastic bottle full of petrol, and unscrewed the lid with his teeth.

'What the fuck are you doing?'

He poured the petrol all over the man, all over his hair, his T-shirt, and his trousers. He heard Wallin choke as some got into his mouth. He placed the gangbang DVD on the back of the sofa so he could see the cover. He walked back to the easy chair as he trickled a thin line of petrol across the carpet. He sat down. Took out a lighter.

'Let's start from the beginning. You made that film, didn't you?'

'It's not illegal to make movies.'

'You arrange orgies where people pay money to degrade prostitutes.'

'Oh, God. It's no worse than what people do elsewhere. And that girl on the cover, she likes it. It turns her on. Call it self-destructive if you want, but she does it for symbolic payment. You're not going to fucking light me on fire, you're not that sick.'

Wallin was panting, breathing through his mouth. The whole room smelled like petrol.

'Where did you film it?'

'At the home of a guy who let us use his flat in return for being allowed to watch. And then I happened to forget a copy at Blue Dreams. It ended up with the rentals by accident. No big deal, everyone has a mask on.'

'Who are the men?'

'All kinds of people. One is an actor. Several lawyers. A former football star. Different people . . . All they have in common is that bukkake turns them on.'

'Tell me about Jennifer. What sort of contact did you have with her?'

'What do you want to know? Like I said, she was there for some of the get-togethers. And she helped me find new chicks sometimes.'

'What about Ramón. How do you know him?'

Wallin was silent for a moment and appeared to be thinking.

'I bought drugs off him.'

'What kind of drugs?'

'Heroin. He and Jenny got hold of almost a kilo – don't ask me how they managed that. I put an offer on half of it. I got it damn cheap because they were starting to panic. They had no idea how they were going to distribute such a large amount.'

Wallin swallowed hard.

'That was why we tried to find out who you are. It had nothing to do with the DVD or some fucking address book. I bought drugs from some unreliable junkies and then you – at least I assume it was you – suddenly show up at Blue Dreams asking about them. It stands to reason I would get paranoid.'

'So what are you doing with the horse?'

'What do you think? I'm selling it. To friends, people I meet out. All kinds of people use heroin in this country. Celebrities. Businessmen. And you've gotta have style to make any money at the end of the line. Can you imagine Ramón at Café Opera? What the fuck was that dude thinking . . . that he was gonna sell it off, gram by gram, out on Plattan?'

'What about John Sjöholm. What does he have to do with all this?'

'He hid the goods for them. In his car. Which was a stupid fucking place to keep it.'

They didn't say anything for a moment. Katz was trying to process the information. Wallin didn't know anything about the address book and the phone numbers.

'Does the abbreviation H.o.P. mean anything to you?'

Wallin stiffened.

'I have nothing to do with that stuff.'

'With what?'

'House of Pain. That's other people, doing that.'

'Like who?'

'I don't know, and I don't want to find out. Rumour has it there's a cop involved.'

'What do they do?'

'Disgusting stuff . . .'

'Do they kidnap women?'

Wallin was silent; apparently he'd decided not to say any more. Katz stood up, flicking the lighter.

'Okay, take it easy . . . I get it . . . Word is, it's foreign women. No one goes looking for them. Chicks who are here without proper papers, girls who walk the streets. And whores whose biggest problem isn't that they're whores, it's that they'll do anything for a fix. They just disappear. And then they're never heard from again. There are these rumours about some sort of fucking *tunnel* . . . That they send them on after a while, to other people, with the same tastes . . .'

'Did Jennifer have anything to do with House of Pain?'

'I wouldn't be surprised. That girl is crazy. I heard she tried to kill her dad when she was sixteen.'

Katz flicked the lighter again, lighting the scented candles that were on the coffee table next to the lines of cocaine. He could smell the vanilla scent.

'Do any of your so-called clients know any more about House of Pain?'

'Maybe . . . The guy whose flat we used, he's the only one I can imagine might know.'

'What's his name?'

'Wiksten or something like that. A young, rich bohemian type. He lives in a luxury apartment he inherited in Öster-malm. He was only watching, like I said. Through a hole in the wall. I sure as hell never thought those things were real, but it turns out they do exist in some old Östermalm flats. Secret peepholes.'

Katz picked up the scented candle and put it down on the petrol-soaked carpet.

'I swear, that's the only tip I have. This guy is pretty god-damn extreme in his tastes. He thought that time was too tame. He showed me a film he had made with some guys he knew. But I couldn't even watch it, it was too fucking much.'

Wallin shook his head.

'They had some kind of gentlemen's club. They called themselves the "Bathing Friends" or something like that . . . I don't know if it had anything to do with this. And he knows Ramón, or rather Jenny. They met in Switzerland, he said.'

'How can I get hold of him?'

'I never got his number. But like I said, he lives in Öster-malm, near Karlaplan. I don't remember the address . . . I swear, if I had it, I'd give it to you.'

'What about Ramón's phone number? Do you have that?'

'It's in my phone, I think, in my coat pocket in the hall. Why?'

His voice had become thick.

'I don't understand what you're doing here. I don't under-stand your weird questions. I never tried to get back any goddamn address book. I don't need an address book; I meet my clients at the bar. I let them know when I've rounded up a couple of girls who are willing to take part in a gangbang or a facial session. I just get paid for a service. Just like I get paid for the drugs. And it's voluntary, all the girls get paid . . . it's all voluntary.'

Wallin had collapsed onto the sofa; he could no longer manage to hold himself up.

'Please, for God's sake . . . you're not going to light me on fire, you're not, right?'

But no one answered. The person he'd been speaking to had already left.

Judging by the first three digits of the mobile phone number, Ramón had a contract with Telia. The phone had probably been destroyed; it was probably lying in a stream somewhere, never to be found, but there was no way for the operator to know that. Katz called customer service early in the morning, gave the number, and pretended to be interested in switching to a plan with unlimited data; he asked if it was worth it, considering the model of phone he had.

'I see on the computer you have an iPhone 5,' said the young woman who had taken his call, thus giving him the only piece of information he needed. 'No problem. I'm guessing you want to stream video and listen to music? I'll be honest with you, Ramón, our new plan is actually better and cheaper than the one you have now. If you're interested, I can offer you a 10 per cent rebate, but you'll have to sign up for a two-year commitment.'

Katz pretended to hesitate and asked to call back in a few days.

A few minutes later he was sitting in front of the computer. The exploit program he'd downloaded from a Russian IRC channel broke through the log-in screen on the 'Find my iPhone' app and tricked the automatic support service to send a temporary password.

Katz typed in the randomly generated combination of letters and hit 'Enter'. He waited for what seemed like an eternity.

Then there was a ding. The phone's whole iCloud was open to him.

After confirming that the phone wasn't broadcasting a GPS signal, just as he'd guessed, he went through the email without finding anything of great worth.

He moved on to the call log, incoming and outgoing calls. The last one was from the same night Ramón died; he had been called by a blocked number at 20.13. The call had lasted exactly two seconds. Someone checking to see if he was home?

Katz looked back through the logs, but the traffic information was only saved for a month. Ramón didn't seem to have been very social. All the rest of the outgoing and incoming calls were to and from a contact called 'J'. Jennifer Roslund, Katz assumed.

He took out his phone and dialled her number, but didn't get through. He tried to imagine where she might be, what had happened to her . . . but he couldn't picture anything.

Only Ramón's most recent activity was saved on his browser. He had googled wholesale heroin prices and clicked his way to a few obscure sites where people discussed drugs and guns, but the older history was deleted and impossible to restore.

He looked at the photo folder. The pictures had been taken within the last year. Jenny was in most of them. Photos from their apartment in Husby, snapshots reminiscent of crime-scene photographs: bags of heroin, syringes. Photos of them injecting each other, pictures of her playing with the snake. And pictures that had been taken out in the country: Jenny standing next to John Sjöholm on a dock by a frozen lake.

Further up the hill was a large villa in Italianate style. The house in the drawing he'd found in the storage locker? Katz was almost sure it was.

He checked the date. The photo had been taken in March.

Then he clicked on through the album. Suddenly there was a picture of a woman in the back seat of a car. John Sjöholm was sitting beside her. The woman had dark skin and was in her twenties. Her clothes were ill-fitting and threadbare. There was something vaguely Indian about her features. She was laughing, as if the photographer had just said something funny. And the photographer was Jenny, Katz thought, because the next picture was of Ramón sitting behind the wheel of the same car.

Katz scrolled on and was soon startled. It was the woman again, but this time she was in a cramped room with bare concrete walls, and she was terrified. The picture had been taken in the dark, with a flash. A steel cage was visible in the background; it was perhaps a metre high and equally wide. Someone had clearly struck her in the face; it was bruised.

The next picture was a close-up of the woman crying in despair.

The photos had been taken in June, before they came into all the heroin. Was this how they'd gathered the money they needed? Delivering women to an organized ring of sex offenders? House of Pain, as Wallin had called it.

Katz couldn't stomach any more. A sense of approaching death hung over the entire scene.

After copying the photos to his computer and logging out of the iCloud, he looked up the name Wiksten in an online directory. There were fifty Wikstens in Stockholm, but none of them lived near Karlaplan. He did a Google search for 'the bathing friends' but the only hits were for a volunteer association that had once founded the botanical gardens in Visby.

On Ziz.com, which was a small social network a bit like Facebook, there was a forum with a similar name – 'Bathing

Friends', without the 'the' – but it was closed to non-members. The photo on its front page depicted a dock on a frozen lake. The same one as in Jennifer's drawing?

He added the name 'Wiksten' to the search and found a hit for an obscure chat site about prostitution where 'Bathing Friends' was mentioned. One member of the discussion, who called himself 'Wik Sten', had uploaded a photo of himself posing with a towel around his hips on a swimming dock. Katz recognized him, though his eyes were hidden by a black rectangle: the young man with a hipster beard who worked at the City Mission's day shelter.

'Had fun with Bathing Friends,' he had written, in response to another member's question about what he had done over the weekend. 'An unforgettable day in the company of nine guys and one girl.'

Magnus, Mona had called him.

He looked up the name online. The first hit was a year-old article from the street magazine *Faktum*: an interview about his work with the city's homeless. Magnus Wiksten-Kylenstråhle stared gravely into the camera. His paternal grandparents were the founders of a well-respected print media company. According to the article, he lived on the interest from his inheritance and spent his time volunteering for social causes. Helping others who were less well-off gave him a sense of purpose, he explained.

Katz minimized the window. He reached for the phone and dialled Eva Westin's number, but she didn't pick up. He opened his email instead. He wrote her a brief message explaining what sort of help he needed.

She woke to a ringing phone. She looked around, unsure, for a moment, where she was. Then the pieces fell into place. Hoffman's bedroom. His side of the bed was empty. Just a tangled blanket that looked like a trailing vine.

The phone was still ringing. She stood up, still tipsy. They had drunk an entire bottle of rum in the course of the evening, and, if she knew herself, the better part of it had ended up in her own belly.

There was a vase of flowers on the nightstand. The crime novels he read lay in a perfect stack on a trendy metal footstool. The wardrobe was open. She could see the row of white shirts and dark work suits, like shed skins.

There was a note on his pillow: 'Had to run an errand. I made breakfast.'

He had drawn a heart at the bottom.

She walked into the living room. The phone had stopped ringing, but something told her the call was important.

Her clothes were in a pile next to one of the beanbags. Her phone was on the floor next to a half-empty mojito.

One missed call from Katz, but she could live with that.

The other missed calls were worse, and there were five angry texts. All were from Ola, and the first one was from the day before. Had she been so smashed that she hadn't heard her phone?

She already knew what the matter was. Her week had started. She was supposed to have picked up the kids from Söder yesterday after school, but she'd fucked up as usual.

She reached for the drink. She took a sip of the room-temperature contents, then put the glass down in disgust. She read the last text, in which he threatened to keep the children away from her until she started therapy and got her shit together.

She dialled his number. Waited stoically to be chewed out. But Lisa was the one who answered.

'Hi, Mum, where are you?'

'Hi, darling. I'm at work.'

'But it's Saturday. You don't work on Saturdays. You promised we would go to Junibacken today, remember?'

'I'm so sorry, Lisa, I forgot again. Did you have to wait a long time for Dad to pick you up yesterday?'

'Erika picked us up in the car as soon as she could. I called from my teacher's phone to say you hadn't come. I tried to call you too, but you didn't answer. I want to go to your house now. Did you clean our room?'

'Yes.'

'Did my new *Kamratposten* come yet?'

Her little girl's innocent voice. She trusted her, would never dream that her mother would lie to her or sleep with her boss instead of spending time with her children.

'I think so,' she said, biting her lip hard. 'I haven't checked the post.'

'Dad wants to say something . . .'

She listened to his scolding, which was surprisingly restrained, probably because Lisa was nearby.

'Okay,' she said when he was finished. 'What should we do now? I can pick them up in twenty minutes. I'm not far away.'

'Come over here as fast as you can.'

'I promise to hurry. I'm really sorry, Ola. I have to improve matters on my end.'

But he only sighed and hung up.

She sat there with the phone in her hand. Katz had sent an email too, she noticed. She called it up. He had briefly explained that he needed help accessing reports about missing prostitutes.

She gathered up her clothes and went back to the bedroom. Still no sign of Hoffman.

She put on her pants, which had black spots of blood in the crotch. She wondered if she should take a quick shower, but there was no time. A used condom lay on the floor, sending messages about the day before.

She reached for the note he'd left. She wanted to write something back, to say that she had to pick up her kids but really wanted to see him again. She looked around in vain for a pen.

She put on her clothes and walked over to the small office, where she pulled out the top desk drawer. One compartment contained an old mobile phone, a pad of Post-its, and a ball-point pen with the logo of the Police Authority. She tested it on a scrap of paper, but the ink was gone. She happened to jostle the phone by mistake as she went to close the drawer. The screen lit up and displayed the most recent incoming call.

Her heart was pounding at her chest like a hammer as she went back to the hallway and into the boy's room.

Here comes Maxi! I'll show you some real speed! said a recorded voice from a toy car she happened to nudge with her foot. All those hundreds of toy sounds she'd heard throughout the years since she had kids, at the strangest times, in the weirdest places . . . Once a faint bleating had plagued her for a whole week before she found a stuffed animal – a bedraggled lamb; an impulse buy from Skansen – caught at the very back of Lisa's wardrobe.

Katz's number was the last one to call the phone. The closest mobile tower was in Liljeholmen.

Å was the initial listed before the phone number in Ramón's address book. Åke Hoffman.

She looked at the bulletin board that hung above the plastic bins of Lego. Football posters stuck to the wall with blu tack, a euro bill someone had drawn on, postcards, and a kid's drawing of a snowman. The boy's childish signature was at the very bottom: LINUS H, AGE 5.

Wiksten lived in a luxury building on Karlaplan, just as Wallin had said, but he was listed under his second last name, Kylenstråhle. Through the panes of glass in the entryway, Katz could see a carpeted marble staircase, Doric columns along the walls, gilded plaster accents on the ceiling, and a reception desk where a uniformed doorman had once received visitors.

The front door was locked. He rang the neighbours' buzzers until someone took mercy on him and let him in.

He ignored the lift and took the stairs to the fourth floor. Three doors led into the apartment. Katz peered through the letter box on the middle door. There was post on the floor. The apartment was dark.

Wiksten had been listed as living at this address since he was twenty. His parents lived in Spain. Wiksten was an only child. He had spent his formative years at boarding schools. In Switzerland, among other places, at the famed Le Rosey. Was that how he'd met Jenny once upon a time? Katz had found a defunct blog among Google's cache trash, written by an anonymous former student, that described various scandals throughout the years involving students from the country's most venerable private school, including visits to brothels in Lausanne and Zurich. Wallin had intimated that this was how Jennifer and Wiksten had met.

Katz jumped as he heard the lift start to move. He went up another half-flight of stairs to the attic. The cables creaked as someone ascended . . . but the lift stopped on the floor below Wiksten's. The rider got off, fumbled with keys and vanished through a door.

No response from Eva yet. Mona, he thought. The women who had disappeared from Malmskillnadsgatan, foreign prostitutes no one missed. He ought to contact her and ask if she had any further information.

Through a window in the stairwell he could see a terrace on the facade, five metres to the left. Katz looked around. The attic door ahead was only secured with a padlock. The handle gave way when he kicked it.

He entered a passageway with storage areas on either side. The doors and walls were made of chicken wire; they enclosed all sorts of junk. Light streamed in from a skylight further on. He grabbed a ladder from along the wall, unfolded it, and climbed up. He unhooked the latches and hoisted himself onto the roof.

He was six storeys above ground. Östermalm spread out before him like a toy land. He saw Norra Djurgården in the distance. The Swedish Radio building, the neighbourhood of Gärdet, and the armed forces headquarters.

A ladder was affixed to the roof. It was for use by the snow-clearers in the winter.

Katz was afraid of heights and always had been. His heart attempted to pound its way out of his chest as he cautiously climbed down towards the snow guards.

And then he had reached his goal. He grabbed the gutter and swung his legs over. He was hanging by his arms directly above the terrace. He saw people down on the ground, like little ants. The traffic looked like it was remote-controlled. He let go and dropped.

Just as he'd hoped, the terrace door was unlocked. The apartment smelled stuffy. Wiksten hadn't been there in several days.

Katz recognized the drawing room from the bukkake film – the crystal chandelier, the ballroom-like space with such a high ceiling that you could play a game of badminton in there.

There was hardly any furniture, and what little there was was covered in sheets. He followed a hall to a bathroom with a gilded baroque mirror. He found the peephole in the wall where Wiksten had watched as ten men ejaculated all over Jennifer. Too tame, Wiksten had thought.

Katz peered into rooms that seemed never to be used and passed a kitchen with empty cupboards. Wiksten's bedroom was at the end of a corridor; it was the only space that seemed lived in. The bed was unmade. There was exercise gear on the floor, some dumbbells and barbells. Dirty clothes lay on a chair.

A computer stood on a writing desk; it was in sleep mode. Katz woke it up.

The hard drive was practically empty. It contained only the standard programs plus a dozen unnamed folders on the desktop. But nothing happened when he clicked on them.

He searched for the cookies stored on the hard drive. He started the browser and went to Ziz.com, then used the information in the cookies to log in.

There were no new photos, no information about their whereabouts. H.o.P. was never even mentioned; it just floated in the background like a creepy feeling . . . The members used aliases when they posted. Occasionally someone used the words *'Fest'* or 'party' as euphemisms for what was going on.

But what they wrote about the women was so horrible he could hardly read it. It was as if language had detached from its usual meaning. *They aren't writing about women,* Katz thought, *but livestock, animals to slaughter.*

The next 'party' was now, he realized, that very weekend.

The date and time were given in a digital calendar, but the address was missing.

Katz logged out, turned off the computer, and stood up. His gaze fell upon a pile of old issues of *Situation Sthlm* on the desk. The top one was open to an article about homeless Roma in Stockholm.

Katz had written something about missing women. It had to do with sex crimes, she thought. With perverted men.

She had a brief flashback to the night before: Hoffman had suddenly grabbed her a little too hard, for a little too long, as if he wanted to test boundaries. She'd asked him to stop, and he had respected that.

It seemed thoroughly improbable that he should somehow be involved; there had to be some other explanation for the fact that his phone number was in the address book. But she couldn't keep her thoughts from moving in that direction.

She remembered a course in criminology she'd taken during her prosecutor training: the lecturer had said that sex offenders sometimes collected souvenirs from their victims.

She started with the desk, since it seemed like the most private place. Top drawer first: office supplies, scissors, a ruler, the phone Linus had answered. On to the next: a couple of tax forms he'd saved, plastic folders containing user's guides, a file full of receipts.

She pulled out another drawer: electronic junk, a screwdriver, old post that had evaded sorting.

The bottom drawer was locked. She picked up the screwdriver and stuck it into the gap, putting all her strength into it as she used it like a crowbar. There was a dull crunch as the wood cracked.

The drawer was empty except for a few unmarked DVDs.

She inserted the first one into the laptop on the desk. She

felt the blood trickle from between her legs, soaking through the toilet paper and into her pants as she pressed the power button and waited for the operating system to load.

She couldn't figure out why she was doing this. Hoffman was a perfectly normal man . . .

The folders were neatly arranged by date. They ran back several years. They had been created at fairly regular intervals, about one new folder per month.

Some of them had been named 'Bathing Friends'. Others were labelled with the acronym 'H.o.P'.

She could hardly bear to look at the images, they were so horrific. They had been taken in a bare room somewhere. They documented acts of cruelty.

She opened more folders, her body stiff as a board and in a cold sweat brought on by fear and disgust. Pictures of a dead woman in one of the cages, emaciated into a skeleton; it seemed they had let her starve to death. More photographs, and film clips, of gang rape and out and out sadism. A woman dangling from a noose on the ceiling.

The tools they used resembled instruments of torture. Close-up images of bawling, terrified women. She noticed the track marks on their arms. Junkies, she thought. That could have been her in a different life . . . The men's faces were not visible; they were only shown from behind.

She went to the living room and found her bag. She looked through it until she found an old USB drive. She returned to the computer, inserted it into the port, and began to copy the material onto it.

The laptop fan started up with an insect-like buzzing. She wondered if there was anything else in the apartment . . . anything else she should look for, and if so, where was it?

She quickly looked through the other rooms. She searched the wardrobes in the bedroom, the laundry basket, the kitchen cupboards, the freezer, the drawers under the work surface. A brief foray through the kids' rooms, but she didn't find anything else.

So she went back to the office, dragged the final folder to the USB drive, and ejected it.

Who were the women in the videos and photos? How did the men get hold of them? She understood that they were women from other countries. Did they buy them from pimps or human traffickers? From Mattson's contacts in the Balkans?

The nausea swept over her again, and for an instant she had the terrifying feeling that she was pregnant, that she had become pregnant by Hoffman, even though she was on her period.

She wanted Katz to be there. Or Jorma Hedlund. She needed someone to talk to, someone she could trust.

'Eva . . .'

She turned around as slowly as if she were moving underwater.

He was standing in the doorway with a bakery bag and a bunch of fresh roses in his arms. The visual echo of a smile was still on his face – the forced smile of a person who wants to surprise his lover with French rolls and cut flowers but instead finds her doing something shameful.

He stared at the computer screen and the terrible pictures, and then at her . . .

She said nothing, avoiding his gaze; she just walked past him with purposeful steps, heading for the front door. She held her bag to her chest like a shield against the evil in the world. The door was locked with the security chain, she saw . . . and she could no longer keep her fear under control; she started running out of sheer reflex.

Maybe this unleashed his hunting instinct. Maybe it was

the sign he was waiting for. He had been standing on the threshold of the office as if petrified, passively letting her walk right by him. But not anymore. Before she could reach the door, he was on top of her, hitting her, kicking her, growling like an animal. Like the predator he was deep down inside.

Katz parked the car on Fleminggatan and went in through the front door of the City Mission. As he passed the day room, a young junkie couple were sitting at one of the tables and eating Salisbury steak. Their children – twin boys around five – were playing with Lego on the floor.

The door to the storage room was open. Katja was at the window, just about to finish a phone call. As soon as she hung up, he asked if she knew where Wiksten was.

'He was supposed to be here this morning, according to the schedule,' she said, 'but he never showed up. I just had to call another co-worker to cover for him. Why?'

'When did you see him last?'

'Yesterday. He came by to pick up the new schedule. But he didn't mention anything about taking a day off.'

'Do you know if he ever went out of town . . . to a country place?'

'To be honest, I don't know that much about Magnus. He works as a volunteer, as you know; he's not an actual employee or anything. I'm happy for all the help I can get around here. But Magnus doesn't usually say much about his private life.'

'Do you have his mobile number?' Katz asked.

'Just his home number; I called it a little while ago, but there was no answer.'

Out in the hall, the junkie dad walked by. He was staggering as if the earth's gravity was stronger than his body could handle; he shouted something to his sons as they played.

'Was that all? There are people out there who need me.'

'Two things,' said Katz. 'Did you happen to see if Wiksten had injuries to his face when he was here . . . or bandages?'

'I don't think so. Not that I noticed, anyway. What's your last question?'

'I'd like to know how a person could go about tracking down a homeless Roma family . . .'

Wiksten was guaranteed to be in the crime database, Katz thought as he walked back to his car – at the very least, there would be old sentences for buying sex. There was no way he could have stayed under the radar for all these years; there had to be something on him, even if it was on the fringes of another investigation. He needed to get hold of Eva Westin to learn more.

He took out his phone to dial her number, but instead he discovered three missed calls from Mona. She had left a message.

He dialled the number to his voicemail and felt his stomach sink when he heard her voice.

She sounded calm and collected as she explained she'd hit rock bottom, the only place where you could get a foothold in order to rise up again. Because she truly wanted to get better. Because she wanted to get her son back.

She was on her way to a private clinic outside the city, she explained. You got to stay in a large house surrounded by nature; she had seen the photos. The form of treatment wasn't exactly on the up and up; it was experimental, still in its infancy, so she wasn't really allowed to tell anyone about it. She was at a petrol station outside the city with Wiksten. She was calling from a phone box while he filled up the car. She'd had to surrender her own phone; she wasn't allowed to bring it along. She apologized for not answering when Katz tried to reach her earlier. She'd had a lot on her plate – contacting the authorities, petitioning to have her son stay with her for a trial period as soon as she worked out a proper living situation. She would be in touch once she was back in town. 'Cross your fingers for me,' was the last thing she said before she hung up.

PART 6

Jorma had managed to shadow the cop for nearly twenty-four hours. He'd bought a GPS tracker at an electronics store and attached it to the car outside the police station with a magnet. Amazingly enough, it hadn't been discovered. He'd followed the cop at a distance in Emir's Sierra. He was cautious, always leaving a gap between them. He lost sight of him a few times but always managed to catch up with him again.

The man had zigged and zagged through the city. He'd visited a few apartments and a tanning salon; he had taken a detour to Värtahamnen, where he disappeared into a shipping store.

He had spent the night at the police station. Or perhaps he had left the station on foot through one of the side entrances. In any case, in the morning he came out through the main doors again and got back into his car.

More visits to apartments, plus a short stop at a Thai massage place in Liljeholmen. Trafficking women, Jorma thought. It matched up with what Leyla had told him.

Late in the afternoon, he went to a cafe on Ringvägen. He met someone inside. Then he crossed the Skanstull Bridge and drove to Enskededalen, where he rang the doorbell at a turn-of-the-century villa and was let in.

Jorma took out his phone and googled the address. No hits. The same went for the Land Rover in the driveway. The person who lived there appeared to have unlisted information. Another cop?

*

He waited until it started to get dark before walking around the house to the back garden. Lights were on on the ground floor, but the blinds were down. There was scaffolding on the gable facing the neighbouring house. The aroma of fallen apples. A bit further on there was a pond; its fountain was turned off.

He rolled up the left leg of his trousers and pulled off the tape that had secured the Colt to his shin. He stuck it into the pocket of his hoodie and walked up to the house, hunching down as he went.

He slid behind the scaffolding, noticing the smell of paint from the freshly painted facade. One of the windows was covered in plastic.

He pulled off the electrical tape. He tore it in two with his teeth and stuck the pieces on the windowpane in the shape of a cross. He took off his hoodie, wound it around his hand, and smashed the glass. All that was heard was a dull crunch. The tape held the pieces in place. He carefully removed them from the window frame, then crawled in feet-first and landed on the floor with a soft thud.

He found himself in some sort of hobby room. A pool table stood in the centre and there were diplomas on the walls, trophies in a glass cabinet – marksmanship awards, it looked like.

Framed newspaper clippings were arranged on a shelf as if they were museum pieces. A fat man was visible in the photographs. Cheeks like a bulldog. In one press photo, he was posing in a uniform full of insignia alongside some politicians; it was some sort of gala event. The man was a cop.

Karl Mattson, read one caption. So this was the man Hillerström had told him about – the handler's boss.

A dark passageway led out of the room. Jorma opened a door and was standing at the cellar stairs. He heard country music coming from the floor above.

No alarm had sounded; he would have heard it when he broke the window.

He stopped in front of the door that opened onto the ground floor. He peered through the keyhole. There was a kitchen on the other side. But no people.

He took the Colt from his pocket.

The country music was still playing. It seemed to be coming from a room further on. He pressed the door handle down and stepped into the kitchen with his finger on the trigger.

No one there. No voices. Just the music.

Too late to turn back, he thought as he headed for a door.

The music suddenly stopped. There was a faint light from the room on the other side. He opened the door. The parquet floor creaked as he took a step inside.

He froze mid-step. He felt something cold on the back of his neck. A voice mumbled something, and then he fell forward and all light vanished.

Katz tried to picture the images as he drove north on the E4, but his mind refused. He could only see darkness and cages. A black lake, birds of prey circling in the sky. But no people.

House of Pain. Mona was on her way there with Wiksten.

The dark-skinned woman in the photographs from Ramón's iCloud, the article in the magazine in Wiksten's bedroom. It was all connected.

He exited the highway at Sollentuna. His GPS updated his directions: *Go straight ahead . . . then take the second exit from the roundabout . . .*

The field assistant at Crossroads, the volunteer organization that helped vulnerable migrants in the EU, had sent him a link with the GPS coordinates. But the man was unsure whether the migrant camp still existed. *These people are frightened; they keep moving, and they have good reason to do so. People threaten them and abuse them. There's not usually anything in the papers, because they don't dare to report the crimes to the police. And also sometimes the police evict them; communities won't let them settle down just anywhere.*

He was getting close. The site was in the nature reserve at Östra Järvafältet. The absurdly friendly computerized voice told him he had arrived. He parked the car at a rest area. The tent camp was supposed to be a hundred metres into the woods.

A piece of frayed tarp was still hanging from a tree, flapping in the breeze. A couple of squares of dead grass indicated where the tents had once stood. Further on was a ditch latrine, a hole in the ground they had used as a toilet.

Katz was startled by a jogger running by on the path. The man stopped, took off his headphones, and shook his head.

'It's such a fucking relief that they're gone! They were shitting in that pit over there.'

He used his elbow to point at the hole in the ground.

'Seriously, they can do that stuff back where they came from. But not here, dammit.'

'What happened?'

'The place burned down a week ago. Wouldn't surprise me if they did it themselves, so people will feel sorry for them.'

The man wiped the sweat from his brow and jogged in place.

'What are they even doing here? You can't go into a shop in this city without tripping over a beggar holding out a cup.'

Katz didn't say anything. He tried to digest the fact that he was too late.

'Believe me, they're going to end up spreading disease. Have you seen how some of them sit there, scratching themselves?'

The man put his headphones on again and made a bitter face, then jogged on into the forest.

Katz clicked on the next GPS link. This place was on the other side of the Skanstull Bridge, at the abutment below Gullmarsplan.

Most of the big camps are south of the city. There's one at Högdal Hills, for example, at the old dump. If you can't find the boy there, you might check under the bridges leading out of Södermalm. They spread out so they don't have to compete with each other. You know, they can't all beg in the same spot, or camp in the same spot. That's the sort of thing that makes people think there's a beggar mafia running everything behind the scenes. But it's not true. These people are just trying to help each other, make sure they're not competing the wrong way . . .

Just before Haga, he changed lanes and drove onto Essingeleden. Stockholm lay before him like a panoramic postcard. He saw the Dagens Nyheter building keeping vigil over southern Kungsholmen, the church towers of Gamla Stan spearing the sky to the east . . .

He got the sense that it was already too late once he came out of the Söderled Tunnel and muddled his way down to Simlångsvägen. He stopped the car at a turnaround and followed a path over to Skansbacken. He could see the camp from quite far away, just under the bridge abutment.

He walked past a temporary wall made of sheets of hardboard. The bridge itself served as a roof. This could have been anywhere in the Third World, he thought, a shantytown in Bombay or Lusaka.

A camping stove stood on a wooden bench. A discarded steel work surface with two sinks had been set up beside it, like a parody of a kitchen. Plastic drums of water. A toothless woman in her forties was sitting on a mattress, making tea on another camping stove. The boy's mother – they looked alike. Two young girls, about ten years old, were playing further up the hill.

'*Le Alexandrus rodáv* . . . I'm looking for Alexandru.'

The woman nodded towards a tent not far away.

'*So mangés lestar?*' she said. 'What do you want with him? He hasn't done anything naughty, has he?'

Katz didn't respond. A barge slipped by in the canal. The hum of traffic. The shrieking of a metro train crossing the Skanstull Bridge. And he remembered the days he'd spent in places like this. The nights when he hadn't found a spot in a shelter and had to sleep outdoors. The times he'd woken to people assaulting him, waking into a nightmare of violence.

The nights he'd been robbed, when people had taken his belongings and pissed all over him. Or the time an obviously mentally ill man had crawled into his sleeping bag as he lay in a multi-storey, totally gone on heroin, and tried to rape him before someone realized what was about to happen and chased the man away.

He sat outside the tent with Alexandru and showed him the photos he'd printed out. He started with the picture of the dark-skinned girl in the back seat of the car. Tears sprang to the boy's eyes.

'Do you know her?'

'Yes . . . it's Mariella.'

'Your sister, right?'

The boy nodded; he couldn't tear his eyes away from the photo.

'Is Mariella a prostitute? Do you understand what I mean? Does she sell herself to men?'

The boy peered up at the bridge abutment. And Katz suddenly saw Benjamin as a child, just a little older than this boy was now, fleeing through Europe with his parents. His sister had vanished, too.

'There they are,' the boy said softly.

He held up the photo of Jennifer and Ramón.

'Who?'

'The people who wanted to rent me from the gang in Husby. I was supposed to pick up drugs for them, in a different city.'

'But you said no?'

The boy rubbed at a spot of dirt on his trousers.

'Your sister knew them too?'

The boy nodded.

'And their friend . . . John,' he continued, 'the guy with the spots on his face. They got drugs for her. Drove her to see clients.'

'Then what happened?'

'She disappeared. One day she was just gone. Because she and Mum fought all the time.'

The boy stopped speaking, biting his lip gently.

'Were they fighting because she walked the streets?'

'And about the drugs. But how else was she supposed to afford it? Returnable bottles?'

The boy flipped through the photos. He stopped at the picture with the villa in the background.

'We were there once,' he said. 'At that house. John took us there. He wanted us to sleep over. It belongs to a police officer, he said.'

Katz was confused.

'They were going to pay my sister if she slept with him and his friends, but she panicked when we turned off the road. She forced John to turn around. She put a knife to his throat.'

Katz's mind was whirling. So that place was owned by a cop, one who knew Wiksten. The boy's sister had got away that time, he thought. But they captured her again later. She had been chosen because she didn't exist . . . because no one would report her missing.

'Do you know where the house is?'

'Not far from here. Maybe an hour by car.'

'Could you find your way there?'

'No.'

'Are you sure?'

'I wasn't watching . . . I was scared.'

'Why did you go along with her?'

'I was supposed to get money too. That was when my sister refused to do it, once she realized what was going to happen.'

Katz swallowed hard.

'I need to find that place. Is there anything else you remember about it, anything special?'

'There were flowers growing in the lake. Big white ones. Do you know what they're called?'

'Water lilies. Do you remember anything else? Anything special about that place?'

The boy was quiet, thinking back.

'John said you could take a boat all the way there. And there was some place nearby with paintings. He'd been there to see them once, along with the girl, Jennifer. There were weird paintings there, he said. I didn't really understand . . . but he said that there were people made of plants.'

Jorma was on the floor, bound to a metal pole behind his back. Steel wire was wound around his neck and arms. A jute sack had been pulled over his head. He could breathe through his nose, but he couldn't speak. Otherwise he would have done so, would have spoken to himself . . . to poke holes in the silence. But it was impossible. They had stuffed a rag in his mouth and covered it with electrical tape.

The air was starting to get thin and warm, as if he were warming it up with his own body heat.

He had trouble swallowing; his mouth was dry as a bone. *Don't hyperventilate*, he thought. *Breathe calmly.*

The cop had knocked him unconscious. The last thing he remembered was the barrel of the handgun on the back of his neck. When he came to again, he was lying in the back of the Land Rover with his hands and feet tied together. They had driven for an hour, maybe a bit longer, out of the city – the sound of traffic had grown fainter. The last part of the trip had been on gravel roads; he had heard the small rocks hitting the undercarriage.

Then they had stopped, opened the doors, and pressed a rag to his face. They knocked him out and carried him in here.

He was falling inside, dreaming of sounds . . . of notes bracing up the darkness, drawing lines through the silence. He dreamed that he was playing the piano in Midsommarkransen, going more and more slowly until every note lasted an eternity. That was why he'd never got hooked on drugs. Whenever he wanted to escape, he did it with music, playing and playing, sometimes for days on end, without eating or sleeping, stepping into a world of his own where nothing could hurt him.

There was such a thing as non-sonic music, he thought. Reading sheet music was enough for the notes to occur in the mind. Beethoven had been deaf as a post when he composed his Ninth Symphony. He had created the chromatics in String Quartet No. 14 in total silence. Music existed as ideas, in a sphere outside people themselves.

This was how he would avoid going crazy, avoid the thoughts of what might happen to him. Play Evergreens by Hoagy Carmichael in his head. Theatre music by Weill. Sonatas by Schubert and Beethoven. Separate the individual notes in the chords. Put them back together again . . .

In his imagination, he placed his right hand on the keys and played a G#maj7. He heard the notes very clearly – G#, C, D#, G – and he took them apart and glued them back together again. Silent music. He changed his finger position and played a 7sus4 in the same key, all fingers on the black keys, but he couldn't hear anything anymore; he was falling deeper into unconsciousness. He felt thirsty although he wasn't awake; he felt hunger in the form of stomach cramps. He thought he heard a sound – a woman screaming in the background – and then steps as someone approached.

When he awoke, the room was bright. He could make out the silhouette of a person through the jute. The person was standing perfectly still in front of him. The cop? But he wasn't sure.

He heard someone whimpering elsewhere in the room.

The room smelled vaguely of human waste. Was it coming from him? Had he soiled himself?

The person walked around and stood behind his back, lifting off the jute sack.

Jorma blinked in the fluorescent light. He was in some sort of cellar. The ceiling was low; there was just enough space for a grown man to stand upright. No windows. If there was a door, it must be behind him. Concrete walls to the right, whitewashed bedrock straight ahead. A dugout shelter . . . or the foundation under a building?

The floor was made of earth and stone slabs. There was a sheen of condensation on the ceiling.

He looked to the left, in the direction of the whimpering. A woman was squatting in a cage. At first he couldn't comprehend the sight. It reminded him of something he'd seen in a movie. A medieval torture chamber, he thought. Or a scene from an evil fairy tale: *Hansel and Gretel.*

She was young. Twenty, tops. Black hair, dark skin. Emaciated, nearly skeletal. The cage was barely large enough for her. She was grasping one of the bars, and her other hand was shielding her eyes, as if the light were painful. Naked. Track marks on her arms and legs. Bruises and contusions from being beaten; poorly healed wounds on her face. Dark spots on the bottom of the cage. From urine, he thought, or blood from her genitals.

He suddenly realized how cold it was and that he was shivering; his body was stiff.

The person behind him cleared his throat. A man. He was breathing calmly. Then he suddenly became aware once again of the tape over his mouth and he felt the panic well up, because he was going to suffocate, because he couldn't see the person behind him, because he couldn't predict what would happen.

He panted through his nose and felt like he was asphyxiating; he was afraid he would swallow the rag they'd stuffed in his mouth.

Calm down. Go inside yourself . . . into the music.

The jute sack fell down over his face again as he struck a seventh chord in his head. A male voice said something, and the woman started wailing.

The rattle of a lock opening. The woman shouted something in a foreign language as she was yanked out of the cage; it sounded like a prayer. She screamed in sheer panic as a door opened and closed behind him.

Pitch dark again. Silence.

He didn't know how much time had passed, but the man was back in the room again. He had lit a candle and placed it on the floor in front of Jorma. He pulled off the jute sack and the tape that had covered Jorma's mouth.

Now he could see who it was. The fat police commissioner he'd seen in the newspaper clippings. Just below average height. Thinning hair. Porous skin, as if someone had rubbed coarse salt into his face. He was wearing pale grey trousers, a checked shirt, and a dark cardigan. He held a revolver in his hand – Jorma's own Colt. He opened it, inserted a bullet, and spun the cylinder before putting it back in place.

'What are we going to do with you?'

The voice was mild, almost friendly. He moved to stand next to Jorma, then pressed the muzzle of the gun to his temple and cocked the hammer.

This is not happening, was all he could think. *It's not possible. I can't die this way.*

The man's finger hugged the trigger. He breathed calmly and began to hum a melody.

Then the man pulled the trigger and the sudden click sounded like an explosion.

The terror must have caused him to pass out. When he woke up again, he was lying on the floor on his stomach, still with his hands and feet tied together. The fat man was sitting on a chair in front of him. He aimed a torch at him. The cage was empty. The woman wasn't there . . . or maybe she never had been. Maybe he had only imagined her.

'You could be dead now. You got lucky. Chance was on your side. What were you thinking? That someone who has spent his career in surveillance won't notice when someone is tailing him? You're the guy who managed to escape after the robbery, aren't you?'

The fat man took a handkerchief from his pocket and wiped his forehead thoroughly.

'You don't have to say anything right now. We'll get all the information we need out of you.'

'Where are we?'

'Out in the country. Can't you smell the forest?'

Jorma turned his head so he had a better view of the room. He saw the cage again, along the far wall. A plastic bucket where the woman had done her business. He smelled human waste again. He hadn't dreamed it. This all had to do with what Leyla had told him, what Zoran had been dragged into.

'Who's the girl?'

'Just a whore . . . Why do you care?'

The cop had risen from the chair. He poked Jorma's chest with the toe of his shoe. He took out the Colt again, spun the cylinder, and pressed the muzzle into Jorma's ear canal. The steel was cold; it felt like an icicle in his ear.

'You're ahead right now, but you could lose at any moment . . .'

He didn't understand what the man wanted from him. Why didn't he just shoot him?

'Honestly, what are your odds of survival? Five out of six is 83.3 per cent. But your odds get worse each time; first 67 per cent, then 50 per cent.'

The muzzle moved to the back of his head. He was playing the grand piano this time, a Sibelius melody Harri had taught him during a period of sobriety when Jorma was nine. He floated away on the music as he'd always done when life became unbearable. If he was going to die today, it would be with piano music in his head.

Another click.

'Two–zero in your favour. You really must give me the chance for a revenge match.'

She never would have imagined that so much violence could be concealed in one person, so much ruthlessness, once the catatonia had loosened its grasp on him.

Hoffman had kicked her in the back and rained blows across her face so hard that her lip had split and one of her front teeth had loosened. She resisted, screaming, tearing at his hands, trying to bite him as he dragged her by the hair across the floor like a ragdoll; he dragged her into the office, where he handcuffed her to the radiator and turned on loud music. He had just turned it down again, as if to test her. His eyes were those of a completely different person. They were unrecognizable, ice-cold behind his dark irises. Unadulterated hatred.

'You don't have to do this,' she managed to say. 'Hoffman . . . it doesn't have to end like this!'

He just shook his head.

'People know I'm at your place. I just talked to my ex. I'm supposed to pick the kids up today, right now, actually . . . I was supposed to be there already; it's my week. Ola's going to wonder where I am.'

He was holding a service weapon; he must have brought it home from the office. He removed the magazine and checked to make sure it was full, then replaced it. His expression didn't change.

'A few more minutes and he's going to start calling my phone. He'll be worried. I told him I— I was here.'

Her stutter was back, the lock in her mind that linked to

her ability to speak. She rarely stuttered these days. She'd hardly had a problem since she was a teenager, living in junkie hell. But then again, she had done it almost constantly back then. Now it only happened when she was under too much stress.

'D-don't do it, Hoffman. Let's talk about this. There has to be sss-sss—'

The words died somewhere along the path from her speech centre and her tongue.

The computer was still on, displaying the terrible images. She could see one of their victims, a skeletal girl hanging from the ceiling by her arms. Hoffman turned it off. She yanked at the handcuffs and heard the metal chain clicking against the pipes of the radiator.

'Shit . . . shit . . . SHIIIIIT!'

The situation was slowly sinking in for him. He was about to panic, and she couldn't let that happen. Panicking was what made people do desperate things.

Win some time, she thought. *Try to speak calmly to him.*

'The DVDs, the pictures – those are from old investigations, right?'

Even she could tell how fake that sounded, how clear it was that she was lying. So she changed tactics.

'I'm prepared to listen to your version of things, Hoffman, and I'll accept it if it sounds plausible. Then we'll work this out together, as best we can . . . They won't come down on you as hard if you turn yourself in.'

'Shut up, bitch! I can't think!'

Squeeze him, but not too hard. Make sure to give him a way out.

'How would you get rid of my body . . . if you shot me . . . and all the blood . . . how would you get it out? My ex will tell the police that I called him from here. They'll put two and two together. If you let me go, I promise to help you, I swear!'

He had collapsed onto the office chair, as if someone had poked holes in him and his air was slowly leaking out.

'Mattson is the one behind all of this, I know it. You only played a minor role. Sarajevo sent me the phone tap logs . . . Mattson helped smuggle women into the country, to brothels, to organized sex rings . . . Some were sent on to other cities, and maybe to Norway or Finland . . . Mattson deposited the money into foreign bank accounts, and he kept some of the women for himself, like some sort of commission . . . He kept them locked up and . . .'

She could smell her own fear, a sour odour rising from her pores as he aimed the pistol at her.

'Eva, you don't know what you've got mixed up in here. You have no idea the kinds of people who are involved in this. Why the hell did you start snooping?'

All she could see was the muzzle of the pistol, that tiny black pupil staring at her. And Hoffman's shadow against the white walls of the office. A character out of an Indonesian shadow puppet theatre. Like the ones she and Ola had seen in Bali . . . the long trip they'd made to Southeast Asia, the kind almost all young middle-class couples took back then, to have an adventure together before it was time to get married and have kids like everyone else.

Perfect moments? she thought as she closed her eyes and waited for it all to end. *Did they exist?* She remembered two such moments in her life. One was on the ferry to Gotland with Ola, on the way to his parents' place in the country. She had been seven months pregnant with Lisa. He had brought her coffee and a chocolate cookie from the cafe. The sea outside the windows perfectly calm. Coffee. Milk chocolate. The child moving inside her. Ola's smile as he rested his hand on her belly. A sunbeam falling on her through the window. Perfection . . . The second time was with Katz in the basement bicycle area in Hässelby, where she used to spend the night when her home life was at its worst. Her virgin shot. Katz had readied the rig, found a vein for her, and injected. That indescribable rush . . . Katz removing the needle. The little trickle of blood that ran down her forearm. The kiss he gave her. The rush into bodily paradise. Perfection.

When she looked up again, he was gone. She heard him in the girl's room. He was searching for something, slamming drawers and wardrobe doors. He'd turned up the music again. So no one would hear her if she shouted.

She yanked at the handcuffs, pulling with all her might, ignoring the pain as the metal cut into her wrists. She found the screwdriver she'd used to break open the desk drawer; it was on the floor, two metres away.

She extended her legs to try to reach it . . . Ten centimetres beyond reach . . .

She could feel its shaft against her foot; her toe slid across the plastic. Then she caught it and pulled it a centimetre closer.

Hoffman was back in the room again. He realized what she was trying to do. He picked up the screwdriver and stuck it in his back pocket.

He was holding a skipping rope. The same kind Lisa had at home, candy-striped with glow-in-the-dark hand grips.

'Don't do it!' she said. 'Please, Hoffman . . .'

But he didn't respond. He just walked up to her and wound it around her neck.

Her vision went black. The pain was unspeakable as her larynx was crushed into her windpipe; she heard the cartilage cracking.

She wanted to scream but couldn't make a sound.

She pictured Lisa and Arvid running towards her in Vasa-parken. This was her week, she knew. Ola had just dropped them off. They were tanned; it was spring or early summer, and somehow they were timeless; all their ages gathered in their bodies. She wanted to remember them that way, take them with her, the boundless love she felt for them . . . the last thing she would think of before she faded away.

Then suddenly the pressure lessened; the skipping rope had fallen to the floor. She looked up.

Hoffman was in a totally different world. He had aged; suddenly he was an old man. It had happened in just a few seconds, like Dorian Gray. His hair looked white. He walked to the desk. Picked up the pistol. Stuck the barrel in his mouth.

His eyes were like two empty wells as he seemed to count down the seconds. He gagged as the barrel touched his soft palate.

Do it, she thought. *Just do it.*

But she knew he was too much of a coward.

If Katz understood Alexandru correctly, his sister had been in the house on at least one occasion before she disappeared. Jennifer Roslund had met her on the street. Maybe they had sold themselves together.

What more did he know? Not much.

He knew the place belonged to a police officer who was an acquaintance of Magnus Wiksten's. And that Ramón and Jennifer had delivered women to a sex ring that often met there. They did it so they could get money to buy a large amount of heroin; they had fantasies of moving up in the world and becoming drug lords. But something had happened along the way, and now they were likely both dead.

There was a place with famous art nearby, Alexandru had said. And you could get there by boat from Stockholm.

People made of plants . . .

Skokloster Castle. Its famous art collection – was that what the boy meant? The Italian baroque painter Arcimboldo's portrait of the Holy Roman Emperor Rudolf II was part of the castle's collection. *Vertumnus*. At first, when Katz found it on the castle's website, it looked like a regular old oil portrait, but if you looked more closely it became clear that his face was made up of many kinds of plants. His eyes were mulberries. His beard was made of chestnuts . . .

He called up Google Earth. He searched in expanding circles around the castle until he had scanned all the buildings within a ten-kilometre radius. Roads wound like snakes through the sleepy Uppland countryside. Meadows, bogs, and cultivated forests. Farms dotted among fields. It was a Falured Astrid Lindgren idyll. Summer cottages. Lake Mälaren like liquid metal, steely grey.

Then he found it: the estate. It was isolated, on a peninsula, several kilometres from the closest neighbour. There was a boathouse and a large villa further up the hill. The aerial image grew grainier the more he enlarged it. But it was unmistakable. This was the house he'd seen in the pictures on Ramón's iCloud.

Five minutes later, he had looked up the property records.

It was called Stensjiö Gård. It was a farm under leasehold. Two hundred hectares of forest and water in the municipality of Håbo. The parcel of land had once belonged to Skokloster. The property was owned by one Karl Mattson . . . the letter M in Ramón's address book?

The torch was still lying on the floor, but the light was growing dimmer as the battery drained. He felt like he was floating alone in a globe of faint light, surrounded by empty space.

The gleam of metal pipes running across the ceiling. Condensation had gathered there. A drop of water fell and landed on his foot. His feet were bare; why hadn't he noticed that before?

His tongue stuck to the roof of his mouth.

He heard the sound again, a faint whimper.

'Is someone there?' he asked.

A moment passed before she answered. Her voice was so faint that he could barely hear it.

'Yes . . . me, Mariella,' she answered in English.

He strained his vision until he could see the gleam of her eyes. He could make out the contours of the cage across the room. She was crouching inside it. Like an animal. A monkey.

'Do you know where we are, Mariella?' he asked.

'In a house . . . in the country. They put me in a cage. Many months now. Women die here . . .'

He turned in the other direction. A workbench. Tools hung from hooks. Hammers, files, socket wrenches, soldering tongs. Parts from dismantled radio equipment. The steel wire had softened up around his wrists.

'Where is the door?'

'Behind you. But it's locked. You not come out alive. And if you scream, nobody hear you.'

The woman began mumbling in a foreign language; he thought it was a prayer – she was praying to God.

'How many people are there in the house?'

'Mostly just the fat man, but sometimes more – ten or fifteen. Sometimes nobody for a week . . . then they leave food and water for me.'

The handler's boss, he thought. *The fat one. This was his place.*

'When new girls come they get rid of first girls. Or send them to other people in the tunnel.'

That word again: *tunnel.* Leyla had mentioned it in connection with the women Zoran had freed.

He stretched his foot towards the torch, resisting the urge to stop when the steel wire cut into his throat, and he managed to stick his toe out one more centimetre and move the torch so it was aiming at the woman. She was lying down now, curling into a foetal position, and her eyes were closed. She was only half conscious. He wondered how long she had left to live.

A few hours passed in which nothing happened. He tried to talk to her, but she didn't answer. His hearing had recalibrated itself until he could hear even the faintest sound. The vibrations of a car driving up to the house. The muffled voices of men in the distance. A car door slammed, and then there was a female voice . . . a different woman; she was shouting in panic on the floor above.

The steel wire had softened even more. He could rotate his right forearm around its own axis. But he couldn't get it loose; his hand was still stuck in the wire. Whoever tied him up knew what he was doing.

He gave a start as the door behind him made a noise. A key turned in it. The lights on the ceiling came on.

It was the blond man this time. He walked around Jorma,

pulled up the chair, and took the Colt from his pocket. He wore a prosthesis over the stump of his little finger, and it looked surprisingly natural with its plastic nail.

'Lost it in the line of duty,' he said as he noticed Jorma's gaze. 'It was bitten off.'

He sat down.

'Shall we continue?'

Jorma felt the muzzle of the revolver against his cheek this time. He closed his eyes. He was panting through his nose like an animal.

'What do you want to know?'

'Who you are and what you know.'

'You first.'

The handler laughed, a short, yelping noise.

'What can I say? We got lucky. What were the chances that I would be the one to pick up the phone when Abramović called? Much worse than your odds right now.'

He cocked the gun.

'A father calls to say that he owes five million kronor to people we know. Ready to spill everything he knew if we could arrange a new identity. We had to get rid of him. But then he went underground.'

The puzzle pieces came together before him; the man was putting it all together for him, telling him how Zoran had tried to work out a deal, confirming what Jorma had suspected – Zoran had been unlucky enough to turn to police officers who were personally involved in human trafficking. When they couldn't get at him in any other way, they made sure he committed a robbery. They killed him, using the task force team as a cover. *What about Leyla?* he thought. They knew she would keep quiet; they would hurt the children if she talked.

'And the security guy . . . Jocke?'

'He solved our problem for us. He thought he was going to go down for the robbery after it failed. He hanged himself.'

'And Hillerström?'

The blond man shrugged. He stood up. The woman upstairs screamed again. Her voice was shrill, filled with mortal fear.

'My boss likes to have fun. And he has like-minded friends. Now it's my turn to ask questions . . .'

He didn't see the point in talking. They weren't going to let him live anyway. Not after the things he had seen and heard.

'I simply want to know what you know. And whether you've told anyone about this.'

'Fuck you!'

'Who have you seen since the robbery? I want names for all of them.'

Jorma snorted up snot and spat it at the man. The man said nothing. He let the saliva run down his cheek. He walked around to stand behind Jorma and grabbed his middle finger.

His finger broke with the sound of a dry stick cracking in two. It was bent 180 degrees back against his hand. At first Jorma didn't feel a thing. His body was in a state of shock.

The handler took hold of the next finger but rapidly let go of it again.

There was a muted report in the house. It sounded like shots being fired. Someone screamed for help and ran across the floor above with heavy steps.

His whole wrist was crushed, limp, pliant, like heated plastic. He still couldn't feel the pain. Jorma pulled his hand up and to the side and found that it slid out of its steel-wire binding. The handler was gone; he'd left the door open in his rush.

His legs would hardly carry him as he walked over to the workbench. He looked around among the objects. He picked up the nail gun hanging from one of the hooks. With his left hand. His right was useless.

Katz drove through a green tunnel of pine forest, and then the scenery opened up and he could see for miles. The scattered deciduous trees were bursting with autumn colour. He startled a hare out of a ditch and watched it zig and zag down the road before executing an amazingly sharp turn and vanishing into a field.

He stopped the car on an old logging road and checked the contents of his backpack before getting out.

There was no breeze. It smelled like pitch and earth. The hot car engine gave off metallic pops.

The house was two kilometres from where he had stopped. The only road to it was private and followed the water's edge. He would be discovered if he approached that way.

The main building was surrounded by nature and had a view of the road. Mattson had inherited the house twenty years earlier. He had bought out his older sister's share and increased the acreage by leasing an adjacent forested lot.

A narrow path led into the woods. If he wanted to approach undetected, this was the best way. According to the map, it was wooded all the way up to the house.

The terrain was more difficult than he expected. Steep rock hills. Thick vegetation. A brook wound between the trees. Katz followed it until he reached a wildlife fence. He no longer knew where he was, or even if he was heading in the right direction.

He followed a narrow path to another rocky hill. He

climbed up it and looked around. He saw a dilapidated hunting stand in a clearing. A mowed swathe for high-voltage
power lines ran in the other direction. Then he spotted
another trail that wound its way down to the lake.

Five minutes later he had arrived. He retreated into the
treeline to avoid being seen. He crouched down and took
out his binoculars.

The road ended fifty metres away at a wooden boom with
a sign that read 'Private Property'.

The sauna and the jetty where Wiksten had been photo-
graphed with a towel around his hips were on a spit of land
that jutted into the lake. There were water lilies growing
there, just as the boy had said.

A Land Rover and a grey hire car stood in the driveway.
The curtains were drawn in the house. It was quiet . . . uncan-
nily quiet.

A movement at the edge of the water caught Katz's
attention. A tall man with blond hair stepped out of a boathouse. He looked around as if he sensed that he were under
surveillance. Then he shook his head, walked towards the
house, and vanished from sight.

Katz moved on, walking up a mound until he came to the
short side of the building. He wiggled out of his backpack
and took two metal thermoses from it; they contained explosive charges made of plain old ammonium-based cleaning
agents. Rickard Julin, of all people, had taught him how to
make them.

He heard a car engine in the distance. A van with tinted
windows was approaching from the road. The driver
stopped. A guard opened the gate, but Katz could only see
his back. The vehicle drove up to the front of the house.

The dark-haired man who stepped out was of a similar age
to him. He walked around and opened the rear doors. He

yanked a woman from the back, holding her by the hair at the back of her head as he dragged her up to the house.

Katz was shocked when he saw who it was: Eva Westin.

He left his current position and moved rapidly along the edge of the woods. He stopped when he was level with the back of the house. He felt to make sure that his pistol was still in his pocket.

A cold sweat had broken out on his forehead. Saliva streamed incessantly into his mouth. If something happened to her, he would never forgive himself.

The fabric curtain was drawn aside in one of the ground-floor windows. A fat man rested his head against the glass and peered out. Mattson.

Katz had taken the time to learn more about him. The man had created one of the county task force teams, among other things, and he had previously been in charge of the vice and narcotic squads. These days he was one of two directors at the county police.

He took out the binoculars and tried to spot Eva. But all he could see was the dark-haired man, who had forced her into the house. He was on the phone with someone.

Wiksten was sitting on a sofa along the wall. He didn't have any wounds on his face as far as Katz could tell. But he seemed nervous somehow. Or excited.

The curtain fell back again.

Squat juniper bushes dotted the mound where Katz was standing. The lawn began two metres below. He would jump down and run over to the side of the house. Start by locating the guard.

He sank to his knees below the closest of the dark windows. He breathed deeply to slow his heartbeat. He moved along the facade, aiming the pistol ahead. He stopped at a rain barrel and peeked out.

There was a man by the boom gate. A bodybuilder type. Probably a cop.

Katz approached a side entrance. A stairway led up to a door with a round window.

He heard screaming from inside the house. A woman was bawling in panic. The darkness rose up in Katz. Pure hatred.

Then he heard an engine again. Another car was coming up the drive. More guests, he thought. The 'party' was about to start. The man who was keeping watch took his post beside the boom.

Katz couldn't wait any longer. He crawled in under the stairs and taped the first bomb to the foundation, the explosive strength aimed out. It would be a violent blast, but it wouldn't cause great material destruction. He had once been trained in this sort of thing – handling extreme situations all on his own. The element of surprise was key. The goal was to create chaos and panic. Fear could paralyze people.

He attached the wire to the blasting cap and twisted the egg timer. He had three minutes.

The car had stopped at the gate. The window rolled down. The guard leaned over. Then there was a dull bang, and the man's legs went out from beneath him.

Katz was bewildered. He left the stairs and ran, stooping, back outside. He crouched down behind the Land Rover and attached the second bomb to its undercarriage. Then he headed for a low stone wall further on.

The gate was open, he discovered when he turned around. The guard was lying at the side of the road with the blood pumping out of a bullet wound in his head. His legs were jerking epileptically.

The car came up the gravel driveway and stopped in front

of the front door. A masked person stepped out, left the door open, and walked calmly up the stairs.

Katz looked at his watch. One minute until the bombs would detonate.

He heard shots fired inside the house. More shouting, men's voices, someone swearing. *Shit, shit, shit* . . .

Thirty seconds passed before the masked figure appeared again, just as calm as when it arrived. No licence plates, Katz noticed as the car started and drove off. But there was another person inside the car; he could see a figure in the back seat.

The explosions that followed deafened him in both ears. Seabirds rose from the water and flew out over the bay. Katz's ears were still ringing as he walked up to the house, aiming his pistol in front of him.

Two violent explosions, one right after the other. Where had they come from? The shouting from the floor above had ceased; all he could hear was a quiet mewling.

'I'll be back,' he said to the woman in the cage.

There was no reaction.

He still couldn't feel his hand. It was as if he had become disconnected from his own body.

He held the nail gun in his left hand as he walked up the stairs.

The door was half open, as the handler had left it. It was a soundproof door with several layers of foam mounted on the inside.

He found himself in a rustically decorated hall. He cautiously rounded a corner and opened a door into a windowless room. There was an empty cage on the floor, just like the one in the cellar, but its door was open. A woman was chained to a hook in the wall by her hands. There was a dog collar around her neck. A food bowl stood on the floor in front of her. She had been blindfolded with a piece of black fabric. He pulled it off. A blonde junkie chick was staring at him in terror. At least she was alive . . . He would have to take care of her later.

His tunnel vision took over. He went into another room. A male body lay on a sofa – a younger, bearded guy. Shot in the head . . . Next to him, in a pool of fresh blood on the floor, lay the handler, with a large hole in his chest.

The fat boss cop was lying in the doorway to the next

room. His intestines were protruding from the bullet wound in his stomach. He was trying to crawl, trying to say something, but his voice didn't work.

Jorma entered yet another room. Black plastic bags covered the windows. Tube lighting cast a bluish glow. There were strange tools on the floor. Two barbed wire nooses. Something that looked like an iron collar or a garrotte. Flecks of dried blood on the floor. A torture chamber, he thought. Fear had eaten into the walls. A rope noose hung from the ceiling.

His legs gave way and he sank to the floor. His vision went black for an instant, and he dropped the nail gun and fumbled for it in the darkness. He was dizzy from forty-eight hours without food or water. He heard approaching footsteps.

It took him half an eternity to get back on his feet again. Then he discovered another door across the room. He managed to drag himself to it and found himself in a kitchen. The steps came closer, stopping in the room behind him. He sank into the gap next to a cupboard and realized that he'd forgotten something – but he couldn't remember what it was.

Katz stopped at the door where Mattson lay. The third victim. He had one room left on the ground floor, the only room he hadn't checked. Mona was okay. She would make it.

He entered a room with veiled windows. He shuddered as he saw the noose hanging from the ceiling. A nail gun lay on the floor. He picked it up and shoved it into the band of his trousers.

Two people were still missing: Eva and the man she had arrived with. They couldn't be far away. The cars in the driveway had been destroyed.

He looked across the room, where a door was ajar.

He opened it and found himself in a rustic kitchen.

Through the window he discovered the dark-haired man on his way to the boathouse. He had a pistol in his hand. He was dragging Eva behind him.

She was exhausted. Otherwise she would have resisted. Hoffman was dragging her by the hair towards a red building at the water's edge.

A wooden gate was open to the road. A man lay in a ditch, shot in the head.

There were burning cars in the driveway. The odour of melted plastic and explosives hung in the air.

Somehow the chronology had short-circuited. She could hardly remember the order in which the events had occurred, nor how Hoffman had managed to get her from his apartment into a car on Hornsgatan. Why hadn't anyone reacted when a woman was bundled into a windowless van by an armed man?

It felt like he'd driven her around for several hours, and she'd heard him swearing on the other side of the thin metal that separated her from the cab. She realized that she had been given a grace period, but it wouldn't make any difference because he would just get rid of her in a safer place.

Then he had stopped here, at a summer home surrounded by water and forest, and dragged her into a room with several other people inside. Mattson was one of them, and there was another man, a slightly younger one . . . She realized that this was where they had recorded the terrible movies. Hoffman exchanged a few words with the others before bringing her into an adjacent room. By that point she was absolutely paralyzed with fear. She knew it would all end there, and she hardly reacted when shooting suddenly erupted in the house. Hoffman had taken her out via a side door, and at the same time she heard two explosions, one right after the other.

'Get in the back!'

They were in a boathouse. He pointed his gun at the motorboat that was moored at the jetty.

'Get in, I said!'

She grabbed the railing and felt her legs give way. Tiny waves lapped at the jetty. The pilings the boathouse stood on were green with algae. Suddenly the door behind them opened.

'Lie down, dammit!'

Hoffman heaved her onto her back and pressed the muzzle of the gun to her face. She blinked at the figure in the doorway. She would have recognized it from a hundred metres away in a crowd: Katz.

He ran as fast as he could. He wasn't thinking anymore. He was just doing what his instincts told him to; he opened the door and stood there.

Eva was lying on the dock. The dark-haired man was pressing a pistol to her temple.

'Hoffman,' she whimpered. 'Don't do it . . .'

So that was her boss. She'd mentioned his name once. It was all connected somehow, although he couldn't discern the pattern yet.

'Put down your weapon.'

Katz placed the Glock on the floor.

'Kick it over or else she dies.'

He did as he was ordered.

'Who the fuck are you? Do you know each other?'

Katz just nodded. It was all he could manage to do. He still couldn't believe that Eva was there.

'You lie down too, arms behind your back.'

The dark-haired man aimed the gun at him. Katz needed more time. He still had the nail gun tucked into the waistband of his trousers. But he had to get closer in order to use it. He needed to divert his attention so he could get it out before the man had time to react.

He lay down on his stomach, turning his head so he could see her. He felt so much love for her, for this grown woman who had fought so hard to be the person she was, or the young woman he'd met a lifetime ago when they were teenagers – all the feelings that had gathered over the years in a meaningless pile that he had never made use of, because of who *he* was. The door behind him was open. Light streamed in as if onto a stage.

Hoffman mumbled something inaudible, staring at them with the gaze of a desperate man. His finger squeezed the trigger. And Katz knew it was too late, that this was the end for both of them.

He turned his face away and closed his eyes. He heard the shot, the report rebounding against the boathouse wall, and felt the spray of warm blood hit his face.

PART 7

Time flew; before they knew it, winter would be here. Katz hated this time of year. The darkness threatened to smother him.

The Hanukkah celebration was advertised in a mailing from the Jewish congregation, the twenty-fifth day of the month of Kislev: '*sufganiyot* and warm beverages, crafts and presents for the children.'

Two thousand two hundred years earlier, when the Maccabees entered the ruins of the Temple in Jerusalem after their victory over the last in a long line of foreign oppressors, they had found a single tiny bottle of oil and used it in the menorah. Incredibly enough, it lasted for eight days . . . and that was why eight candles were lit in the candelabra, one for each day.

To his own surprise, he had dug out the old silver *chanukiah* with its Star of David; it had once belonged to Benjamin and, he guessed, Chaim and Sara before him.

He had polished it, placed it on the kitchen table, and purchased candles at the Jewish Centre on Nybrogatan. He had to go through two security queues with metal detectors to enter the shop and perform his errand. He took note of the guards patrolling the puny asphalt playground of the Jewish School; they were paid by the congregation since the public viewed them as unnecessary. Security had been increased because the Israel–Palestine conflict had reached a new fever pitch, and you had to answer for it even if you were a schoolkid who lived in another part of the world.

Perhaps this was just an attempt to find his way back to an everyday routine, though it manifested itself in the form of a diversionary tactic.

Shortly after his visit to the Jewish Centre, in any case, he finished the translations of the Russian military publications and began a long-awaited consulting job for Viral Tech, a British antivirus firm that appreciated his talent for analysing malicious code. Katz mapped out the idiosyncrasies of a new Trojan faster than anyone had expected and received a fee large enough for him to take a few months' holiday.

For a while he toyed with the thought of travelling out of the country, of leaving the darkness and the battlefield behind, but the enthusiasm he had initially felt for this idea soon died out.

The only trip he ought to take was to Skogskyrkogården, the cemetery, to grieve. But he couldn't even bring himself to do that. Instead he sank deeper and deeper into his depressing Katzness. He isolated himself, hardly ever leaving his apartment.

The newspapers were still writing about the incidents in the house in a surprisingly sober fashion; perhaps it was too macabre, far beyond what the general public might be interested in. An affront to good taste, even for the press.

The police had dug up the entire estate around Mattson's house, plus parts of the surrounding woodland, in their search for corpses. But they had only found one: the remains of a woman of around twenty-five, lying in the only spot the cadaver dogs had pointed out, in a ravine some distance into the woods. According to the medical examiner, she had been strangled with a strip of plastic and buried three years earlier. Her identity was still a mystery. Mattson's ring hadn't taken any risks. They had chosen their victims with care.

There were still a great number of questions hanging in the air: the masked person who had calmly walked into the house and shot four people to death – what had that been all about?

No one else had shown up at the country home that evening; an alarm must have gone out to all the members of the network. The forum had been shut down the same night. Maybe it would pop up again somewhere else, but in a safer place, on a darknet somewhere.

The 'tunnel' that Wallin had mentioned . . . did it exist?

Perhaps Mattson's house had been just one of many stations.

In the nineties, in the infancy of the internet, Katz had followed the development of the dark web on behalf of the armed forces. The hidden cyberworlds that lay far beyond the horizons of the regular web. The embryo of what would become a rubbish tip for all the crap that existed in their wired world. Anonymous online criminals who logged in behind walls of proxies, selling drugs and weapons, protected by the Tor servers' centrifuge, where IP addresses dissolved into thin air. Digital marketplaces where people ran wholesale trade using cloned credit cards and dumps. Cyber-activists who confused their battle for freedom with net anarchy and furnished impenetrable web hotels for paedophile rings. Online laboratories where people wrote custom malicious code. Foreign intelligence services, the Mafia, terrorists. Katz knew he would never find the answer there. It was too big, too vast, full of hidey-holes where people vanished without a trace.

But during his sleepless nights after the incidents in the house, he clicked his way there anyway, down into the darkness, to places that weren't indexed by the search engines. *A person could find anything there,* he thought, *the 'tunnel,' networks where humans were bought and sold like livestock by people just like*

Wiksten and Mattson, spread all over the world. He could only see the tip of the iceberg. He could only hear the digital echoes, the screams of women and children.

One afternoon he got himself together and tracked down Alexandru. The boy had moved to a caravan camp in Nacka along with his mother and two newly arrived relatives. Mariella and his younger siblings were back in their home village in Romania.

Katz was welcomed with tea and cookies in the caravan they had been able to take over from a previous inhabitant. The boy asked him a little about what had happened in the house, and Katz answered as best he could.

'How is Mariella?' he asked when the boy seemed satisfied.

'Some friends helped her travel home. She's living with my grandma now. She says she's going to quit the drugs. Until then she's *marimé.*'

'Unclean? For how long?'

'I don't know . . . maybe a few months. And she also needs to rest after everything that happened.'

Katz didn't want to imagine what the girl had been subjected to during her months of imprisonment, but he knew one thing with certainty: she had been lucky. They had found her just in the nick of time.

Mona. She had been lucky as well. And she had turned her luck into an even greater conviction to make a break with her old life. She had left Stockholm a few weeks earlier. She was given a spot at a treatment home in Dalarna, not far from the town where her son lived. She had called him one evening to tell him about it, sounding shockingly unaffected by everything she had gone through. She was a survivor, just like him. It would take more to break her.

'The police were here again before she left,' the boy went on. 'But she couldn't tell them any more than she had already. That Jennifer and Ramón sold her to those men. She didn't mention you either, just as you asked. Thanks for finding her . . . and thanks for helping me with Miro. You had a chat with him, right? Because I never saw him again after that.'

Outside the caravan windows, two haggard men were sorting returnable bottles, large ones here, small ones there. They appeared to be in their fifties, but they were probably only half that old. It was difficult to imagine that they preferred this life over going back to their homes. But so it was, and in the end that explained everything.

'What happened at the last place you lived?' Katz asked. 'In the forest?'

The boy lowered his eyes.

'They came in the night, poured petrol on our tents, and set fire to them.'

'Who did?'

'*Gadjé* . . . foreigners, Swedes. Luckily, we weren't there. It was too cold to sleep outside that night. The imam in Husby let us stay in the mosque. In the morning, when we went back, everything had burned and they had carved swastikas into the trees.'

Katz accepted a fresh cup of tea, which the boy's mother poured out of a thermos. He marvelled at how clean the inside of the caravan was, and that it was even possible to keep it so clean considering there was no running water.

'What happens now?' he said. 'How long will you stay?'

'*Si te dikása maj anglé.*'

'"He who lives shall see . . ."'

The boy smiled at him.

'Your Romany just gets better and better. And you know what? I'm going to start at a real school after Christmas.'

He slept poorly, without dreaming. Dreamless sleep: he hated it; it reminded him of his junkie days. A dreamless sleep was an imitation of death; it disavowed memory.

He could have been dead too. He had expected to die in the boathouse, as he lay on the floor and felt the spray of blood hit his face. Or when he was under attack in the apartment. That hadn't been Wallin, as he'd first thought, nor was it Wiksten. He had seen Wiksten's corpse as he walked through the house; there hadn't been any bite marks on his face.

Had he sent someone else? But who would it have been?

The cemetery. When he closed his eyes, he pictured the chapel, heard the cantor singing, the prayers, and someone crying in despair. He knew he had to start the process, knew he couldn't put it off any longer. He ought to visit. He should have done it long ago.

The days grew shorter. The first Advent lights were lit in the windows of homes. The address book was still in the locker along with the bukkake DVD and the remaining packs of heroin. Katz's plan was to get rid of all of it, but for some reason it never happened.

Jorma Hedlund called a few times and wanted to get together. They had only seen each other once since the events in the house, to make sure their stories matched in case they were called in for questioning. But Katz kept finding more excuses to avoid seeing Jorma.

He just tried to get time to pass. To kill it.

Time and again, his thoughts went to Skogskyrkogården. The ice-cold wind blowing outside the chapel. The black-clad funeral-goers. The crunch of the wet gravel under his feet as they walked towards the gravesite. The rows of stones whose inscriptions meant nothing to him. And the image of the boy at the very front – an orphan at far too young an age – leaning over the rectangular hole, bordered by piles of earth, dropping a flower onto the coffin. What had he been thinking? He didn't know . . .

He went down to his cellar storage unit again, taking out the moving box from which he had rescued the Hanukkah candelabra. A box of decorations was all he had left of them. Somehow, during his years on the street, he had managed to keep it safe. It had spent time in the attics of various acquaintances, at Jorma's place, among others, at storage facilities, and for a while, in a rock shelter that belonged to MUST, the military intelligence and security service . . . the safest place a homeless junkie's valuables could be.

Skogskyrkogården. The small Jewish section, he thought as he stood with their wedding rings in his hand . . . He really ought to visit. Go to their graves. Try to grieve for them for the first time in his life. Maybe he should bring Eva? He didn't want to go alone.

During the first week of December, something happened to rouse him from his lethargy. He got a call from Boris Epstein's youngest daughter, Miriam. Her father had something he wanted to give Katz; it would be best if he could visit.

It was eleven in the morning when Katz arrived at the apartment in Sundbyberg. The woman who answered the door was about his own age. She was wearing a checked skirt and a modest white blouse that was buttoned up to the throat. She looked like her father – the same high forehead, the same lovely brownish-grey eyes.

'How nice that you could come. Dad is getting worse by the hour. Please, come in. I'm Miriam.'

Katz followed her into the kitchen. She put aside a planner that was lying on the table, full of notes written in neat script.

A doctor came out of a room further on and removed a pair of disposable gloves before walking over to greet Katz.

'I've given him more insulin,' he said, turning to Miriam. 'He's beginning to perk up a little. Don't give him any whisky, no matter how much he begs for it.'

'I promise I won't.'

'Dad is a walking list of geriatric diagnoses,' she went on once the doctor had left. 'You should see his medicine cabinet – he could open a pharmacy.'

She gave him a curious look.

'He's told me about you, or rather about Benjamin. He

wanted to give you something, he said, a *memory*, before it's too late.'

A bell rang from inside the bedroom. And then a faint voice called her name.

'To everyone's surprise, it's not cancer or his heart that's getting him,' she sighed as she stood up. 'Instead it's the most recent addition: ALS. The tests came back a week ago. He can hardly swallow anymore. It's a dreadful disease. People starve to death, or they suffocate when their lungs stop working. Hold on for a second, please. I'll tell him you're here.'

When Katz entered the room, Epstein was lying in a hospital bed with an electronically adjustable backrest. An IV bag hung from a metal stand; two different tubes ran to the port on his wrist.

'Benji's boy,' he said with a trace of a smile. 'You look like him, you know . . . your troublesome father. You have the same demeanour, like an undertaker with a toothache.'

A religious text written in Hebrew lay on the nightstand.

'My daughter is trying to lead me onto the right path before it's too late,' Epstein slurred as he noticed Katz's gaze. 'That girl is the exact opposite of her father. She lives by the rules. She keeps kosher. She goes to the synagogue more often than the rabbi does. And to the *mikvah*, the bathhouse, once a month.' He gave an ironic wink. 'I heard her on the phone with the Chevra Kadisha, the funeral organization, this morning. You'll have to start practising the *Kaddish*, Danny . . . Not long left now.'

With difficulty, he reached for the text on the nightstand and lifted it up. Underneath it was a photo album.

'I dug this out of my cabinet after you were here last time. I took a walk down memory lane.'

About two dozen photographs were glued onto black paper. They depicted Benjamin and Epstein sixty years earlier. In one of them, they were standing outside the Nalen restaurant next to a poster of the Benny Goodman Orchestra. Several photos were from the boxing club in Narva; they were posing with their gloves on, in a fighting stance. Two of the pictures were a little older; they had been taken outside Central Station. Benjamin was holding a suitcase; he was dressed in a pale felt hat and a tweed suit. Taxis outfitted with wartime wood-gas units could be seen in the background. Next to Benjamin was a grey-haired man twice his age but just like him in looks. Chaim. Katz's grandfather. He had never seen a picture of him before.

'Taken in February, 1944,' Epstein said. 'Benji was on his way to Berlin and then to Vichy in France, all the way down to the Spanish border, to try to find out what happened to his sister. Europe was under German occupation, and your father was a Jew. But nothing was impossible for Benjamin Katz. He had some sort of congenital deficiency – he didn't understand fear . . . I suppose you could say he had contempt for death, or maybe a death wish. Berlin was *Judenrein*, as they called it. Goebbels had ordered as much the year before as a gift to his beloved Führer. And Benji walked around that city with a fake passport, looking for Hannah.'

'Someone must have helped him.'

'He didn't say much about that either. But the Swedish armed forces were involved somehow.'

Katz was struck dumb as he tried to digest this information.

'After the war he made some further attempts behind the Iron Curtain. He went to the Baltic states and the DDR, among others.'

'Did Dad tell you anything else about those trips? If he received official help, it must be documented somewhere.'

'You'll have to visit the archives. But I'm afraid the most important documents are classified.'

'What about Chaim? You knew him too. Didn't he ever say anything?'

'Only by insinuation. He believed that they found out what happened to his daughter in the end – that she wound up in a so-called *Freudenabteilung* in a concentration camp.'

'A brothel?'

'That might be putting it too kindly, since those poor women were gassed after a certain number of months. But there was a persistent rumour that said someone in Vienna had reported her to the Gestapo, and that this same person had something to do with those establishments. Benjamin made a promise to Chaim that he would track him down and avenge her. But the rumour was false. It turned out to concern an entirely different woman.'

Katz considered the photographs. He only owned four pictures of Benjamin, and just as few of his mother. Those photos, a few books, and the decorations in the moving box were all that was left of them.

'There may be some people who can help you,' Epstein said in a voice that was growing weaker and weaker. 'A historian at the Swedish Army Museum, among others. Mikael Stern. I wrote a letter to him after you visited me last time. He has access to certain archives that aren't meant for the eyes of mere mortals. Call him. He's expecting you.'

There was a knock at the open door. Miriam was standing in the doorway with a tray of medicine in her hands.

'Sorry to interrupt,' she said. 'But it's time for Dad to follow doctor's orders.'

She placed the tray on the nightstand, then walked to the

window and cracked it, letting in the raw December air. Katz noticed the syringe that lay next to the packet of sterile gauze.

'My daughter is a nurse,' Epstein said, eyes closed. 'It's very practical. After all, the doctor can't be here all the time.'

She opened the plastic packaging of the syringe, and drew clear fluid into it from a medicine bottle.

A thought was about to come loose inside Katz. At first it was so faint that he barely sensed its presence, but then it became clearer, as if some sort of logical formula were slowly detaching itself from the room.

Jorma waved at the three people standing in the glass entry-way. Leena had her arm around Kevin – a grown man now, with his own place in Rågsved. And there was Aino, in the wheelchair, with the vacant stare of a person on her way into the fog. Kevin jokingly gave him the finger. The guy was not unlike Jorma himself as a young man. He was a cocktail of fragility and explosiveness. He only hoped that Kevin wouldn't make the same mistakes Jorma had. Leena had hinted that he was starting to hang out with the wrong crowd.

The kid was his second-highest priority now that the worst of the danger had passed. He was planning to take him out to the movies one evening, but there were a couple of other things he had to deal with first.

The trio in the entryway of the Finnish retirement home in Fisksätra was the closest he would ever get to a nuclear family, he thought as he backed out into the driveway and nearly sideswiped the sliding door of a delivery van, from which a young woman was unloading cartons of Karelian pierogies. Aino's wrinkled hand waved back, then slowly sank onto the armrest of the wheelchair. The question was, did she even know who she was saying goodbye to? She was more and more forgetful with each visit. The most recent relapse had affected her language. She was forgetting words in a way she never had before – mostly Finnish ones, strangely enough.

Happily, there was no unfinished business between them, he thought as he watched them disappear in the rear-view mirror. He had no reason to blame her; she had done the

best she could, trying to survive with a psychopath for a husband, protecting her children to the best of her ability,
getting a divorce when she realized there was no other way
out, just as Leena had done ten years ago when she realized
things had gone too far with Kevin's dad . . . His anger flared
up at the mere thought of his sister's ex. Apparently he'd
contacted Leena again, in a threatening sort of way. Perhaps
he would have to rearrange his list of priorities and put that
idiot closer to the top, like maybe in third place, or even
higher if he kept up the harassment. The thought of Kevin's
dad made his adrenaline jolt twice as high as it already was.

As he drove through the roundabout before the motorway, he fished the business card from his back pocket. He'd
got it from Katz when they met a few weeks ago. On the
afternoon they had gone through what had happened and
updated each other on what they had experienced.

He dialled the number as he drove onto Värmdövägen,
squeezing the phone hard when the voice came on the
other end.

'Yes?'

'It's me again. Hedlund. I have a six o'clock appointment
. . . Is it okay if I come right now?'

'I'll have to check the calendar . . . hell yes. You're welcome
anytime. Until four o'clock. After that it gets pretty busy.'

He followed the early-afternoon traffic back to the city. The
first snow had started to fall, heavy and wet. When he discovered a cop car sitting at a service road, he reflexively
slowed down. But they had nothing on him; he would make
it through this time too.

He had finally dared to move back to his apartment in
Kransen and was slowly starting to let down his guard,
return to his regular life. The investigation into the missing

armoured-truck robber had been shelved. The criminal police had other matters to attend to. Like trying to figure out what had really happened at Mattson's house.

He had played the piano like a madman for the first couple of weeks. He had even gone down to Aulos to buy new sheet music. Some complicated pieces by Prokofiev as well as the piano part of Mahler's Fifth Symphony. He drummed the first measure of the melody against the wheel as he passed Sickla and drove into the dark mouth of the Söderled Tunnel.

As long as no new evidence was unearthed at the crime scene, he was safe. He hadn't even told Leena about the robbery. He didn't want anything to leak further to Kevin. The kid needed good role models. And he would be one of them – not the man he had been, but the one he would become. He had made up his mind. He had half a million kronor left in the safe deposit box in Huddinge. Funds on which to build a new life. Since last week, the other half of the money was in an account in Cyprus, in Leyla's name. To help Zoran's kids in the future. She would soon receive a letter from a lawyer in Nicosia, written in such a way that she would believe it was Zoran's money, something he had arranged for her behind her back.

He blinked in the daylight as he drove onto Huddingevägen. Deep-rooted exhaustion, he thought as he continued towards his destination. He wasn't sleeping well at night. He had dreams about the incidents at the house.

He had been hiding in a space in the kitchen, still in shock over everything that had happened, when a person suddenly entered . . . and walked past him and vanished into the garden. Katz, he realized with a thirty second delay. He had watched as Katz ran down to the boathouse. And in the midst of his confusion over finding his best friend there, he must have realized that Katz was in danger.

He returned to the room where the corpses lay, took the Colt that was still in the handler's grip, and rushed down to the boathouse.

The door was open. He heard people talking inside – a voice ordering Katz onto the floor – and he realized that something terrible was about to happen and that there was no room for error.

In his dream, he opened the cylinder of the revolver again and again to check the ammunition. The handler and Mattson really had been playing Russian roulette with him. There was a single bullet in the cylinder. It was aligned with the bore.

Connected to the boathouse was a jetty. He cautiously approached the window and peered in. He saw what he needed to see and didn't hesitate as he lifted the weapon. He had one chance, and he had no intention of squandering it.

Eva had stayed behind to meet the first squad car. They would sync up their stories later, they decided; the main thing was that he was never there, or that at least, officially, she hadn't seen him. He and Katz left the house together; they walked through the woods and left in the car.

He had arrived at his destination. He parked the car across the street and peered up at the third floor. Drawn curtains. No one could see in. There was nothing to suggest what was really going on. The man was waiting for him. He was looking forward to it. He would just park in a safer spot.

The view from the roof of the apartment building had to be wonderful. She could have seen the neighbourhoods of her youth from up there.

Their last stop had been Hässelby Gård on the other side of the motorway – the white high-rise in the city centre where she lived with Rita and Jonas during her teenage years. But she had been born a bit further south, in Blackeberg. Their flat in the complex on Drachmannsgatan, which had been paid for by social services, was only a stone's throw from the luxury buildings of Södra Ängby, but the line between the two areas had been as sharply drawn then as it was now.

That had also been her older brother's last address in Stockholm. Roger had been given away when he was ten; he ended up with a new family and never came back. He was in Skåne, Rita said, one of the few times the topic arose, but that was an unsubstantiated rumour; they had never heard from him after his move.

Geographically speaking, her mother hadn't gone very far in life. Råcksta was one of the few parts of Stockholm where you could still get an apartment via the housing authority, and the rent was likely half what it cost in the city proper.

The antennae sticking out from balconies made her think of a spaceship that had been forced to make an emergency landing.

At least she didn't have to worry about the time. She had been on leave for over a month while her colleagues in homicide and the human-trafficking unit tried to make sense out of the chaos.

She couldn't count the number of hours she'd spent in questioning. She was one of the key witnesses in a mess she was starting to suspect would never be untangled. She had told them everything she knew about Hoffman and her own investigation, minus certain details that could compromise Jorma and Katz; she had handed over the material she had received from her colleagues in Sarajevo; she had made sure that the criminal police got in touch with the Bosnian police; she had done what she could to help with the huge puzzle. But what more did they have to go on than witness accounts? The only information they could get from Mona, the Roma girl Mariella, and Eva herself had to do with people who were dead, who could no longer be interrogated. The evidence from Mattson's house led nowhere. Hoffman's CD-R discs and the backup she had loaded onto her USB drive had been destroyed. He had got rid of them on the way to the house.

She followed the investigation out of the corner of her eye, via her contacts at the police station. Two kidnapping investigations and five for murder – for the five people in the house in Håbo – had been launched. They did know that Mattson was involved in human trafficking and that his connections led all the way down to the Balkans, but that was where the trail ended.

The trafficking had been a separate matter, she thought as two young women with pushchairs passed her car, *and the sex ring was yet another.* Mattson, Hoffman, and Wiksten had used some of the smuggled women for their own private purposes. They had brought others in on their own, some with the help of Ramón and Jennifer Roslund and another man, now dead, by the name of John Sjöholm.

But who else had been involved? They would likely never know.

In any case, someone, or several people, had cleaned up after themselves with a vengeance. The police still had no clues about the person who had done the shooting in the house, and something told her it would stay that way.

At least she had managed to keep Katz and Jorma out of the investigation. The weapon with which the latter had saved her life was untraceable. Jorma had promised to get rid of it as soon as possible.

She sighed as she dug her phone out of her bag. She was planning to call and say she had arrived, but instead she pulled up the few photos she had of the children. She hadn't seen them in a month. She hadn't had the energy.

Arvid smiled at her with his missing teeth. Lisa seemed sceptical in a blurry photo taken the previous summer in the archipelago. *Children of a hopeless mother,* she thought. Just like her.

Her first thought was that the woman who opened the door couldn't be her mother. Rita was sixty-seven, but the person who stood in the doorway, watching her through a pair of blue eyeglasses, looked at least fifteen years older than that. She was wearing black leggings and a knee-length grey wool cardigan. A pair of Dr Scholl's sandals and no socks. Her hair was thin and white, though some patches of her scalp were bald.

She made a gesture that Eva interpreted as a signal to come in.

The apartment was small, maybe forty square metres: two rooms and a tiny kitchen. She caught a glimpse of a bedroom through an open door. A pink teddy bear sat on the cro-cheted bedspread; the bear seemed familiar. There were prescription bottles on the nightstand.

The living room smelled like old cigarette smoke. A nearly completed puzzle of Stockholm City Hall covered the coffee table. A Sweden Democrats election poster was tacked to the wall.

'What are you doing here, anyway?' Rita asked as she sat down in an easy chair near the balcony door. 'I thought it was a joke at first, when you called.'

She offered her a cigarette from the pack, then lit one herself after Eva shook her head, but she let it rest in the ashtray.

'It's been a long time since I saw you,' she said.

Her eyes seemed far away, just as they had when Eva was little. Rita had always kept a filter between herself and the world – so she could tolerate it, Eva assumed.

'Twenty-four years. When I turned eighteen. At the treatment home in Vilhelmina. You came to visit with a probation officer. They let us take a walk by ourselves. You were in bad shape. I remember you asked if I had any drugs.'

Her mother seemed to search her memory, but came up empty.

'That was the last time, on my birthday. I stayed up there until I finished *gymnasium*. Then I started studying at Uppsala. I never got back in touch. You didn't either.'

Her mother picked up the cigarette again but let it burn down.

'So how are you?'

'Good.'

'And you have kids, you said on the phone.'

She couldn't remember mentioning anything about Arvid and Lisa, but apparently she had.

'Yes, one girl and one boy. They don't even know you exist.'

Her mother gave an awkward laugh.

'I understand you work as a lawyer.'

'A prosecutor. How did you know that?'

'Dad told me . . . You saw him.'

'I didn't see him. He called. And that was more than ten years ago. I don't know how he got my number. We spoke for five minutes before I hung up on him. I think he was in prison. Do you have contact with him?'

Her mother smiled a Rita smile, just the corner of her mouth. Eva was slowly beginning to see her mother clearly. But she felt nothing, not even disdain.

'It's been just as long since I saw him.'

'Were you the one who left, or was it him?'

'Both of us. It just wasn't working anymore. The way we were living, we were about to kill each other.'

She seemed to relax. She changed the subject and began chatting about her life on disability. She had started attending church, the Pentecostal one in Vällingby, not because she was a believer, but to meet new people. And she didn't drink as much anymore because she had liver trouble.

'Bet you'd never have guessed that.'

'That you go to church or that you try to stay sober?'

'Church. People care about each other. Some of the ladies come over to check on me sometimes. It's nice to have company . . . and no one judges me.'

She went to the kitchen to make them some coffee and returned with cookies she must have bought for the occasion.

'I have to say, I was surprised to hear from you. I didn't expect it. And I don't deserve it.'

'How insightful of you.'

'At least I'm not blaming anyone but myself.'

She poured the coffee into mugs, putting two sugar cubes into her own and stirring it. Her hand trembled as she put down the spoon.

'So you don't know why you're visiting?'

She didn't say anything, because she truly didn't know. Or was there something she wanted? To be reminded of where she came from, so she could finally start to appreciate all she had? The children. Jorma and Katz. Her colleagues. Maybe even Ola.

When she looked up again, her mother had dozed off in the chair. She had suffered from a form of narcolepsy since her teen years. When Eva was a child, Rita would fall asleep just like that, sometimes in the middle of a conversation.

She walked into her mother's bedroom. She observed the view of Vällingbyvägen and the Grimsta Forest. The silhouette of Hässelby further to the north-west. The neighbourhood where she'd become a young woman, fallen in love with Katz, and lived the most destructive and perhaps also the most beautiful years of her life.

She picked up the stuffed animal from the bed. 'Eva', read the label on its back, but the marker was so faded that the letters were hardly legible. The bear had been hers once upon a time. Her brother had given it to her for Christmas.

She had only been three when he disappeared. A skinny blond boy who had been born with birth defects because Rita mixed Thalidomide and barbiturates during her pregnancy. She had panicked after a few days on speed and vodka and tried to fall asleep on the sedative the doctor had prescribed. After her delivery, her addiction got even worse.

She had looked up to her brother, eight years her elder; she still remembered how he tried to play with her on the kitchen floor in Blackeberg, and that he took care of her when Rita and Jonas were gone, which was sometimes several days at a time. A boy without arms with parents without feelings, as she'd once tried to explain it to a befuddled friend in law school. But it had seemed normal to her at the time. All the bizarreness that made up her everyday life. She hadn't thought it was strange at all back then.

She walked over to the nightstand and read the prescription labels. Codapane. Diazepam. Stilnoct. A whole buffet of painkillers and anti-anxiety medications.

On one red bottle was the word 'Temodol'. Chemotherapy. She ought to have guessed by the bald spots where her mother's hair hadn't yet grown back.

Rita was still sleeping when she returned to the room. Her abdomen was swollen under the cardigan, Eva realized. Maybe it was her liver? She looked at her bare feet in the Dr Scholl's. Her toenails were well manicured; they were the only part of her appearance she had always taken pains with. The nail polish was a shade of pale pink, the same as her fingernails. And she remembered other moments with her, when she had been sober and Jonas was in prison. At those times she had been happy, laughing; she'd tried to play with Eva and take care of her. She would place Eva on the bathroom stool and paint her little girl's nails, toes and fingers both, and she would let Eva pick the colour, but she always chose the same one as her mother had.

She felt lighter as she opened the front door and walked along the asphalt path towards the car park, as if she had been relieved of a burden. It was a sunny day. The snow that had fallen during the week had melted.

She got behind the wheel and took out her phone. Katz had called. She hadn't seen him since the incidents at the house. She had only spoken with him briefly, on the phone, about the situation with their alibis. She closed her eyes and pictured him as he was back when they were teenagers. The handsome, dark-haired Jewish boy with the inscrutable eyes and strange last name. She remembered the joy she had felt, the butterflies in her stomach each time she saw him.

Then she dialled into her voicemail and listened to his message. The puzzle began to take shape before her eyes, and it contained new pieces she hadn't known existed.

108 people die every minute on earth, Jorma thought. *Every hour –
6,480. Every day – 155,520.* What did one more matter? Especially
if it was a total pig.

It was a thought experiment. But the fact remained: if the
worst happened, he needn't have a guilty conscience.

He looked around as he waited. The flat consisted of two
separate apartments that had been joined. That was why
there were two kitchens and two bathrooms, and mirror-
imaged floor plans. He was in some sort of waiting room.
All that was missing was a queue number.

A guard was zapping from programme to programme on
a TV in the front kitchen. Or maybe 'guard' wasn't the right
word. Someone who kept an eye on the operation, made sure
that money changed hands smoothly, that no fights broke
out. *A Russian*, he thought. *Or a Serb.* The prison tattoos on
the man's arm were full of Cyrillic letters.

An Asian girl was sitting on a sofa, rubbing skin cream
into her calves. She looked like she hadn't slept – or, for
that matter, left the flat – in a week. There were two
more women in the flat, two rail-thin blondes; he had the
idea they were Poles. The whole concept was thoroughly
organized. You could make an appointment online or over
the phone.

He wondered if the other tenants in the building realized
what went on here. The guy had presented him with a whole
menu of options when he called, complete with a price list
and everything, before he took off to fetch the girl. *Berne.*

That was how the man introduced himself. His letter box in Kransen only listed a last name: Lindberg.

Berne was the one who had opened the door when he rang with the prearranged signal. He had tossed his dreadlocks and said that Jorma should wait there until he returned. The guy was high as a kite and didn't seem to recognize him. His girl was on a home visit to a john, he'd explained . . .

Jorma's gaze slid on across the room. It was an incredibly bluesy place. Depressing wasn't the half of it. Bare walls. Cheap IKEA furniture. One of the rooms he peeked into didn't even have a bed. Just a mattress with a fitted sheet and an Oriental rug hanging on the wall.

He heard a key in the front door. He saw his neighbour girl as if through a tunnel. Her empty eyes. Berne was standing behind her; he took off his black North Face jacket and hung it on a hook. He nodded at the guard type guy, who had stuck his head out of the kitchen. He took hold of the girl's arm and shoved her into the bathroom.

'Wash yourself,' he said in English.

They were alone in the room now, he and Berne. It was astounding that he didn't recognize Jorma. It was also astounding that he had let him in on the basis of a single phone call.

'So what does it cost again?' he said.

'That depends on what you want to do. Regular fucking?'

Jorma nodded neutrally. He guessed he might as well do what he'd planned right away. Solve the problems in the correct order.

'Give me two thousand kronor and you do anything you can think of with her. But I don't want to have to take her to the hospital.'

The girl walked out of the bathroom. She was wearing

only pants and a bra. She made some sort of thrusting motion that was probably supposed to be sexy. He wanted to cry.

He fished two thousand-kronor bills out of his inner pocket and handed them to Berne. He received a spliff-yellowed smile in response.

'Okay. You can use the room at the end of the hall. Have fun...'

He followed the Thai woman down the hall. Someone had punched a hole through the plaster wall – traces of a fight that had got out of control.

A twin bed stood along one wall. At least the sheets were clean. The girl sat down on the edge of the bed, took off her pants, and dropped them on the floor.

'You want massage first?' she asked in English.

Her voice was childlike. How old was she? Eighteen? Twenty? He wondered if she recognized him.

He shook his head. Thought of the Roma girl in the cage at Mattson's country home. Of the porn filming session Katz had told him about. The shipment from Poland Leyla had described ... the women in the truck, the ones Zoran had rescued. He thought of all the pigs in the world.

He took out his wallet again. He took out another wad of cash, another ten thousand kronor from the safe deposit box in Huddinge.

'Where is your passport?' he asked in English.

'No understand.'

'Thai passport?'

'Berne took it away.'

She glanced nervously at the wad of bills ... and then she accepted it and stuck it under the mattress.

Berne. What kind of fucking awful person was he? Who the hell did he think he was? God? Did he think he owned people? There was nothing worse than a pimp; he hated them. He pictured Leena as she looked when she was twenty; if this sort of thing had ever happened to her, he would have killed the bastard.

'What you want from me?'

'Nothing. Just wait here. The money is for your plane ticket . . . I'll be back soon.'

His neighbour looked at him in surprise as he stepped into the waiting room.

'Did you forget something?'

'Oh, no. Just need to take a piss.'

The guard was sitting with his back to him as he entered the kitchen. He hadn't seen or heard a thing.

He fished the adjustable spanner from the shaft of his boot. He took two steps forward and brought it down right on the back of the guy's skull. Someone must have turned down the volume on reality. He didn't hear a sound, not even when the man tumbled to the floor with blood pouring down his bull-neck, knocking the TV over as he went.

The pool of blood on the floor was spreading. It caught up with a crumpled receipt, which floated on top of the viscous fluid. The man wasn't moving; his feet were just twitching slightly. He was wearing tattered trainers. His socks were the same shade as his blood. A cigarette was smoking in an ashtray on the table where the TV had been.

He walked back to the waiting room. One of the Polish women appeared suddenly, and she screamed at the top of her lungs when she saw him. His hands and shirt were spattered with blood. But his reality was still on mute; he just saw her mouth moving, like that of a fish in an aquarium.

Berne had stood up. He backed up against the wall, palms out, talking, shaping his mouth into words . . . but they just fell to the floor, popping silently against the linoleum.

Jorma opened the window, let in some air, and breathed deeply.

'What the hell is going on? Are you fucking crazy?'

The sound was back. He socked the man in the face, then added two or three blows of the spanner. Berne crawled into the corner. He kicked him in the gut and watched him fall over sideways.

The man was white as a ghost. His whole body was trembling. A vein was throbbing hysterically at one temple. It looked like a larva, or like there was a parasite writhing under his skin. He kicked him in the face. The man's nose smeared across his cheek. He no longer looked human. He was like a painting by Picasso; his facial features had become crooked and strange, an experiment in Cubism.

'Get up!' he said. 'Out!'

He pointed at the open window.

'What the fuck? What's wrong with you? We're three storeys up!'

His voice was thick; Jorma could see shards of broken teeth between his torn lips.

'You'll break both your legs or your back and be in a wheelchair for the rest of your life. It's either that, or this.'

He had taken the Colt from the shaft of his other boot. There were no bullets in the cylinder. He had used the last one on Hoffman. But the man in front of him didn't know that. He hit him in the face with the spanner again and heard something crunch.

'Out, I said . . . You have five seconds.'

His dreadlocked neighbour's face was streaked with blood. Trembling, he crawled over to the window and managed to stand up. He sat down on the sill and swung his legs out. He turned around, tossing a quick glance at the muzzle of the revolver. And then he jumped.

Some late hollyhocks were blooming along a south-facing wall. Dormant grapevines draped the pergola. The garage was freshly painted. A can of paint stood on an electrical box.

There was a greenhouse in one corner of the garden. Katz remembered the summer cottage his parents had rented on the island of Värmdö for a few years in the late seventies. His mother had spent all her time in the greenhouse there. She had grown tomatoes, kept citrus trees in pots, and had a large olive bush that she harvested in late autumn. Katz had loved to spend time with her there. He would sit for hours on a flower box and watch as she cared for the plants, watering them with the enamel watering can, genuinely happy for the moment, calm in a way he wasn't used to seeing . . . happy because she could spend time there with just him. Benjamin never visited the greenhouse; it was her sanctuary.

He walked by the empty pool and over to the terrace, peering into a drawing room through the glass partition. It was dark. An alarm box connected to a security company was mounted by the door.

By the time he returned to the front of the house, a man had appeared outside the very similar house next door and was watching him suspiciously over the fence.

'Are you looking for someone?' he asked.

'Beata. But she doesn't seem to be home.'

The man was in his forties. He was holding a tennis bag and glanced anxiously at his watch.

'She's at work, would be my guess. At Danderyd Hospital. And who are you?'

There was a beep as the man aimed a key at the garage door, and then a metallic whine as the door opened.

'Danny Katz. I know the family. It's about her daughter, Jennifer.'

The man shook his head as if the very name gave him the willies.

'I haven't seen her here in several years. Just Eric.'

The person who had been walking towards them on the golf course, Katz thought. He looked like Beata, but Katz had drawn the conclusion that it was because they were together, because he was her lover. She couldn't have been more than twenty when she had him. Eric Söderberg. Her son. Jennifer's half-brother.

'Was that all?' the neighbour asked.

'Do you know what time she usually gets home?'

'Well, if you know her, all you have to do is call and ask.'

The neighbour didn't move. Apparently he wasn't planning to leave until Katz had gone on his way.

'The house is connected to an alarm service,' he said. 'Just so you know. And that's true of all the houses in this neighbourhood.'

Katz walked around the neighbourhood until he had arrived at the house with grounds that backed on to Beata's. He had an hour before he was supposed to meet Eva Westin in town to see what information she had for him.

How was it all connected? He had given Beata his business card when he met her at the golf course. He had told her he suspected Ramón had been murdered. Beata didn't want to take any risks, so she'd sent her son to Katz's place. That was the simplest explanation. Eric had been waiting for him while he took the detour to John Sjöholm's car and discovered their second victim . . .

The carport was empty. Katz opened the front gate and followed the gravel path around the house. He climbed over the fence just behind the greenhouse and looked around. The neighbour was nowhere to be seen.

Then he opened the electrical box with the screwdriver he'd brought from his car. He turned off the main current and walked to the cellar door. The alarm box had gone dark. It was easy to pick the lock – it was an ASSA model from the early eighties.

He started on the ground floor. The kitchen. Beata's bedroom with its double bed and cloistered atmosphere, the living room with a fireplace and New England-style furniture.

The first floor was dominated by an office. Medical literature on the bookshelf. Most of it was about anaesthesia and surgical assistance. Two shelves were taken up by books on addiction. All kinds of addiction – alcohol, drugs, gambling, and sex. There were several books about twelve-step programmes and the Minnesota Model. Books about co-dependence and Family Anonymous, an approach Katz was familiar with from his own NA experience. The bottom shelf contained a row of books about the sexual abuse of children.

He followed a hallway until he found himself at a door adorned with a Nirvana poster. Jennifer's girlhood room. Stuffed animals and dolls were lined up along the head of the bed. An empty terrarium stood on a bureau.

He cracked the wardrobe door. The suitcase he'd seen in Husby was on the floor inside. The clothes she had been wearing were arranged on hangers.

A parent demanding a promise of revenge from a son,

Katz thought as he glanced around the room, just as Chaim had demanded of Benjamin once upon a time. The pieces had fallen into place when he saw Miriam preparing a syringe to inject medicine into Epstein's arm . . .

Beata had brought Eric along to the apartment in Husby. Ramón – the man Beata assumed was the latest in a long line of her daughter's pimps – had been doped up on heroin. She was an anaesthesia nurse; she knew exactly what to do. First she sedated him, likely with something she'd brought from the hospital. Then she injected the overdose into his arm. She watched him die before they took Jennifer away with them.

But where was Jennifer now?

On the windowsill were photographs of her as a child, with Eric and Beata. A loving family, Katz thought; you could tell from their expressions, the way they were holding each other, the atmosphere around them – that elusive thing called devotion.

He pulled out the top desk drawer. Drawings. Recent ones. Self-portraits of Jennifer on a hospital bed, observing herself in a mirror. Another pencil drawing, finely detailed, of her brother as he stomped a snake to death. The animal he had learned to associate with his little sister's life as a junkie.

Katz moved on to the basement. He passed a hobby room with a couch and chairs and a TV, turned left down a hallway, and suddenly found himself in something that resembled a doctor's examination room. The setting of her most recent self-portrait.

A county-hospital stretcher stood along one wall, covered with a paper sheet. There was an IV stand at its head, with a bag of nutrient replacement hanging from one of its hooks.

An adjustable lamp hung from the ceiling. On the floor was a bottle of hand sanitizer.

Through the glass doors of a medicine cabinet he could see sterile compresses, syringes, gauze, blood pressure cuffs, and an otoscope. A dozen boxes of methadone with labels from Danderyd Hospital lay on the top shelf.

A metal hatch had been installed in the far wall; it was one metre high by half a metre wide. It locked from the outside by way of a large padlock. The key hung from a nail.

It took a moment for his eyes to adjust to the darkness. He guessed that this part of the house had once been equipped to house a boiler.

A chamber pot stood on the floor next to an empty wine bottle. A camping table held a couple of plastic forks and plates with scraps of food.

On the far side of the room he could make out a bed.

Had they been keeping her locked up here since the night they killed Ramón?

He looked at the body that was lying under the blanket, its back towards him. The even breaths. The light brown hair across its shoulders. At first he thought she was asleep, but he was mistaken.

'Mum?' she said without turning around.

'What can I do for you?' asked the attendant behind the archive desk on Agnegatan.

She briefly explained her errand.

'Three hits,' he muttered after entering the search terms into the computer. 'Would you like me to bring out the material?'

'Yes, please.'

The attendant opened the door behind him and vanished in among the sixteen thousand shelf-metres of old investigation materials that went by the name 'criminal archives'. Five minutes later he was back with the closed cases in a trolley.

'Here you go,' he said. 'Take as much time as you need.'

She sat down at one of the reading tables, opened the top folder, and began to page through it.

The first police report on Carl-Adam Tell had been made in the early nineties, shortly before his divorce. It concerned Beata Roslund's son from a previous marriage: Eric Söderberg. The boy, fourteen at the time, had told his mother that Tell had wanted them to watch pornographic films together. He hadn't dared to refuse.

Beata Roslund had filed the report. A psychologist had talked to the boy. Beata had been present, and according to the transcript she prompted her son to such an extent that in the end she was asked to leave the room. They had watched porn, nothing more, the boy maintained, speaking in a recorded interview that was later transcribed. Tell hadn't made any sexual advances; they had each been sitting in their own easy chair in the basement hobby room in Vallentuna to watch the VHS tape. According to the boy, the pornography they watched was extremely violent. His stepfather had asked if he liked what he saw.

Tell, in an initial interrogation, had denied the incident ever happened. He didn't own any pornographic films, he said; he opposed anything degrading to women and he respected his stepson – he would never in his life think of subjecting him to such abuse. He denied even being alone with the boy on the night in question. The whole family had been at home.

When asked why he thought the boy might make up such a story, he responded that they ought to ask his wife. According to Tell, Beata Roslund was behind the whole thing. She was trying to get revenge on him. Their marriage had been on the rocks ever since an infidelity came to light a few months before.

It had been word against word, Eva thought as she sat in the bright light of the reading lamp, listening to the attendant whistle as he worked at the photocopier a few metres away. The police had followed up once the divorce became reality. So Beata Roslund's husband had not left her after all, as she had told Katz – she herself had pulled the plug. She had demanded her ex-husband be interrogated again.

She browsed on . . . Beata Roslund had claimed her ex-husband frequented prostitutes and sex clubs that organized orgies, and that he had done so throughout their marriage. She considered it a miscarriage of justice that the two of them had been awarded joint custody of their daughter.

She opened the next folder. The second report, made seven years later. This time it concerned Jennifer, who had been nine at the time. According to Beata Roslund, the girl had returned from spending the autumn break with her father in poor psychological condition. When she pressured her daughter into telling her what had happened, she said that Tell had brought her to a house in the country one evening. To an orgy involving several men and women, in which the women had been sexually degraded. According to Beata, the girl was given sleeping pills and put to sleep in a separate room, but she woke in the middle of the night when the orgy was in full swing. Her father had found her and brought her back to the room, where she went back to sleep. When she woke up the next morning, they were back in Tell's flat in Norr Mälarstrand. When Jennifer asked about what had happened the night before, he told her she had just been dreaming.

Like a witches' ride to Blåkulla, she thought as she turned the page. Or was there something to the accusations? Had Mattson's country home already been up and running back then? Or had it been somewhere else? *The tunnel*, she thought, *the one both Jorma and Katz had mentioned?* But no names showed up in the investigation, since Tell categorically rejected all the statements as wild fantasies and even filed a counteraction against his ex-wife for slander. Word against word once again, and the investigation was laid to rest. Though sympathies lay with the man's side of things. The story just did not seem reliable. According to the testimony of an expert witness, they could not rule out the possibility that the girl had fabricated the memories, perhaps with the help of her mother.

The ex-spouses did not have much contact. An enclosed report from social services stated that they didn't even see each other on the sporadic occasions they handed over their daughter into the other's custody; a court appointee took care of that. On paper, the girl was supposed to spend every other week with each parent. But Beata Roslund did everything in her power to obstruct the agreement.

What was her motivation . . . revenge? Genuine hatred? Or incidents that really had occurred?

She stood up, walked over to the counter, and returned the materials to the attendant.

'You said you got three hits,' she said.

'The third file was opened a year ago,' was the response.

'So?'

'The investigations you'll find in here are all more than fifteen years old . . . archived before digitalization. You can pull up the third one on the guest computer. Or on the intranet. You're with the Economic Crime Authority, right? I recognize you. It's too bad about that Hoffman.'

She ignored the looks she got as she walked down the hall. She hadn't visited the office in six weeks, but it felt like a year. She got a cup of burned coffee from the break room and glanced quickly at the closed door of Hoffman's office. His nameplate had been removed.

As soon as she was inside her office, she navigated to the server and read the report.

Carl-Adam Tell had been found near his boat at Norr Mälarstrand, drowned, just over one year earlier. The body, which was found ten hours after his death, was autopsied as a matter of routine. Tell had had large amounts of alcohol and sedatives in his blood. The accident had happened late at night, a few days before the boat – a 50-foot catamaran – was to be stored for the winter. There were no witnesses to the incident. He had probably slipped on the deck, hit the back of his head on the railing, and been knocked unconscious before falling overboard. At least that was how the medical examiner explained the swelling on the back of his head.

She leaned back in her office chair and looked out the window at the bare trees around Kungsholm Church.

Had they started with him? The first victim in their orgy of revenge. Had they tracked him down when he was on his boat late at night while heavily under the influence? Had they hit him in the back of the head with a hard object and thrown him overboard? And bided their time for almost a year before they got Ramón and John Sjöholm? All the men they hated for hurting Jennifer.

But what about what happened at the house? The shootings?

She brought up the weapons registry to see if Eric Söderberg was listed in it, or if he was a member of a shooting club, but got no results.

'They do it out of love,' she said as she reclined on the camp bed in front of Katz. 'As if I don't have free will. And you should know . . . Mum is vindictive. She always has been.'

Her voice was strained; she was in withdrawal.

'They'd had enough, I guess. All the hate they've stored up inside throughout the years – for the men they think have used me – it needs to find an outlet somewhere.'

She absentmindedly scratched at her arms. Lovely arms, Katz noticed, lithe and muscular. In another life he would have been attracted to her.

'The treatment centres have never worked for me. Mum lets me stay here when I want to, despite the terrible thing I did to her. I have a key. Beata's only rule is that I'm only allowed to come at night, when the neighbours won't notice. God knows how many cold turkeys I've done in here. It might sound sick, but the padlock . . . it's voluntary.'

She didn't seem surprised to see him there. As if she had somehow been expecting a visit in her self-imposed prison. She had told him about the murders of Ramón and Sjöholm as dispassionately as if she were talking about people she'd never met. It had all gone down much as Katz had guessed. A mother's hatred for the men she considered to be exploiting her daughter. A son's loyalty. And she had also confirmed that she, Ramón, and Sjöholm had delivered women to the network.

Magnus bought sex from me in Switzerland, when I lived there. He used to do some sick fucking shit to me.

Wiksten had recognized her when she showed up at the shelter with Ramón. He'd offered them a large amount of money if they could procure what he wanted. That was the money they had used to buy the heroin.

Without batting an eyelid, she told him about the women they'd tricked, saying that they would drive them to see rich clients, a simple job, and they even paid them in advance. Then they would deliver them, high, to the house.

There was something wrong with her, Katz thought as he listened. Something had happened to her to transform her into the person she was.

'Did Mum tell you about the accident?' she asked.

She sat up on the camp bed. Placed the empty wine bottle on the camping table. Put on the robe that had lain on the floor. The skin of her thighs was covered in goosebumps.

'When I was sixteen, Dad took me on a road trip through Europe. He stopped at a rest stop outside Frankfurt. We had been driving all night, from Stockholm, and he only made one stop along the way – at a roadside brothel where he knew the owner. He did what he always did at those places. Afterwards he was tired . . . drunk. He lay down in the back seat. I knew how soundly he slept. The key was in the ignition. All I had to do was start the car. I drove the car back up the same exit ramp we'd taken and hit the accelerator as hard as I could.'

She stopped talking and scratched her arms.

'Afterwards no one could tell which car had come from which direction. There were no traffic cameras on that particular stretch of motorway. And it was night-time, too dark for anyone to get a clear picture of what had happened. They took for granted that the guy in the Porsche had been driving against the traffic. He was only nineteen and had been convicted of careless driving before. And of course they couldn't question him, because he was dead. But Dad knew the score.'

She grew quiet. Reached for something on the table; a drawing pad, Katz saw, and a pencil.

'He broke off contact with me after that.'

'But you saw him again?'

'You know how it is; a junkie always needs money.'

She started drawing. She stopped and measured him with her thumb in the half-light. The lead rasped against the paper.

'The last time, Ramón came with me. We ended up fighting. I don't know exactly what happened, because I was super fucking high, but Ramón hit him in the head with something . . . and then we made sure he fell overboard.'

She held up the drawing for him. It was the start of a portrait of the two of them together. They were in this very room. Katz had his arm around her shoulders. Comforting her, it looked like. Both were nude.

'You took something from him before you left.'

She licked her thumb and erased something from the paper. Nodded.

'Yes. An address book.'

'The numbers . . . whose are they?'

She looked at him placidly.

'Contacts, I think . . . at the different stations.'

Her eyes were glassy. She had stood up and was hugging her own body.

'I have memories from my childhood, from other houses, in other cities. I saw things I wasn't supposed to see. I understood things that were impossible to understand. Dad never touched me . . . but I realized who he was, what he and his friends were up to. We kept the address book for security, in case something happened to one of us. We didn't even dare to keep it at home.'

She stopped talking and pulled a plastic bin from beneath the camp bed. Packs of heroin. A few syringes. The drawing had fallen to the floor. Katz's face had been rubbed out.

'At Mattson's house . . . someone came in and executed four people.'

Katz noticed how the words got stuck in his throat, how the draw was coming back to him, just as strong and as unpredictable as always.

'It wasn't Mum and Eric, if that's what you're thinking. An alarm was sounded. Someone or some people decided to amputate an injured limb from the greater body. Cut it off. That's how it works.'

Her lovely, clear blue irises seemed to see right through him.

'Hoffman, Mattson, and a bunch of other people whose names you'll never learn . . . Dad knew them all.'

Her voice stopped, as if it had faded into the haze of his abstinence. And she wasn't looking at him, he realized, but at the person behind them.

'The tunnel,' she whispered as the beam of a torch lit up the room. 'Dad was the one who created it.'

She couldn't reach Katz. His phone was dead; it went straight to voicemail when she called. He was supposed to show up over an hour ago.

She instinctively knew that something was wrong.

She dialled Jorma's number as she stood inside the cafe and watched the daylight disappear. She heard that slight Finnish accent that would never fade, even though he was born and raised in Sweden.

'Is something wrong?'

She explained as best she could. She told him about Katz's call, and how he'd asked her to look up a few things about Jennifer Roslund's family.

'I'll be right over,' he said. 'Where are you?'

'In the city. Outside Ritorno.'

'Great. I'll be there in fifteen.'

They drove towards Vallentuna, which was the best option she could think of for the time being. Katz hadn't mentioned where he was, but, considering what he'd asked her to look up, it seemed plausible that he'd gone there. The suburbs marched past outside the window, getting fancier and fancier the further east they drove.

They turned off just before Väsby, followed the GPS directions towards Täby Kyrkby, and turned north again, approaching the nouveaux riches neighbourhoods.

They parked the car outside a shop five hundred metres from the house and walked the last little bit. Glowing Advent stars hung in windows. She pulled her coat tighter around her body.

Small, meaningless fragments of thoughts were whirling inside her head. She had a bad feeling about this . . . really bad this time.

They approached the house, a white, two-storey brick villa on a cul-de-sac. Skeletal trampolines on the neighbours' lawns. The bare trees. A thin layer of snow that had piled up in little drifts in front of garages.

A car was carelessly parked by the pavement.

The house was dark; the front door locked.

They followed a paved pathway to the back of the house. Neither of them said anything. They couldn't say why, but both knew they didn't have much time. She wiped a snowflake from her eye, blinked, and saw an empty pool with a grey tarp covering it, a greenhouse reflecting the last of the daylight, the metal door of an open electrical box that was mounted on the tar-paper wall of the garage.

The massive picture windows were dark. But Katz was somewhere in there, she was sure of it.

There was a dull crack as Jorma kicked in the glass terrace door. He carefully stuck his hand through the shards of glass and unlocked it. He paused briefly before opening it . . .

'Did you bring the Colt?' she asked.

He shook his head.

'I got rid of it. Didn't think I'd need it anymore.'

No sounds or movements as they walked through the living room. Their eyes slowly adjusted to the dim light. They rounded a corner and found themselves in a kitchen. Their eyes swept across the furnishings: the kitchen table, the chairs, the potted flowers on the windowsill. A set of kitchen knives, sorted by size, hung from a magnetic strip above the counter. One was missing.

The room was oddly quiet. No hum from the fridge – it was as if a fuse had blown. She hit a light switch, but nothing happened.

The scents of another person's home made her lose confidence. She had the sense of having taken a wrong turn, of being out of place.

'You check upstairs,' she said to Jorma. 'I'll keep looking down here.'

She moved on to a narrow passageway that led to a basement door. She suddenly heard sounds from downstairs – glass breaking as something fell to the floor. She couldn't keep herself in check any longer; she opened the door and called Katz's name, but there was no answer.

Jorma's footsteps on the first floor. Hadn't he heard it? She ought to go and get him, but her instincts told her there wasn't time.

A damp odour struck her as she walked down the stairs. The basement was faintly lit by the street lamps outside.

She was in a hobby room. She turned on her phone's torch function and shone it around. There was a set of furniture around a glass table. A television stood on the sideboard, and under it was an open shelf: an old VCR. This was where they had watched porn together, Tell and his stepson. Orgies, ones Tell had filmed himself.

There was a draught in the room; a door was open. She felt dizzy, as if the world had shrunk down to a narrow hallway with darkness on both sides.

It felt like she was moving through a wind tunnel, like the air was pushing against her at ten times its usual strength. She turned off her phone, followed a hallway towards an open sliding door, and glimpsed a hospital stretcher and an overturned cabinet. Plastic-sealed syringes lay among the shards of glass on the floor.

She peered in through the open door but could barely interpret what she saw. She only perceived movements and strange shadows, like a person about to go blind . . . A man, she thought, straddling another man. Pulling a sharp object out of his body. Raising his arm, taking aim.

Katz had no time to react before the man's foot struck the back of his neck. He was flung forward and saw a palette of exploding colour as he tumbled about and landed with his back to the wall.

The light from the torch bobbed on the ceiling. At first he wasn't sure where he was. Then the room arranged itself again, according to its particular grammar. Jenny shouted something incomprehensible as her brother yanked her out of the room. He was bigger than Katz remembered. Nasty scars from the wounds on his face where Katz had bitten him . . .

'What did you do to her?'

Katz tried to get up, but his legs wouldn't obey. Eric had something in his hand. And Katz knew what it would feel like when the object slid into his body, the blade of a fillet knife, like a thin slice of concentrated heat.

'Let him be, Eric!'

'Shut up. Get out of here. Mum will be home any minute.'

The blade flashed in the beam of the torch. Katz managed to twist to the side; the first slash missed his face by a millimetre.

He managed to throw a punch, striking as hard as he could, but he missed. The hand and the knife rose up again. Katz took purchase against the wall and heaved himself up. He fell through the hatch and landed on the floor in the sick room, then got to his feet again.

Jennifer was gone; he felt the draught from the basement door. Eric slashed at him again, slicing a hole in his jacket.

The medicine cabinet crashed to the floor as he backed into it, in full panic mode. Shards of glass crunched under his feet. Katz managed to wriggle out of his jacket and wind it around his forearm for protection. Eric was stabbing at him wildly; the tip of the knife pierced the layers of fabric and cut open his skin just below the elbow.

Katz's back was to the wall. He heard the other man's heavy breathing. The knife came at him so fast he had no time to react. The blade sank into his shoulder, just below his collarbone, and was pulled back out again.

The pain was otherworldly. Blood filled his armpit and soaked into his shirt. He heard the cry of a terrified animal and realized that the sound had come from him. Urine ran down his thighs; his bladder must have released.

His arm would no longer obey him. The sinews were torn. He tried to kick, but the signals from his brain couldn't reach his body. Saliva flooded his mouth; he swallowed and swallowed and had the sensation of drowning in his own spit. His vision went black and he fell to the side.

When he came to again, Eric was straddling him and aiming for his neck. Time slowed down, moving like thick glue.

The torch was on the floor across the room. Its light had grown fainter; the batteries were dying. Time started back up again. He reflexively twisted to the side as the knife sliced down. The blade missed his throat but slid into his armpit instead, entering his body at an angle and wedging itself between two ribs.

Let it be stuck there . . . No more stabbing . . .

It had punctured his lung. There was a squeak every time he took a breath. Katz was no longer thinking, he was just fighting the pain. He locked onto Eric's arm with both hands, pressing the man to his body, and felt the tip of the knife scrape between his ribs.

The light of the torch was nearly gone, and they were fighting in darkness, silently, intently.

Someone called his name as if through a kilometre-long tunnel. Sounds, other people in the house. He knew he was hallucinating, that his fear of dying was making him hear voices.

He pulled harder at the hand that held the shaft of the knife. Eric was fighting to prise it loose. That squeaking from his ribcage – as if he had grown gills.

Don't let him stab again . . . Keep the blade in me . . .

He tried to fight, one minute, maybe two, but his strength was petering out.

He could hardly see anything anymore. Just the shape of Eric's body, like a black shadow on top of him. And the knife as it came out of his armpit and flew up again.

Then he suddenly heard a noise – the sound of footsteps walking on shards of glass. It was as if he had developed night vision out of the blue. He saw a person picking something up off the floor near the door, and rushing at them from the side. Single-mindedly, no fear. He watched as, all in a single motion, Eva tore the plastic from a syringe, took aim, and jabbed at Eric's face from below.

There was a second's delay before the roar of pain. Blood dripped down into Katz's face. The body on top of him relaxed. The needle had gone straight into the man's eye.

Epilogue

Christmas, 2013

Through the chapel windows he could see grey snips of the December sky. A cantor was singing in a powerful tenor. The coffin was in the centre of the room, with mourners on either side of it. Epstein's daughter, along with her closest family. Frydman, from the synagogue on Sankt Paulsgatan. Another couple of men Katz recognized from the Orthodox congregation.

Was it time to say the *Kaddish* now? Or was that at the graveside?

Katz glanced discreetly at Miriam, trying to see if she had a *kerija* – a tiny tear in her clothing; believers wore these as an expression of grief. The week of *shiva* would start as soon as the funeral was over. The mirrors in her home would be covered, and meals would be eaten on the floor. A candle would be kept burning around the clock.

Epstein had died two days earlier and was handed over to the professionals at Chevra Kadisha, the Jewish funeral service. The body had been ritually washed, dressed in white trousers, a white shirt, a white coat, and a *tallit* – a prayer shawl – although Katz doubted that the old man had owned one.

Earth from Jerusalem lay under the pillow where his head rested. The congregation read *Tziduk Hadin*, just like the last time Katz was here, three decades earlier. The prayers were the same. Frydman, he faintly recalled, had been present that time as well, wearing a black hat – could it be the same one he had on now?

As the service continued, more memories flickered by. The terraced house they'd lived in when Katz was ten, in the Märsta area, for just one year because his father made enemies with the neighbours. He remembered the badminton net in the little patch of garden out the back . . . Benjamin, shirtless and with a cigarette in the corner of his mouth, as he explained in German how to serve. Yiddish was reserved for jokes and scoldings. Swedish was for everyday use. German was for instructions. His mother, in the hammock on the veranda with a glass of orange juice in her hand, a sunhat shielding her face.

Later that summer, they had sent him to Glämsta, the Jewish summer camp in the archipelago. *'Dos ayntsike ort in Shvedn vu du vest kenen filn zich normal iz inem dush,'* as Benjamin laconically put it in Yiddish. The only place in Sweden where you'll feel normal in the shower! Apparently he had hoped that some time among other circumcised boys would give Katz's own Jewish identity a boost. Lessons in religion and Jewish history, the yearly Maccabiah athletics competition, the flirting between teenagers who came from Jewish families all over the country, sneaking cigarettes at the 'secret cave', and the gossip around the kiosk where they gathered in the evenings. But Katz had felt like just as much of an outsider there as in every other situation. He didn't even fit in as a Jew, he thought.

The next summer he went to Glämsta for the second and last time in his life; his visit ended early. Not far off, on the same island, there was a city-run summer camp where less well-off Stockholm families sent their children. Incidents had occurred throughout the years: someone had spray-painted swastikas on the buildings that belonged to the Jewish organization, and there had been fights down by the beach.

During the second week after Katz arrived, an older boy from the city camp messed with a religious boy from Skåne, Adam Lewinski. It was at night, at the grill site the two camps shared. The older boy, a large blond type with his hair in a ponytail, had torn the yarmulke from Lewinski's head in order to impress a couple of girls, and he tossed it into a bush. Lewinski had been frightened, so he found his cap and left.

Katz had lingered at the grill site as it grew dark. He heard the guy with the ponytail telling one of the era's more common anti-Semitic jokes to his friends: 'Know how you get six million Jews into a Volkswagen? Two in back, two in front, and the rest in the ashtray.'

When the guy went to take a leak, Katz followed him. He found a fist-sized rock along the path. He waited until he had opened his fly and started pissing, then took five steps forward and tapped him on the shoulder. As the guy turned around, he smashed his teeth in.

The boy was still standing. Katz struck again, this time hitting the side of his head. Blood sprayed from his temple, cascading onto Katz's clothes. When the guy collapsed to the ground in front of him, Katz calmly dropped the rock and walked away.

That same evening, he was questioned by the Norrtälje police. The guy he assaulted had barely survived the attack. But Katz didn't say a word; he just vanished inside himself, staring blankly at the cops as they tried to get a confession out of him.

Benjamin picked him up the next day; he slugged him in the ear in front of three horrified Jewish youth leaders, tossed him into the back seat of the car, and drove away. He didn't say a word to Katz for the whole trip back to Stockholm, he just chain-smoked cigarettes and muttered curses to himself in Yiddish: *Di alte nevayle . . . a goj hot majn zun opgenart . . . a shlak zol dir treffn, shtinkendiker shmok . . .*

When they parked outside the house, he turned around and gave Katz a look he had never seen before: chilly, distant, as if it belonged to a completely different person.

'You have to be colder,' he said, and his voice had been that of a stranger too, of another man. 'More clinical, Danny. You let someone see you . . . that was your mistake.'

The first of many investigations into Katz's psyche had been performed shortly thereafter. No one talked about all the alphabet-soup diagnoses back then, but he'd had them all. Violent tendencies with psychopathic traits, he had later read about himself in one of the social services documents. *Just like Benjamin,* he thought. That was where the darkness came from.

The service was over. Strong men from Chevra Kadisha carried the coffin to the gravesite. Katz followed, last in the procession.

The stately pines that shielded the southern Jewish graveyard from sunlight, the damp gravel paths, the rows of headstones with inscriptions in Hebrew. Names that sounded so familiar from his childhood: Gleichman, Kessler, Goldberg, Stern, Herz, Konig, Farber, Weiss, Gordon, Mosesson, Silberstein, Rubin, Blumenthal, Perski, Klein, Swartz, Fuchs, Lazar . . . and somewhere, further on, in a spot he no longer remembered: Anne and Benjamin Katz.

The coffin was lowered into the ground with ropes. One by one, the mourners walked up to pour three shovelfuls of earth over the dead.

Katz had left the procession to take a seat on a park bench nearby. He was observing everything from a distance when a man suddenly showed up and sat down beside him.

'We've never met. My name is Mikael Stern.'

The man was in his sixties. His face was ruddy; he had sideburns and pale blue eyes. He reminded Katz of someone, but he couldn't figure out who it was.

'Maybe this isn't the right time . . . but here, in case you want to contact me. Boris told me you have questions about your father.' The man handed him a business card. 'It's easiest to reach me at my work. I'm the head of research at the Army Museum.'

Katz looked out across the gravestones, the wall that separated this area from the Christian side, the funeral-goers in the distance. The nearly ninety-year-old David Frydman, supported by his grandchildren, or maybe great-grandchildren, was shovelling earth onto Epstein's coffin.

'There are about thirty reports on your father in our archive. All of them were written by the C-Bureau, one of the armed forces' intelligence services during World War II. It was run by Carl Petersén, if that name means anything to you. They're incredibly interesting.'

The man had lowered his voice. And Katz suddenly knew who he reminded him of. Lynx. The intelligence officer he'd met a single time in Santo Domingo, the man who'd tried to recruit him into his organization. He'd been impressed by Katz's knowledge of languages, by what he knew about computer programming and the dark parts of the internet, by what he'd managed to learn about Lynx's group by hijacking the administrator account for one of the armed forces' servers . . . But for Katz, that had just been another aspect of the hunt for Joel Klingberg, the businessman who'd tried to frame him for a murder Joel himself had committed.

'I don't know what Boris had time to tell you, but your father's life was like no other. Especially what he got up to during the last years of the war. The material is classified. If you want to move forward with this, both of us will be breaking the law.'

The man straightened his *kippah*, which had gone askew, and fastened it on one side with a kirby grip.

'Why would you do that?' Katz asked.

'Break the law? I have my reasons.'

The man stood up with a friendly smile.

'Do you know where they are laid to rest, by the way, your parents? In the other direction, past the chapel, in the glade.'

He took leave of Katz with a slight nod and retreated back to the graveside.

The stone was small, as if it didn't want to attract attention. It was in a glade, just as Stern had said. Katz had never seen it before. It had been erected a few months after their deaths. It was made of polished black granite. A Star of David. Their names, and birth and death years. That was all.

To the left there was another spot, an empty one. Had they purchased it for him? Jewish burial plots are eternal.

Katz placed the silicate stone he'd taken from the gravel path on the grave. Never flowers at a Jewish gravesite. No living things with the dead.

The sky was as inconceivably grey today as it had been that time three decades earlier. He had been first in the funeral procession, supported by people he could no longer remember, watching the coffins lowered into the ground, before he disappeared into that merciless period, into the institutions, the youth homes, a different life.

A stab of pain coursed through his right armpit where the bandage pressed against the sutured stab wound. He had survived against all odds, thanks to Eva.

What about Hannah? he thought as he stood before the

headstone. His father's sister, who rested in a grave in the sky. What had happened to her?

He pictured Eric Söderberg and Beata Roslund at the Kronoberg jail. The preliminary investigation was well underway; in a few months they would appear in court on charges of homicide and attempted homicide, and he himself would be called as a witness. Eric had lost the sight in his eye, but, amazingly enough, the needle hadn't caused any other damage.

Jennifer's whereabouts were still a mystery. Maybe she had left the country.

What about his grandparents . . . what had happened to them in Israel?

He had never got to know them; he hadn't even got to know Anne and Benjamin. The people he tried to conjure up were strangers.

On his way back to his car, he stopped at a storm drain, took out the business card Stern had given him, and let it drop between the bars.

Why dig up the past? Why look for the dead when he was there among the living?

And it struck him that this thought was very Jewish.

Katz spent the last few days before Christmas working out. He got up early, ate breakfast, walked to the gym at Alviks Torg, and methodically went through the various muscle groups, station by station.

The soulless hit parade streaming from the loudspeakers, the TV screens with their morning soaps and talk shows on mute, the women half his age on the treadmills – it all reinforced the sensation of living in a void – the same void he was trying to kill.

He ate lunch in the tennis restaurant around the corner

and had two cups of coffee to top it off before going back to the gym and doing a final round with free weights. In the afternoon, as the last daylight faded away – these were the darkest days of the year – he was back in his apartment, where he ate an early dinner and watched TV for a while before turning out the lights and going to bed.

The nights were full of dreams, but he couldn't remember what they were about. Just their general mood. The sensation of falling, of dropping through a pitch-black shaft.

He didn't have any jobs awaiting him, so he avoided the office, didn't bother to check his email, and didn't accept any calls, although he listened to the messages of the ones he'd missed.

Eva Westin asked if he wanted to celebrate Christmas with her. Her children would be going up to the mountains with their dad. Jorma Hedlund sent a rival offer. Katz was welcome to come to his sister Leena and her son Kevin's place if he liked.

He didn't respond. He just kept going in the same circles: sleep, food, workout, sleep.

One evening he took the metro into the city. He got off at T-Centralen and took the escalators up to Sergels Torg. It was the last few hours of the Christmas rush, the twenty-third of December. Harried people were weighed down by bags of wrapped presents. The scents of *glögg* and roasted almonds floated in the air; Christmas music poured out of shop speakers. A Peruvian orchestra in traditional clothes was playing pan flute music on Plattan.

Katz stopped at one of the advertising columns. He took in what others didn't or wouldn't see: the homeless, the junkies, the drug trafficking that went on day and night, since misery didn't exactly have set business hours. People in irritated withdrawal, talking shit with each other. Toothless junkies nervously checking their phones. Prostitutes washing up in the public toilets . . . Katz took a mental lift back to the time when Sergels Torg had been the centre of his world, the place his life revolved around. He looked over at the glass vestibule, where two plainclothes cops tried and failed to blend in with their surroundings, the bathroom where he had cooked junk and shot up more times than he could recall, the discreet door into the search-and-seizure room where the cops had taken him again and again, to stick a gloved index finger into his anus, searching for drugs.

He kept moving to avoid attracting attention, going up to Åhléns; he made a round through the lowest floor of the department store before returning to Plattan and doing what he'd come there to do.

He didn't bother to work out on Christmas Eve. A new snow had fallen during the night. The sun was peeking out. The day was fairy-tale beautiful.

Katz stayed in bed for a while before getting up, taking a shower, and going down to his office.

For the first time in a month, he started up his computer. He went to the Blue Dreams website and found that it had been made with an old version of Adobe Dreamweaver. It took him fewer than ten minutes to get past the firewalls and trace the server. It was somewhere in Russia. It seemed to specialize in offering services to the porn industry; a hundred or so companies used it.

Not long after this, he was engrossed in the source code of a DDoS program. He updated the style of the code so it would better suit his purposes, and he eliminated a few bugs. The average computer user would never notice that the hard drive had been recruited for an attack. It would just run a little slower than usual when the botnet program started up.

Katz typed in the last few commands. It would take several hours for the traffic to increase and for the program to take full effect. He pictured thousands of porn surfers sitting at their computers . . . the shock on their faces when the sites they were using went black under the massive pressure of a DDoS attack.

He stayed at the office until lunchtime. He vacuumed and sorted through papers and office materials. Last of all, he checked his email.

He had fifty unread messages in his inbox. Most of them were work-related; some were Christmas greetings. The only thing that captured his interest had arrived that very day. A Canadian Hushmail.

The sender's address was randomly generated.

Katz clicked on it. There was no text or attached files. The message field was blank, aside from a stamp-sized photo of a lynx.

Lynx, he thought. What had the man said on the only occasion they had met, in the dark, on a luxury yacht in Santo Domingo? That he had a friend who was about to wind up in trouble?

Had he meant Jorma? Or Ramón?

But it had been too cryptic at the time; the whole situation had been too chaotic . . . There was no guarantee that there was any connection between the events.

And yet he knew: this was a greeting.

He turned off his computer, opened the safe, and took out what he needed.

The sun had vanished by the time he returned to his apartment. Snow was falling once more over western Stockholm. There was no traffic on the streets. The Christmas celebrations had begun.

*

At three in the afternoon, Katz sat down on the floor of his bedroom. Before him, on a towel, lay everything he needed. The spoon. The lighter. The pack of five-millilitre syringes he'd bought at Plattan. The little pack he'd taken from the safe.

He shook the powder into the spoon and mixed it with water; a third of a bag, a tenth of a gram, tops. When he was using, he had burned through five grams in two days, a pack per dose.

The veins in his arms constricted as the scent of warming junk spread through the room. His body remembered what was coming. Time would stop at last, expanding horizontally instead. The emptiness would fill with meaning.

The phone rang from his nightstand. Eva Westin, he saw on the screen as he placed the cotton ball in the spoon and sucked the solution into the syringe.

He let it ring. He pulled the scarf tight around his upper arm, tapped away the last few air bubbles, and pressed the plunger against the dose.

Snow was falling outside the window. He heard music somewhere in the building: Bach's Christmas Oratorio.

His years on the run would soon be over.

He aimed the needle at his arm, at a twenty-degree angle, towards his heart – *always towards the heart*. The correct angle. Not too sharp, otherwise there was the risk of going through the vein.

That tiny, rubbery resistance before the tip penetrated the skin. He was sweating and freezing in turns.

Katz hesitated with the needle a centimetre into his arm, mechanically pulling back the plunger to see if he could get a flash.

The snow was falling harder. Like a dance outside. White crystals in the dark of Christmas.

A ding from his phone, where Eva had just left a message.

The blood was dark red; it flowed slowly into the syringe. He pulled off the tourniquet with his teeth and injected.

The rush hit him like a flood of relief. And far off in his consciousness, Katz could feel how strong the drug was. Very strong . . . *too strong*, he had time to think, before his pulse disappeared and the world went black.